Dear Reader,

As I write this letter, Thanksgiving is two weeks away. My house is decorated with autumn leaves. The scent of a flickering cinnamon and apple candle is floating through the house. And I'm stocking my pantry with chocolate chips, canned pumpkin and a variety of spices, not to mention walnuts, pecans and almonds, with a lot of baking in mind for friends and loved ones.

We had a little snow here in Idaho last week. The stores are decked out with beautifully decorated trees. I'm making wish lists for my grandchildren and hoping to find just the right toys for them at just the right price. It's definitely beginning to look a lot like Christmas—and to sound like it too! Soon I'll be listening to Perry Como, Bing Crosby, Andy Williams and others singing carols. *A Midnight Clear* will give you a pretty good hint of which old tunes I love the most. The songs and hymns of Christmas always bring a smile to my face; they lift my spirits—sometimes, in fact, they make them soar!

As you read *A Midnight Clear,* I hope you'll find yourself singing carols right along with Margaret, Shelley, Diane and Beverly, the lovely, generous friends who live on Newport Avenue in Marble Cove. No matter what time of year you read this heartwarming story—winter, summer, spring or fall—it's my fondest wish that you'll find yourself in the Christmas spirit, that you'll carry the true meaning of Christmas in your heart, and that you'll laugh—maybe shed a tear—and cheer for our Marble Cove ladies as they experience one adventure after another.

Merry Christmas!
Patti Berg

Dedication

For Melanie…
beautiful daughter; best of friends;
a blessing in my life.
I love you.

And, as always,
for Bob.

A Midnight Clear

PATTI BERG

Miracles of Marble Cove is a trademark of Guideposts.

Published by Guideposts
16 E. 34th St.
New York, NY 10016
Guideposts.org

Acknowledgments

Every attempt has been made to credit the sources of copyrighted material used in this book. If any such acknowledgment has been inadvertently omitted or miscredited, receipt of such information would be appreciated.

Cover and interior design by Müllerhaus
Cover art by Jeremy Charles Photography
Typeset by Aptara

Printed and bound in the United States of America
10 9 8 7 6 5 4 3 2 1

Chapter One

"O Holy Night, the stars are brightly shining..."

Margaret Hoskins stood outside in the chilly late-Monday morning breeze, bundled up to the nth degree, singing along with Bing Crosby, whose crooning reverberated through the CD player sitting at her feet. Oh, how she loved the holiday season, and with Christmas just weeks away, that joyful passion was flowing from her heart to her hand as she painted the little town of Bethlehem on her art gallery's plate glass window.

The scene was beautiful, the ancient buildings and nativity captured in soft shades of blue and white. The manger took center stage, of course. The donkey and lamb she'd painted in true-to-life colors looked splendid, as did the Magi and their camels, Mary, Joseph, the shepherds, and, of course, baby Jesus. For good measure, she painted a little drummer boy with wide and sparkling brown eyes looking on the scene in absolute awe.

She wasn't out to win the *Marble Cove Courier*'s Best Christmas Window contest, and she definitely wasn't going to campaign for first place. That wasn't her style—she wasn't that competitive. But she truly felt her window was far and away better than any of the others on Main Street. While other shop owners had had their windows decorated with bright and shining snowmen and Santas, red-nosed reindeer, decorated trees, and presents galore, her window captured the true meaning of Christmas, God's Gift to the world.

Some people might forget what the season was all about—but Margaret would not.

After checking for moving vehicles, which were few and far between this time of year, she stepped back into the center of the nineteenth-century cobbled street and contemplated the nearly completed scene. Resting the tip of her paintbrush handle against her lip, she concentrated on the babe wrapped in swaddling and lying in a manger, wondering what else she could do to highlight the holiness of the Christ child. A moment or two passed, her thoughts a jumble of ideas. And then she knew the answer. His simplicity was enough; people gazing at the painting of baby Jesus would know without help from any additional touches of paint that He was perfect.

Unfortunately, the star wasn't. It needed something more.

Glitter? A touch of gold? Silver?

Walking back to the window and the pots of paint she'd set up on a small table outside the Shearwater Gallery, she dipped her brush into a glittery silver and dabbed and stroked additional paint onto the wondrous star, singing once again. Her alto voice blended with Bing's rich baritone in a heartfelt if not always skillful duet.

"Fall on your knees! O hear the angels' voi—"

"Good morning, Margaret!"

She nearly jumped out of her faux-fur-lined snow boots. Somehow she'd managed to yank her brush away from the glass before the bristles and silver paint scraped unceremoniously across her window. She spun around to find Reverend Silas Locke, long-time minister at Old First, the oldest church in Marble Cove, the serious look on his scholarly face belying the twinkle in his eye.

"Morning, Reverend." Margaret brushed a windblown lock of her short, thick gray hair behind her ear, taking a deep breath to still the rapid beat of her heart. "Pretty day, isn't it, in spite of the cold and the clouds starting to roll in?"

"And lovely singing," the reverend added, a gleam in his dark brown eyes.

Margaret laughed. "You're talking about Bing's singing, not mine. Right?"

"I beg to differ. Maddie Bancroft will be trying to recruit you for our choir if you don't watch out." Reverend Locke grinned as he shook his head. "It was your singing that drew me down to this end of Main Street.

"I'm meeting Charlotte Vincent and the rest of the Christmas Stroll committee at Captain Calhoun's for lunch. Would you like to join us?" Reverend Locke turned the collar up on his worn black wool coat. "Since I let the Chamber of Commerce talk me into organizing the lobster-trap tree building, we've got a lot of details to go over. There's nothing like a hot bowl of chowder to stimulate ideas."

Margaret lightly smacked her forehead with the palm of her hand. "Goodness. I nearly forgot we'll be building the tree and decorating it in just a couple of days."

"Yes. Wednesday's the day, starting bright and early," Reverend Locke said. "Allan's already volunteered to move traps from the wharf to the square. He and Adelaide promised to be ready at the crack of dawn."

"You know I'll help in any way I can."

"Not to worry, Margaret." Reverend Locke tucked his bare hands into the pockets of his wool navy peacoat. "We're not about to let your talents go to waste. Just show up sometime during the day and we'll put you to work decorating buoys."

"Just as long as I don't have to climb the tree to stack traps on the very top. I did that often enough when I was younger and braver."

"Well, some poor soul—and it won't be me, either—will be climbing pretty high." Reverend Locke smiled ruefully. "I've been reminded numerous times by several residents that Marble Cove needs to top the record for tallest lobster-trap tree."

Margaret laughed, but when the reverend repeated his lunch invitation, she shook her head. "Lobster chowder sounds mighty good, but I need to finish this window, make a wreath to hang on the door, and get started on my Christmas cards." She smiled. "I got a late start on them this year, but just wait until you see what I've designed. They're rather special, if I do say so myself."

"Well, if it's half as nice as your Christmas window," Reverend Locke said, "it'll be worth the wait. I'd best let you get on with your work now."

And with that they exchanged good-byes. Margaret turned back to her painting. She cleaned her brush and again dipped it in the shimmering silver paint. She had to get the Star of Wonder correct before she stopped for the day.

"*Chestnuts roasting on an open fire...*" The clanging bell on one of the fishing boats in the harbor and the screech of seagulls flying here and there looking for scraps of food drowned out Margaret singing along with Mel Tormé. Detective Fred Little, her next-door neighbor, honked as he drove by in his blue Toyota pickup. Margaret gave him a wave and then glanced at the star again. She sighed. It still wasn't right, but it was long past time to give up. Tomorrow was another day.

After taking her paints, the table, and her CD player into the studio at the back of her gallery, Margaret locked the front door, made sure the Closed sign faced out, and went to work on her wreath. Half an hour later she tucked one last piece of dark green balsam in with the fir and pine she'd gathered in the nearby woods after church yesterday, then sorted through the seashells she'd found hidden in tide pools and scattered on the beach. With her hot glue gun in hand, she was just about to create an angel out of pure white scallop shells when a faraway foghorn captured her attention. Another one, farther away, answered.

Deep calleth unto deep, she mused, remembering a Psalm. She prayed the sound wasn't signaling a ship in distress. She stepped out onto the sidewalk, the icy, salty mist from the sea instantly wrapping around her, nearly chilling her to the bone. Looking past the houses on Newport Avenue—her own celadon-green Victorian farmhouse included—she could see two ships far out on the water, looking like ghosts in the thick fog. They seemed perfectly fine, not the least in distress. Maybe they'd just been calling out a friendly greeting to each other.

She covered her mouth as she yawned, her eyelids suddenly feeling heavy, not all that much of a surprise since she hadn't slept more than a wink or two. Of course, who wouldn't toss and turn after seeing the inexplicable, eerie photos she'd been shown after attending the Advent service at Old First last night?

Oh, those photos.

It was an acquaintance of Beverly's who'd brought them to their attention. He'd come running toward them after they'd left the church, waving his hands like a man who'd just witnessed a horrific accident and needed help.

Jeff was out of breath when he reached them. "There's something odd at the lighthouse," he'd told them, or at least that's what Margaret thought he'd said. "Something strange."

Had he seen the lights beaming out through the windows high up in the tower? Margaret had—several times that year. So had Shelley, Diane, and Beverly, even though the lighthouse had been decommissioned in the fifties and was no longer fitted with a lamp or any other apparatus that could transmit light.

Had Jeff seen lights too? she'd wondered.

But Beverly had asked him point-blank if he'd seen something—something extraordinary.

Jeff shook his head. "I didn't see anything but the sun setting. I was just trying to capture the sunset and the lighthouse, but that's not all that showed up in my photos."

He'd held up his digital camera so they could all look at the viewing screen.

Margaret herself was always taking pictures of the tall, abandoned white tower that stood out on the promontory. And she didn't see anything at all unusual when Jeff showed them the first dozen or so snapshots he'd taken. With what had to be a professional camera—the kind Margaret would love to have—he'd caught the lilac, rose, and peach colors streaking across the sky, the light blue of day rapidly darkening with each shot. But his camera had caught even more. The images of something else. Something unbelievable.

"It's not what I saw," he said, his hands shaking as he held the camera. "It's what showed up in my photos." The display showed a close-up of the top of the old lighthouse.

Margaret looked long and hard. She shivered, not from the cold, but from what she saw. Swirls of ethereal light shone all about Orlean Point Light. They'd looked like apparitions, something straight out of a ghost story or a movie. "Ghosts."

But Beverly had whispered, "Angels."

Angels? Really? Margaret was surprised to hear skeptical Beverly say this.

Margaret turned her head, looking south to the rocky promontory where the lighthouse stood. At the moment, it was partially shrouded in fog. Tall and stalwart and—

Wait. Was that a glint of light? She was sure she'd seen a quick flash through the windows that stretched all the way around the lantern room at the very top of the tower.

She shook her head, closing her eyes for a moment. It had to be a figment of her imagination. A strange manifestation caused by thinking too much about the lights.

Or could it be an angel, as Beverly had said? A beacon of light, of hope, that was calling out to her, asking her to come to the lighthouse? Perhaps to help someone in need?

Margaret felt a pair of little arms wrap around her legs, and she looked down to find three-year-old Aiden Bauer's bright blue eyes and freckled face smiling up at her. She lifted the child into her arms and turned to find his mom, Shelley, pushing a stroller toward her. Shelley and Dan Bauer's fifteen-month-old daughter Emma was bundled up in a knitted pink cap, sound asleep.

"What's brought you out and about this afternoon?" Margaret asked the young, pretty blonde who lived across the street from her. Aiden squirmed out of her arms, too rambunctious to stay put longer than a handful of seconds.

"I had to deliver some of my mini cranberry tarts to Josie at the Quarterdeck Inn. Poor woman's been down with a cold and didn't have the energy to bake anything for her guests' afternoon snack."

"You didn't bake them this morning, did you?"

Shelley sighed and nodded. "I even used my on-the-fritz oven. I'll be so happy once my new kitchen's finished so I can do all the baking for my Lighthouse Sweet Shoppe at home. Using the Cove's kitchen after the restaurant closes at night is getting old." She smiled. "But you know what they say. A girl's gotta do what a girl's gotta do."

"Isn't that the truth." Margaret laughed lightly. "I think poor Josie's been doing far more than a person ought to do too, redecorating the inn mostly by herself."

"I couldn't agree more," Shelley said, "but, oh my, the Quarterdeck is looking absolutely amazing. Oh! Speaking of the Quarterdeck, did you know Jeff Mackenzie is staying there? I don't know about you, but—"

"Mama." Aiden tugged on his mother's coat, interrupting her midsentence, keeping Margaret from finding out what Shelley had against Beverly's photographer friend—or acquaintance, the term Beverly insisted on using for him. "Can we give Miss Margaret her tarts?"

Shelley cupped her son's cold and wind-chapped cheek. "Thanks for reminding me, honey."

"I could heat up some leftover coffee," Margaret said, glad to have a little company. She could easily put off going home for another half hour or so. "If you don't mind it a little strong."

"Actually, I wanted to speak with you anyway," Shelley said. "About the photos Jeff Mackenzie showed us last night."

"Oh yes." Margaret nodded slowly. "The…angels."

"I couldn't sleep much last night, thinking about what we saw in those photographs." Shelley's words came out in a flurry.

Margaret held the door open for her friends, locked up again, and led them back to her studio. While Shelley shrugged out of her pale pink, full-length down coat, Margaret quickly heated a mug of very dark coffee, then set it on a small corner table. She pulled a bucket of crayons out of a storage cabinet, along with some large pieces of newsprint she kept on hand, and sat Aiden down on the floor to draw her and his mom some pretty pictures. Just when Margaret relaxed in a chair, ready to settle down for a nice chat about the photos, Emma began to fuss.

Shelley plucked the blanket off the toddler, pulled her into her lap, and kissed her pretty pink cheeks before settling her down on the floor beside her brother. The little girl was instantly on her tummy, a fat red crayon in hand, helping Aiden with his picture, making squiggly lines all over the paper.

Margaret turned to Shelley. "Now, let's talk about the photos."

Shelley shook her head and rolled her eyes. "They've been bugging me since Jeff showed them to us last night, and I've just gotta ask. Do you think they're real?"

Margaret hadn't even contemplated that question. "They looked real. Or as real as angels or ghosts—or mysterious beacons of light—can possibly look. Have you asked Diane and Beverly what they think?"

"I tried to get ahold of Beverly first thing this morning," Shelley said, "and Mr. Wheeland told me that she and Diane had gone to Augusta to do some Christmas shopping. But I have the feeling they were just as shocked by the photos as I was."

"We were all shocked, Shelley. I don't think any of us expected to see photographs of the lights; as far as I know, no one's ever captured them on film." Margaret pinched off a bit of crust from the minitart Shelley had given her. "But I've seen the lights. You've seen the lights. Why shouldn't they show up in Jeff's photos?"

"But if Jeff Mackenzie's photos are real, I mean honestly and truly real, the world will soon know—and believe—that some unknown and unseen force is making lights shine from the top of the tower, when we all know there's no bulb, no candle, no source in the dome that can give off light."

Shelley had gotten herself so worked up over the photos that she swallowed a gulp of the coffee, then grimaced at the taste. Margaret had been right that it was strong. Shelley reached for a packet of sugar and stirred it in.

"If Jeff releases those photographs, and if people believe what they see," Margaret said, all of a sudden feeling completely uncomfortable, "Marble Cove will be overrun with people hoping to see the lights."

"Can you imagine the ghost hunters who'd show up here?" Shelley gripped her mug even more tightly. "Or producers of some of those paranormal TV shows? I don't want that. But..."

"But what?" Margaret asked. She took another bite of the cranberry tart, hoping the sweetness would help calm her sudden foreboding.

"Well," Shelley said hesitantly, "the first time we met Jeff, he was up in the top of the lighthouse shining a flashlight down on the water. It's like he was trying to pull a fast one, as if he'd heard the stories and was trying to make unsuspecting people think there really are mysterious lights."

"But we've seen them, Shelley," Margaret emphasized. "Even though Fred Little questions our sanity sometimes, we've all seen them."

Shelley nodded. "True. But maybe he's trying to make the naysayers believe there are magical lights for reasons that aren't exactly on the up-and-up."

"You mean trying to profit on their gullibility?"

"Exactly. And now he pops up with photographs of odd lights fluttering around the lighthouse. Maybe he's doctored his photographs to make them look like angels or ghosts are flying around and then put them back in his camera to show us."

"I suppose it's possible," Margaret said. "Creative people can do just about anything with computers these days. But I don't want to believe Beverly's friend is involved in something nefarious."

"I don't want to believe it either. But what do we know about him, other than the fact that he's good-looking? And Beverly won't tell us anything other than she met him years ago."

"She must have her reasons for being so secretive." Margaret swallowed the last bite of her tart. "And let's face it, Beverly's never been big on sharing all the ins and outs of her life."

Shelley pushed out of her chair, crossed to the sink, and dumped out the last of her coffee. "I admit I've got a skeptical streak that's a mile long. My mind was racing, thinking about the photos and whether or not I've really seen the lights. Kept me awake all night—that and our old boiler grumbling and groaning all night long. Try as he might, there was nothing Dan could do to settle it down to putting out heat instead of noise."

Shelley glanced at her watch. "I'd better get these kiddos home." She gave Margaret a quick hug, then bundled up Aiden for the walk home and tucked Emma back into the stroller.

Standing at the door, Margaret watched as Shelley and the children crossed Main Street's cobblestones. When they were safely on Newport Avenue, Margaret turned to look at the lighthouse. Dark clouds were dipping down, almost touching the domed roof. The wind had picked up and she knew the storm wasn't far away. She should go home, maybe take a nap, or buckle down and work on her Christmas cards.

But she couldn't. Even though she'd seen only one glint of light, she felt sure the lighthouse had called to her nearly an hour ago. She had to go there now.

She just hoped she wasn't too late.

Chapter Two

Margaret wound her bulky knit scarf around her neck and over her chin as she wandered along the weatherworn boardwalk, the sound of her footsteps drowned out by the roar of the waves. A gust of wind and sea spray slapped her from the top of her hooded head to the tips of her booted toes, nearly knocking her off the boardwalk. It felt as if the sea were trying to keep her from going to the lighthouse, but she wouldn't be stopped. She'd been summoned. There was some reason she had to go there; soon she hoped to know what that reason was.

Walking as fast as the icy boardwalk would allow, she looked off in the distance toward the two-hundred-year-old lighthouse that had saved many a ship from crashing on the rocky shore, but didn't see any more flickers of light. She really should go home, get out of the cold, but her curiosity wouldn't be satisfied until she stood beneath the lighthouse, looking for any sign of trouble.

At long last she neared her destination. The lighthouse no longer guided ships, no longer saved the lives of sailors or fishermen. Now it served only as a place for taking pictures, relegated to a few paragraphs in New England tour books and maybe an occasional mention in a coffee table book about lighthouses.

Heaven forbid it should ever draw curiosity seekers looking for ghosts.

If Orlean Point Light could talk, she could easily imagine all the wonderful stories it would tell. Perhaps it might even offer up the full truth behind the words *I'm sorry. E.M.* carved into the stone at the base of the tower.

They couldn't ignore those words, and their detective work led them to an elderly man named Edward Maker—the mysterious E.M.—who'd lived in the lighthouse with his mother and father back in the thirties.

As she cautiously walked up each slippery step, she thought about Mr. Maker. The mysterious lights were enough of an enigma without wondering what had possessed Edward Maker to carve "I'm sorry" into stone.

Now Shelley had created a new mystery in Margaret's mind, one involving Jeff Mackenzie.

And those unbelievable photos.

Margaret sighed. She should be thinking about Christmas cards and decorations and buying gifts, but here she was, making a dangerous trek up to the lighthouse, completely caught up in the mind-boggling secrets of Orlean Point Light.

Halfway up the stairs, Margaret caught the glow of the moon cresting on the horizon, the first trace of its light shimmering on the rippling Atlantic. She'd seen the same sight thousands of times, but each time was like the first.

She aimed her camera, wishing for the umpteenth time that she had one with more bells and whistles, and lost track of how many photos she took. When the moonlight hit the waves crashing on the rocky promontory, she snapped those pictures too.

Suddenly, out of the corner of her eye, she caught a different flash of light. It came from up above. From the lighthouse!

She spun around and started to fall, one foot sliding off the step and down to the one below. She latched on to the handrail and held on for dear life, catching her balance before she could plummet down the stairs to the rocks below.

She took one deep breath and then another. Again she saw a flash of light above her. Like Morse code, the light seemed to be telling her to stop dawdling and get to the top. She was needed.

Turning off her camera, Margaret ignored everything else around her and took each and every stair as fast and as safely as her short legs would allow.

She saw him when she reached the top. A young boy—maybe eleven or twelve—sitting on one of the benches the city had placed around the lighthouse, so tourists and townsfolk could sit and enjoy the views of both the lighthouse and the sea.

He was bundled up in a dark blue parka, but she could see wisps of blond hair fluttering over his forehead as he stared at the lighthouse for several moments, then tilted his head down and wrote or drew in the notebook resting on his lap.

He didn't seem to be in any dire need of help. Instead, he seemed quite peaceful, and in spite of the wind trying to catch and carry away the paper he was using, he looked completely focused on what he was doing.

Margaret stood at the top of the stairs, holding onto the railing, and watched him quietly. For long moments his yellow pencil flew over the paper, and then he stopped. He chewed on the eraser end of the pencil, tilting his head this way and that as he studied the lighthouse. What could he be thinking?

Margaret wished she could see more than just his profile, but dusk had arrived, and in the growing darkness, she found it tough to tell if he was smiling or crying. Or maybe, just maybe, his face was filled with wonder, as if he, too, had seen the lights.

"Hello there," she called out at last, her voice mixing with the sharp cry of seagulls circling overhead and a ship's horn coming from somewhere out on the ocean. But he'd heard her. His head whipped around, his eyes wide—with fear?—when he spotted Margaret walking toward him.

"Mind if I join you?" Margaret asked, stepping off the boardwalk and skirting rocks and tufts of tall brown sea grass. "It's getting dark, but if you don't mind, I'd like to sit on the bench beside you and watch the moon. It's pretty, isn't it?"

He didn't answer. A backpack that appeared to be full of school books rested beside him on the bench. He reached out to grab it, pulling it close to his side. Was he making room for Margaret to sit down? Or was he getting ready to run? She was a stranger, after all. Smart boy. She couldn't even remember the number of times she'd told her daughter "*Never talk to strangers, no matter how nice they might appear.*"

And now...she was the stranger.

"Do you come here often?" Margaret asked, hoping the friendliness in her voice might calm his nerves. "I've never seen you before."

Oh dear. He was frowning now. He *was* afraid.

"I have to go." He pulled the strap of his backpack over one arm and the notebook slid off his lap, falling open when it hit the ground. One of his papers caught on the wind, and it sailed up into the air. He tried to catch it with no luck.

"I'll get it for you."

Margaret raced after the paper, dodging back and forth as it flew a jagged course through the air. She jumped for it a time or two, but it eluded capture. It headed east toward the cliff, zigzagging all around. Margaret was running out of breath, but at last the sheet of paper came to a sudden, jolting halt against the wall of the lighthouse. She latched on to it and spun around to face the boy. "I got it, thank goodness."

But she was speaking to thin air. The boy had set off on a run.

"Wait! Don't you want your paper back?" Margaret called after him.

He didn't stop, didn't turn around. Seconds later, he disappeared into the deep, darkening forest of pine, balsam, and fir.

With the paper still in her hands, Margaret plopped down on the bench where the boy had been sitting. She leaned over, elbows resting on her knees, while she caught her breath.

She stared at the lighthouse, at the glass windows high atop. They were completely dark. Not a speck of light shone through them. No beacon. Just the reflection of the moon.

"So," she said out loud, talking to the lighthouse, "was this a wild-goose chase you led me on? I really should have been home writing letters inside all of my Christmas cards."

Leaning back, Margaret took another deep breath. Wind and salt spray stung her cheeks and dampened the paper in her hands. She should have ignored it when it was ripped away from the boy. She should have attempted to talk to him instead. She hoped she hadn't made a big mistake.

When her breathing had calmed and her heartbeat had slowed to normal, she looked at the paper in her hands. A big red *B+* was in the upper right corner of a math quiz, but through the handwritten calculations she could see the faint lines of something on the other side. She turned the paper over.

Margaret gasped. It was a masterly sketch of the lighthouse, with two lights beaming down: one on a boy sitting on a bench; the second shining on an older woman standing at the top of the stairs—a woman wearing a parka and snow boots, with a camera slung around her neck.

Chapter Three

Shelley dashed for the ringing telephone, hoping to catch it before Aiden, who'd been trying to "help" his mom all afternoon—a very long afternoon. It seemed like days had gone by since she'd taken tarts to Josie at the Quarterdeck Inn and stopped to chat with Margaret about Jeff Mackenzie and the photos he may or may not have doctored. But that had been a mere four hours ago. It was dinnertime now, just after five o'clock, and she was nearly worn out.

She slipped in the milk that had sloshed over the top of Aiden's cup when he swung around in his chair at the sound of the phone, but managed to right herself. Unfortunately, she was too late to catch a bowl half full of macaroni and cheese her little boy accidentally swept off the kitchen table in his rush for the phone. It landed upside down on the floor, and the gooey concoction splattered across the old and dingy linoleum. As if that wasn't bad enough, Emma, who'd been sitting peacefully in her high chair was now screaming at the top of her lungs.

Chaos…again.

"I'll get the phone, Aiden," Shelley shouted, just as he reached for it with hands drenched with milk and sticky cheese sauce. Somehow she got to it first and tried to steady her breath.

"Shelley speaking. How may I help you?"

"Here's paper, Mama." Aiden held up the tablet that she'd been using to take orders, which had come in right and left for the last couple of hours. At the rate things were going, she'd be drowning in work before the holidays were over. Somehow she had to keep her head above water.

She struggled to hear the man on the other end of the phone, hoping she'd caught each question.

"Yes, Dr. Spangler, I have a wonderful recipe for dog and cat treats. The way Aiden's dog Prize snatches them out of our hands and gobbles them down, I'm positive they're delicious."

"They're great," Aiden hollered, hanging on to his mom and listening to her every word. "Prize likes them. So do I."

Shelley desperately tried to hear the vet, Leo Spangler, over Emma's wails, Aiden's cheery banter, and the sudden moans and groans of the ancient boiler downstairs in the basement.

"Sure, I can make individual gift-wrapped packages of them for you to give out as Christmas presents. Let me put together a quote and I'll call you back first thing tomorrow."

As soon as she hung up the phone and gathered Emma into her arms, the toddler's tears and cheese-coated cheeks rubbing against Shelley's, her mind spun with ideas for packaging the dog and cat treats. Somewhere she was sure she had rubber stamps in the shape of paw prints. They'd look awfully cute stamped on small white paper bags in all the colors of the rainbow. They'd need some glitter, of course. It was Christmastime, after all, and a healthy dose of glitter made everything look extraspecial.

While she warmed some milk to put in Emma's sippy cup, she stood at the sink, staring out at the gentle snow that was falling in the backyard, while she cleaned her own cheeks, then Emma's cheeks and hands with a soft washcloth. Once Emma was back in her high chair, giggling at Prize, who was lapping up the milk and macaroni from the floor, Shelley blew a lock of her long blonde hair from her eyes. It wasn't even six o'clock, but her energy was running out fast. Not a good thing, since she still had baking to do at the Cove this evening.

"I'm going outside, Mama," Aiden shouted, loud enough for the neighbors to hear. She'd had just enough time to see that he'd put on his boots and coat before he and Prize had run out back, slamming the kitchen door behind them.

At last. A few moments of peace and quiet, but still so much work to do.

Shelley grabbed a roll of paper towels and got down on her hands and knees to clean up the mess before taking a mop to the floor. She was nearly finished when the front door flew open and the wind blew in her husband Dan, not to mention a chill. Before she could offer Dan a smile or even blow him a kiss, Aiden and Prize flew in through the back door, with not only wind and cold, but mud and snow-crusted shoes and paws.

"Daddy! Daddy!" Aiden jumped into his father's open arms. It was such a special sight to see, one Shelley never tired of, although she winced when father swung son around and around, Aiden's legs flailing in midair, his feet coming within inches of a few of the cherished lighthouse knickknacks she'd been collecting for years.

She smiled at her husband; he blew her a kiss. They rarely had time for much more than that anymore, not with the little ones and the dog, with Shelley's baking business, and with Dan working at the docks, helping Margaret's husband Allan with some of his woodworking, and preparing frames for future *giclée* prints of Margaret's paintings—though the work had not been as steady as Margaret had hoped. Still, Dan was a hard worker. Even though there were times when she was frustrated about their financial woes, she loved him just the way he was, faults and all, especially in moments like this, when he was tussling with Aiden, who was already the spitting image of his sandy-haired dad.

After tossing a handful of soggy and cheesy paper towels in the trash, Shelley ran a dishcloth under cold water—apparently the boiler wasn't working quite as well as it should. She might not get the floor mopped until tomorrow, but it definitely needed a little extra cleanup before then. She was wringing out the rag when Dan came up behind her. His hands slid around her waist and even though he was a full head taller, he leaned down and nuzzled her neck. "You look tired," he whispered.

"I've cleaned up umpteen messes today—spilled milk, spilled juice, spilled cereal, most of which Emma managed to toddle through or sit in, which meant an afternoon bath in addition to the one I gave her this morning after more of her breakfast ended up in her hair than in her stomach." Shelley laughed lightly, turning in her husband's embrace. "But all in all, it wasn't such a bad day."

His eyebrow quirked as it did so often, when he wasn't sure he believed her. "Wish I had an ounce of your patience."

"I try to take a deep breath when I get frustrated. That usually seems to help. That, and a lot of quick prayers."

Dan cradled her face in his wind-chafed and callused hands and kissed her. He'd been very loving lately, especially since Thanksgiving, when his father had given Shelley a wondrous gift—the promise of a new kitchen by spring; a kitchen fit for a queen. Dan's dad would be buying the materials, both men would do the building, and Dan and Shelley would somehow find the money to buy all the new appliances. It would be so wonderful once the kitchen was up and running. Thank God the owner of the Cove was allowing her the use of their kitchen after closing time. All she had to do was keep them supplied in baked goods to serve their customers—a pretty fair trade-off.

Shelley broke away and dropped to her knees again to mop up the floor with the dishcloth. Dan poured himself a cup of coffee and leaned against the counter, watching his wife work. "What's for dinner?"

Shelley looked up meekly and shrugged. "Macaroni and cheese…from a box. The kids and I already ate, but there's plenty left for you." When Dan winced, she added, "I should have thrown something into the slow cooker this morning, but I didn't think the day would end up so busy. On top of all the messes"—she blew out a sigh—"the phone rang off the hook."

"Not bill collectors, I hope."

Shelley frowned. "You know I pay the bills on time, Mr. Bauer. We may be struggling financially, but I will not do anything to mess up our credit rating."

"Then please tell me it wasn't my mom, giving you her well-meaning thoughts on the design of your new kitchen?" He winked.

Shelley shook her head and laughed. Her mother-in-law did have a habit of calling at the most inopportune times, and she never kept her opinions to herself. But the phone calls had been good, not bad.

"Actually, I received seven orders for Christmas pies, Yule logs, decorated gingerbread men, and just a few minutes ago, Dr. Spangler asked for an estimate on dog and cat treats—in decorated bags, no less."

"How will you have the time?" Dan asked skeptically. "It's not like you can wave a wand and make all those things magically appear."

"Thankfully, Aiden and Emma both went down for a nap right after lunch, which gave me time to put together an organizational chart detailing exactly what I have to do and when."

"Sounds like you're going to be gone from home even more than you have been."

"It won't be like this forever."

Dan ran a hand through blond hair that needed a good cut. "Sure wish you were going to have that new kitchen before Christmas."

"I do too, but I can make it all work. Well, *we* can make it work," Shelley said. "You'll have to watch the children every evening and I might have to work long after midnight the week before Christmas."

"You'll drop, Shelley." His concern was etched on his face. "You can't go on like this, day after day."

Shelley climbed up from the floor again. "I can and I will. I have to. My baking business means so much to me, and we're finally starting to bring in some money from it. I won't let it fail just because I'm tired."

Dan stood quietly, contemplating all she'd said—she hoped. He sipped his coffee as she rinsed out the dishcloth, then walked to the stove. She lifted the lid on the pot of macaroni and cheese and dished up a bowl for Dan. "There is something else I can do," Shelley said, afraid to look Dan straight in the eye. "Something I've been thinking about a lot the past few days."

"What's that?" Dan asked, taking the bowl Shelley offered him.

"I'd like to hire someone to help me."

Dan raised his eyebrows. "You want a housekeeper?"

Shelley shook her head in frustration. How could he possibly think she wanted a housekeeper? "Between the two of us," she said, her voice low so she wouldn't disturb

Emma, who had fallen asleep in her high chair, or Aiden, who was watching cartoons in the living room, "we can take care of the house. It might never live up to your mother's white-glove expectations, but I love the lived-in look of our home."

He chuckled. "You can't fool me, Shell. You like the lived-in look as much as I like working the graveyard shift on the docks." He looked at the mess on the kitchen table, the pile of dirty dishes in and around the sink. "Truth be told, we could use a housekeeper around here."

"We could, but we don't need one, Dan, not when we're both fully capable of at least trying to keep up with the mess."

"I'm already working extra jobs, snatching up anything that comes along to keep the wolves from our door. I don't have time to play housekeeper too."

"And I do?" Shelley found herself gritting her teeth.

Dan opened a cupboard door and pulled out a bag of potato chips. Shelley knew he hated to argue and dreaded long, thoughtful discussions even more. But they needed to talk, even though he probably thought their dustup was over.

She turned slowly. Took a deep breath. "Actually, it's not a housekeeper I was thinking of hiring."

Dan held a chip close to his mouth. He swallowed. "Then what?"

She drew in yet another deep breath, steeling her nerves. "A baker. Someone who wouldn't mind taking directions from me, because it is my bakery, after all."

"That's crazy, Shell. Hiring a baker would eat up most every penny of your profit."

"Not if I get more orders," she fired back, her words probably more testy than they should have been, but she couldn't help it. "More orders that I wouldn't be able to keep up with all on my own."

Dan rolled his eyes. That was the biggest mistake he'd made in weeks.

"I know you sometimes think my bakery is just a hobby, but it isn't. It's a business, a growing business, and I don't know how much longer I can keep it up all on my own."

"I told you in the beginning you couldn't run a bakery all on your own, and you said you could."

"I can. I just need some help."

"Well, there's no money for help, not if you want fancy new appliances for your kitchen. Not if you want—" He shook his head. "I'm gonna watch TV with Aiden." Dan stalked out of the room.

Emma woke with a start and knocked her sippy cup off the high chair's tray. It bounced across the kitchen floor, just as the boiler let out a loud groan.

Shelley fought back the tears that were threatening to flow. She didn't have time to cry, not now. Maybe later, after she cleaned up the dinner dishes, got the kids ready for bed, and went to the Cove to start her baking—without a stitch of help.

Chapter Four

Snowflakes smacked the windshield of Diane Spencer's car, nearly blinding her as she drove through the dark. What on earth had she been thinking? Making the long drive to Augusta for a Christmas shopping excursion had been pure insanity. She should have called it off after seeing the weather reports that clearly indicated a nor'easter was blowing in and the brunt of it would hit in the early evening. But no, she'd had a long list of people to find just the right gift for, and she'd been looking forward to spending the day with Beverly.

Eight shopping hours later she was completely done in. The drive home couldn't end soon enough. But right now, with Beverly leaning forward in the passenger seat, trying to find something on the radio other than static, all Diane could think about was getting home to soak her achy feet in hot water and Epsom salt—one of her mother's sure cures—eat yet another microwaved dinner because she wasn't much of a cook, then climb into bed and with luck get a good night's sleep, something she hadn't gotten last night.

For the first time in hours, her thoughts drifted to those amazing pictures Jeff Mackenzie had shown her and her friends last night. She rubbed her tired eyes, wishing the snowflakes weren't so mesmerizing, looking like those angelic apparitions in Jeff's photographs.

Their mysterious origins had captured her imagination and given her fodder for the latest cozy mystery she was working on. She still found it hard to believe she was a real, honest to goodness novelist, with three books sold to a big New York publisher. By April the first book would even be in print, for sale in bookstores, and she'd be doing book signings.

"There. How's that?" Beverly asked as she adjusted the radio station, then lifted her coffee cup to her mouth. "A little 'Jingle Bell Rock' is just what we—or you, I should say—need to combat this horrible weather." She turned the volume up slightly.

"Flares along the sides of the highway might be a better idea, anything to keep me from running off the road and driving into a ditch."

"Want me to take over? I've driven this road so many times since I came to live with Father that I pretty much know it by heart."

"Thanks, but I'm fine. Really."

The snowflakes grew bigger, hitting the windshield in a whirling dance. After a few minutes, Diane slowed to nearly a crawl, following the taillights of the vehicle in front of her, and saying a prayer of thanks that there weren't a lot of other cars on the road.

"I'm beginning to think we should have spent the night at your place in Augusta," Diane said, leaning close to the steering wheel and even closer to the windshield, although she doubted that would give her a better view as she drove through the stormy night.

"We probably should have, but, well, Jeff asked me to have coffee with him later. And I hate leaving Father all day and then all night, especially when he's got a cold. He sounded awful when I called him at noon."

"Try giving him some lemon balm tea," Diane said, pulling one of her mother's old-fashioned cold and flu remedies off the top of her head, while keeping her eyes glued to the road. "If you don't have any lemon balm, I always have it handy. Or you might want to try a concoction of lemon juice, ginger, garlic, vinegar, and a touch of cayenne. I know it sounds terrible, but it works wonders."

Beverly chuckled lightly. "Where on earth did you find that cold remedy?"

"My mom," Diane said, remembering her late mother's sweet and loving face, the twinkle she'd always had in her eyes, and her gentle ways. "She was a firm believer that cod liver oil would ward off any old germ that might be floating around, and at the first sign of a sneeze or cough, she'd use me as a guinea pig to try out old-time remedies she'd read about in the books she checked out at the library."

"And how many of those old remedies are you working into the books you're writing?"

Diane found herself laughing, in spite of the treacherous road stretching out in front of her. "I prefer having some poor, unsuspecting person ingest the wrong part of a puffer fish or step on a golden poison frog. And poisons! Cyanide and belladonna may have been overdone, but they're perfect if written about in just the right way."

Diane caught a glimpse of Beverly's smile out of the corner of her eye. "What's wrong with a simple shot in the dark?"

"Too easy for fiction. Real life is another matter entirely."

Diane chattered on, sharing little-known facts with Beverly and tucking away one thought after another into the recesses of her brain—ideas she might be able to use in a book. It made the drive easier and kept her mind off the frightening aspects of the blizzard and the nearly obscured road.

Beverly twisted around in the seat, her leather-gloved hands folded serenely in her lap. "Thanks for insisting I go shopping with you."

They'd made quite a pair: Beverly, with her sleek, dark brown shoulder-length hair that seemed to never have an out-of-place lock, had dressed to the nines in charcoal wool slacks and a coat that nearly matched, a raspberry-colored cashmere sweater and black leather boots, all of which must have set her back a pretty penny; and Diane in jeans, hiking boots with scuffed-up toes, a white cotton turtleneck, and a hunter-green fleece vest. They were so different, yet their friendship had been steadily growing.

"I can't believe you've spent the past ten years doing your Christmas shopping online," Diane said. "Look at all you've missed. Kids lining up to see Santa. Moms on a grand prix rush from one store to another, all of them looking for the hottest deal. Hungry babies crying to be fed." Diane laughed. "And then there's the fun stuff: trying on jewelry, because you have to get yourself a gift too. And finding a quiet spot in the food court to enjoy good conversation with a friend, or discovering that perfect something for a loved one, something that's not even on your list, something you never even thought about."

"I never felt I was missing out on anything. But I did have fun today." She was silent for a moment as she watched the hypnotic snow flitting over the windshield.

"My job's given me a lot of satisfaction," Beverly continued. "I've always liked working at the State House, meeting dignitaries, briefing the governor on fiscal issues. I don't even mind those times when I have to work twelve or fourteen hours a day."

"I have to do that on occasion," Diane admitted, wishing it weren't the truth. "If I get behind on my writing and have to play catch-up, which happens all too frequently, I have to hole up in my office and pretend there's no other world outside, just the one I'm writing about."

Beverly sighed. "As much as I wanted to go shopping during my life with Will, I didn't have time. I started buying cocktail dresses and all of my work clothes online, and when that turned out to be successful and easy, I started buying gifts too. When your nose is already stuck in a computer, it's easy to pop over to your favorite store and order a pashmina scarf or something for one of your husband's golfing buddies.

It's not exactly shopping with a friend, but it makes life fairly simple."

Simple or not, Diane didn't think she could ever buy gifts online. It seemed impersonal.

A big rig whizzed past Diane's much smaller car, all eighteen wheels splashing muddy snow on the windshield just before she reached the turnoff for Marble Cove. Relief flooded through her when she saw the familiar sign of Marble Cove Community Church, her church home. At last she spotted the Christmas lights decorating the homes on Newport Avenue. They were home at last.

"Want to come in for a bit? Say hello to Father?" Beverly asked, when Diane pulled into the first drive on the right, stopping as close as she could to the steps leading up to the welcoming porch of the old Victorian.

"As much as I'd love to," Diane said, "my mind is on warm slippers and a roaring fire, and possibly falling asleep on the sofa. Besides, you have a da—" Diane caught herself before finishing the word *date.* "You have dinner plans with Jeff, and you don't need me hanging about while you're trying to get ready."

"I wouldn't exactly call it a date." Beverly pulled the hood of her coat over her head. "We're having coffee at the Cove. That's all, and it's not like he wants to talk about anything personal."

"No?" Diane asked, finding that difficult to believe.

"No. He wants to talk about the lights that appeared in his pictures, and I want to discuss them too." She laughed lightly. "Call me cynical or maybe suspicious, but I want to make sure he didn't doctor up the photos."

"He wouldn't do that, would he?"

Beverly shrugged. "I don't know. I hate to think he'd do it, but"—she sighed—"I don't know him all that well. He was Will's acquaintance, not mine, and until he showed up here in Marble Cove, I hadn't seen him since…well, since the day Will drowned."

"He seems nice enough."

"Maybe." Beverly smiled, as if just remembering something special about Jeff. "I have to admit, he's pretty handsome. But I'm not at all interested in a relationship—not with him or anyone else. Not now, anyway. I have my father to care for and a demanding job and…I'm just not all that comfortable being around him."

Beverly was protesting too much, looking for excuses to stay away from Jeff Mackenzie. At least that was Diane's guess. But Diane could relate. Two years later, she was still uncomfortable with the thought of dating or being alone—out to dinner, at a movie, a sporting event, or just about anywhere—with a man, no matter how nice or handsome he was.

⋆ ⋆ ⋆

Beverly loved the tasteful blue lights trimming the eaves of the house, the doors, and the windows of her father's home. She'd wanted to hire a professional to hang the lights, but her father wouldn't hear of it, so they'd done it together the day after Thanksgiving. Beverly had made hot cocoa from one of her mother's recipes, which called for a dash of cinnamon, although she used sugar substitute instead of the real thing to keep her father's blood sugar from spiking. When they were finished, the old Victorian looked like a fairy-tale house come to life. Though she had not grown up in the house, it was welcoming and comfortable, and she'd settled in with her father far easier than she'd ever imagined possible.

In just a few months of living here, she'd fallen hopelessly in love with Marble Cove. If only she could live *and* work here. Telecommuting had been a godsend, but making that hour-long drive to the capitol building in Augusta to attend weekly meetings was wearing on her. Oh, how she wished she could find a job here or strike out on her own.

Someday...maybe.

She opened and closed the front door quietly, catching the scent of pine from the Christmas trees she'd decorated in both the living room and her father's library, the place where he liked to relax and read. Together they'd hung wreaths and draped the fireplace mantels with fir, and even now her father was burning the cinnamon-and apple-scented candles made by a local craftswoman. Soon there'd be presents under the tree. The only thing missing was her mother. She'd been gone way too long, and Beverly still missed her dearly.

She'd never thought she could share her deepest secrets, her worries, and cares with anyone other than her mother, but she'd shared some with Diane. She was becoming the sister she'd never had. In time she was sure she'd feel the same about Margaret and Shelley.

And then there was Jeff. He'd shared a part of her past that she wanted to forget, that horrible day on her husband's sailboat. The day Will had drowned. Seeing him again brought that day back full force, when she'd worked so hard to forget, or to at least tuck it far away in the back of her mind.

She wished she hadn't agreed to see him tonight.

"I'm home, Father."

Except for the smooth sound of Nat King Cole's voice coming from the stereo in the library, the house was rather quiet. She set at least half a dozen bags on the hardwood floor in the entry, dropped her gloves on a marble-topped antique foyer table, and hung her coat on the hat rack.

"Father?"

Beverly headed straight for the library when he didn't respond, her boots thudding on the oriental carpets and wooden floors as she made her way past the staircase, through the living room, and down the hallway. She heard one of her father's old LPs drop onto the turntable and the arm of the record player swing back into place. There was a bit of crackly static before Andy Williams started to sing "Sweet Little Jesus Boy," and she saw her father sitting in his favorite leather chair, a hardbound copy of Charles Dickens's *A Christmas Carol* open in his lap, with one hand resting on top.

She might have worried that he'd drifted off to his heavenly home to be with her mother, if his mouth hadn't dropped open, emitting one long and deep snore. Grabbing one of the multicolored afghans her mother had crocheted over the years, she spread it over her father, hoping not to wake him, then backed out of the room.

"Don't know why you're trying to be so quiet."

Beverly stopped when one of her father's eyelids cracked open and he tilted his head toward her. "I thought you were asleep."

"Only dozing, or trying to." His eyes were open wide now, and he shifted gingerly in the chair. He coughed a few times, grabbed a tissue, and blew his nose. "This cold's getting the best of me, and if that isn't enough, I took a dive off the step stool while getting this book down off the top shelf."

Beverly was at his side in an instant. "Are you all right? You didn't break anything, did you?"

"Only my pride." He shook his head in frustration. "Either that step stool is getting wobbly or I am. Unfortunately, I think it's the latter."

"You should have waited until I got home if you wanted a book from the top of the bookcase."

"I'm far from incapacitated, my dear, and if I waited for you to do everything for me, well, I'd go out of my mind." He patted her hand, put his book on the table beside him, and pushed himself slowly out of the chair. His legs nearly folded up beneath him, and Beverly grabbed on to his arm to give him support.

She worried so much about him. Earlier in the year she'd feared the worst, that he might be in the beginning stages of Alzheimer's. That's why she'd rented out her home in Augusta to a coworker and moved in with him here in Marble Cove. It was Diane who'd suggested he might be having ministrokes, and she'd been right. He was doing so much better now, with the prescribed medication alleviating most of his memory loss and confusion. He was pretty much back to himself, almost as sharp as a tack, just as he'd been when Beverly was growing up.

But he was seventy-nine, and she couldn't help but worry. Falls could be dangerous. "Are you sure you didn't break anything?"

"Might have bruised my hip. Maybe my shoulder. But nothing that won't mend with a little rest. I'll just go get myself some aspirin. Pain should be gone in no time."

"Why don't you sit back down and let *me* get the aspirin. I need to fix dinner for you anyway, and Diane suggested I give you a special drink that's sure to cure your cold."

"I don't want you going to any fuss. Just pop something in the microwave."

"It's no fuss, Father. Besides, I need to eat too."

"Thought you had a date."

"It's not a date." Why did everyone think it was? "And even if it was, it's been a long day, I'm bushed, and I'm going to give Jeff a call and suggest we get together some other time."

"Don't you dare cancel on account of me," her father said, bracing his hands on the arms of the chair as he lowered himself back down. "I don't need a keeper."

"I'm not. I've got a bit of a headache and there's a budget report I need to study before a nine o'clock conference call tomorrow."

Her father's dark gray brows knit together above his ultrathick glasses. "You're not making excuses to get out of going out with Jeff, are you?"

"No. Not at all," she muttered, as she headed for the kitchen to get aspirin for her father and to make a quick call to Jeff.

But maybe she was making an excuse. It was much easier than trying to figure out how she truly felt about Jeff Mackenzie re-entering her life.

* * *

Diane hadn't felt this kind of utter loneliness in months, but after a day of shopping with Beverly and now, standing at the kitchen window eating a steaming bowl of microwavable sesame chicken and rice, she missed her late husband. Two years without him hadn't been enough to ease the pain of loss, or to make her feel totally comfortable on her own. Now, with the snow falling outside and the wind whipping at her little cottage that sat just a long stone's throw from the ocean, she missed him.

Terribly.

There was such a huge hole in her heart. Would it ever heal?

Although she'd had a fabulous time with Beverly today, she missed the way her husband had held the packages while she strolled through one store after another. "What about this?" he'd asked her once, holding up a crystal cat playing with a ball of yarn. "Think Jessica might like it?"

Diane remembered laughing at her tall and good-looking blond husband. "That's the same crystal cat you picked out for her last year."

Eric had laughed then too. He'd been so helpless in the shopping department, but he'd been perfect in every other way.

When her English lit professor husband had his nose buried in his books, he was all seriousness. When he put the books aside, he became another man completely, full of warmth and laughter. They could sit across a table from each other and play Scrabble for hours on end, both of them coming up with arcane words that normal people couldn't possibly know, each of them hoping to end up with the highest score in the time limit they'd set for their game. Sometimes they'd take in a movie matinee, eat popcorn and jujubes, then go out for thick and juicy hamburgers afterward and maybe a hot fudge sundae.

Diane sighed, spooned the last speck of sesame chicken into her mouth, let Rocky, her Yellow Lab/golden retriever mix lick what was left of the sauce, then rinsed out the bowl and put it in the dishwasher.

At least she hadn't eaten it straight out of its own recyclable dish.

Eric would have loved helping her write her cozy mysteries. He'd had a warm place in his heart for Agatha Christie's

Hercule Poirot and always tried to outguess the little Belgian. But he was rarely successful. "How on earth does Agatha Christie come up with so many twists and turns, Diane?" Eric had asked, a puzzled look on his face after finishing one of Christie's books. "The woman was absolutely brilliant."

And she wrote *so* many books, even while going on archaeological digs with her husband in the Middle East. She was truly amazing, and Diane couldn't help but wonder if she could come up with as many red herrings and twists and turns in her own books. She certainly hoped so; her publisher would no doubt buy even more books in her series if she turned in something spectacular.

Heading for the living room with Rocky shadowing her every move, she put a new log on the fire and listened to it crackle and pop as she curled up on the sofa with notebook and pen.

"Twists and Turns," she wrote at the top of a new page, then jotted down notes: *1) Avant-garde guests at an uppity party given by a filthy-rich heiress.* No, no, that wasn't right. She crossed out heiress and changed it to: *society matron. Someone who looks as if she's just stepped out of a 1930s movie—like Myrna Loy in* The Thin Man.

Liking that idea, Diane expanded on the scenario. *A shot in the dark.* She chucked, remembering Beverly's comment in the car. No, definitely not. Too cliché. Poisoned wine? Stabbing? A poisoned dart? One of those golden poison frogs or a puffer fish? No, not this time. Chewing thoughtfully on the end of her pen for a moment or two, she finally smiled and scratched out another note. *Poisoned dart shot from a century-old South American blowpipe. Poison used: curare.*

As she flipped to a new page, her cell phone rang. Her children Jessica and Justin usually texted her. Her thought processes were going at such a good clip, and if she ever wanted to be as good or prolific as Agatha Christie, she knew she should ignore the ring, but that wasn't her style. She grabbed the phone from the coffee table. "Hello."

It was Margaret Hoskins, who lived next door in an old Victorian farmhouse that was at least three times the size of Diane's cozy cottage. "Allan made a lovely pot roast with all the trimmings for dinner tonight, plus those double chocolate brownies that you're so crazy about. There's far more than the three of us can eat. Will you join us?"

Diane put a hand on her stomach. The low-on-calories, high-on-sodium frozen dinner hadn't come close to filling her stomach. Still, she'd been gone all day and needed to play catch-up on her writing. "Thank you, Margaret, but—"

"I saw the lights this afternoon," Margaret said, interrupting Diane before she could decline the invitation. "I went to the lighthouse, and I may or may not have stumbled across a young boy who needs help. I need to show you what he drew. It's pretty amazing."

Margaret wasn't any more forthcoming than that, and Diane loved a mystery. Ten minutes later, her pen and notebook left all alone on the coffee table, she knocked on Margaret's door.

Chapter Five

Dan is making an extraspecial Christmas present for Shelley," Allan said, dishing up his second helping of the potatoes, carrots, and onions that had simmered to perfection in the pot roast's juices. "Just don't go telling Shelley." Allan laughed. "Dan says he's never been able to keep his gifts for Shelley a secret. She hunts through closets and drawers and even his truck and the garage, trying to figure out what he's gotten her. But this Christmas is going to be different. Her gift's hidden in my shop, and it won't come out until Christmas Day."

"You aren't going to keep it a secret from us, too, are you?" Diane asked, curiosity plain as day on her face.

"Let's just say he could easily become a master cabinetmaker if he wanted to. I've never seen a man take to woodwork the way he has."

Margaret smiled across the table at her husband, who was now explaining the fine art of hand tooling furniture vs. machine tooling furniture and the intricate nature of crafting inlaid wood. He'd changed a lot in the looks department since they'd married nearly forty years ago, but so had she. Her hair was short and gray now, not long and carefree. Allan was balding and looking like a Mainer more and more every day, his cheeks red and chapped from the wind, his neatly trimmed beard white as the snow falling outside.

He'd always been a great CPA—so had she, for that matter—devoted to his work and the people he worked with. But he was so much more content working with wood, just as she was happier painting. It was a shame that some people had to wait until late middle age to find their true niche in life.

"Daddy and I are going to make a snowman tomorrow," Adelaide said, breaking into the conversation. She might have Down syndrome, but she was the light of her parents' eyes, the blessing God had given them later in their lives than they'd ever expected.

"With a corncob pipe and button nose?" Diane asked, turning her smile on Adelaide. Twenty-five-year-old Adelaide only frowned, trying to understand what Diane meant.

"She's talking about the song 'Frosty the Snowman,'" Margaret prompted her daughter. "Do you remember the words? 'With a corncob pipe and a button nose, and two eyes made out of coal.'"

Adelaide giggled, her brown eyes sparkling. "Now I remember," she said slowly. "I like that song."

"I like it too," Diane said. "Once you and your dad finish the snowman, you'll have to come over and get me so I can come outside and take pictures of it to send to Jessica and Justin."

Diane was such a dear and had been a wonderful addition to their Newport Avenue neighborhood when she'd moved to Marble Cove five or six months ago. And she'd taken to Adelaide right away.

"I bet I have an old scarf you can wrap around his neck," Margaret said, "and some big, crazy-looking buttons that you can put on him to make him look like he's wearing a shirt."

"And if you don't have a hat," Diane stated, "I have a whole collection in my attic."

"Do you really?" Margaret was surprised. She'd never pictured Diane as a hat person.

"I used to pick them up at secondhand stores when my kids were little," Diane said, folding the cloth napkin Adelaide had set the table with. "Jessica loved to play dress-up with her friends, and sometimes Eric, Justin, and I would get in on the act."

"I like Jessica and Justin." Adelaide scooted back from the table, and only then did Margaret notice that her black-and-white cat Oreo was curled up in her daughter's lap. "Are they coming for Christmas?"

Margaret thought she saw Diane's eyes pool with tears. Over Eric, no doubt. She couldn't imagine a Christmas without her own beloved husband.

"I hope so. They said they would try their hardest to get away."

Over brownies topped with ice cream and even chocolate syrup, which was a far richer dessert than Margaret needed, they chatted about the holidays, about the wreaths Margaret liked to make for her friends, one of which already hung on Diane's front door, and about the building of the lobster-trap Christmas tree on Main Street.

"It's a tradition you're going to love," Margaret said. "I thought it was rather silly when Allan and I moved here, but now, well, Christmas wouldn't be Christmas without it. Just wait and see."

A few minutes later, their stomachs full and cups of coffee in hand, Margaret and Diane retired to the living room, the heart of Margaret's home, while Adelaide and Allan cleared the table and washed the dishes.

"Thanks so much for inviting me to dinner," Diane said, sinking down into a big and well-worn leather chair with a Navajo rug tossed over the back.

"My pleasure."

As Margaret crossed the room to retrieve the picture she'd rescued at the lighthouse that afternoon, she wondered if her friends considered the bright and eclectic decorating inside her home at odds with her paintings, which were mostly traditional seascapes and landscapes, flowers and shore birds. They were full of passion—as one Boston critic had said—but soft and subdued. She hadn't shown the wilder side of her paintings to the world just yet. There had to be a right time, but until then, she'd keep them tucked away in her studio.

She opened her desk drawer and pulled out the file folder where she'd placed the boy's picture, not wanting it to end up torn or any more wrinkled than it already was. Sitting down on the leather sofa across from Diane, she set the folder beside her, picked up her coffee, and said, "As I told you on the phone, I saw a beacon from the lighthouse this afternoon. I was at the gallery, finishing up my holiday window, and at first I thought my eyes were playing tricks on me, that maybe I'd seen a reflection off a freighter or the sun glinting off someone's window. But it wasn't all that sunny today, and dark clouds were coming in when I saw it."

Diane leaned forward, as if this conversation needed to be spoken in hushed, secretive tones. "You don't have to convince me that they're real. I'm a firm believer in miracles."

"Then you truly do believe the lights are a gift from God?"

"Absolutely." Diane lifted Oreo into her lap when the black-and-white ball of fur rubbed against her leg. She sank her fingers into the thick coat and, as if she knew there was something more Margaret wanted to talk about, said, "You mentioned seeing a young boy when you got to the lighthouse." Her gaze turned toward the folder sitting next to Margaret on the sofa. "I've been dying to know all evening what it is he drew. Goodness, Margaret, if you keep me in suspense much longer, I'd say you should start writing mysteries too."

Margaret lifted the folder, but didn't open it. Not yet. "It was so terribly cold out this afternoon. The wind had picked up and the waves were crashing against the shore. It really was a horrid time to venture up on the promontory, yet this young boy—maybe eleven or twelve, I'm such a terrible judge of age—was sitting on one of the benches studying the lighthouse. And drawing."

"Do you know who he is?"

Margaret shook her head. "I thought I knew nearly everyone in Marble Cove, but I've never seen the boy before, and considering the look on his face when he saw me, he must have thought I was the devil incarnate or a madwoman about to snatch him up and throw him over the cliffs."

Diane grinned. "I can't imagine you giving either of those impressions to anyone, no matter how wild their imagination."

Margaret laughed. "That might be a bit of an exaggeration, but when I tried to talk with him, he ran off and disappeared into the woods. But he did leave this behind." She opened up the folder, looking again at the pencil drawing, before handing it to Diane.

"It's beautiful."

"It could have been sketched by a master, or someone on the verge of being a master. But he's drawn two beacons of light too. And look what—or who—it's shining on."

Diane studied the drawing, her eyes narrowing slowly. She raised her head, staring at Margaret with the same amazement Margaret had felt when she'd first looked at the picture.

"You?"

Margaret nodded. She didn't understand it. Not at all. He couldn't have seen her before sketching her picture.

So how had he created her so perfectly, right down to the camera hanging around her neck?

"I don't know why I think this, but he needs help, Diane. I'm sure of it," Margaret said. "But I don't know who he is, and I don't know how or where to find him. So what am I going to do?"

Diane gave Margaret a smile. "If God wants you to help him, He'll make a way."

Chapter Six

It was nearly 2:00 AM, Wednesday, when Shelley left the Cove. The air was crisp and calm, and her boots crunched through the snow as she trudged home. A smattering of stars and a sliver of moon peeked through holes in the clouds. She loved nights like this; she just wished she wasn't so tired.

Most of the homes on Newport Avenue were dark, even her own, but the lights were on in the room Diane used as an office. Shelley could see Diane's silhouette through the window, looking as if she was sitting at her computer, taking advantage of the night's stillness to work on her book. She'd wave at her friend, try to catch her attention, if she wouldn't look like a madwoman. And really, she didn't want to disturb Diane in the middle of the night.

She breathed in the icy air, watching the fog surround her when she exhaled. She was exhausted from baking up a storm all evening, rushing through her work for fear the storm that had raged off and on since late Monday afternoon would take out a power pole and leave her in the dark. The snow had stopped falling a good hour ago, but each step she took through at least a foot of powder was so grueling that she felt like she was wearing concrete boots. She couldn't wait to climb into bed, tuck her head against Dan, and fall fast asleep.

Her quaint two-story bungalow was quiet when she walked inside, her boots left on the porch to avoid leaving puddles on the floor. She stepped gingerly over Aiden and Emma's toys, wishing Dan had picked them up after tucking them in for the night, or at least before he'd gone to bed. They weren't worth fretting over though. She swept up a G.I. Joe action figure, a small red fire engine, and a stuffed puffin that would have squeaked had she stepped on it. She dropped the toys into a basket at one side of the room, and gave Prize a pat on the head when she came into the living room to investigate the disturbance.

"Need to go out?" she asked the rapidly growing pup.

Prize's tail wagged, and an instant later, she raced for the kitchen door. Shelley let her into the backyard, keeping the door open just a crack to keep cold air from coming in. Downstairs in the basement the boiler groaned, not as loud as it had earlier in the day, but the noise was definitely annoying, and a little ominous. The thought of the antiquated heating system going belly-up sent a chill up her spine. Now was not the time to have to put money out for a new one when every extra penny they earned was being set aside to buy appliances for the new kitchen.

God will provide, she told herself.

Prize pushed through the door, her wet paws skidding across the floor. The puppy lapped up a healthy amount of water from her bowl, then padded off to Aiden's room to keep a watchful eye on her master.

Shelley took a quick look around the kitchen, expecting to find a microwavable popcorn bag on the counter or dirty ice cream dishes in the sink, but the counters were spotless, the sink empty. Her smile widened. Dan was trying hard.

She patted her mouth, stifling a yawn, and could still smell cinnamon, ginger and sugar on her fingers. She'd baked three pumpkin pies for the Cove, plus a big batch of lobster-shaped gingerbread cookies for Captain Calhoun's Crab and Lobster House. Oh, but she wished she was standing in her new and much-improved home kitchen right this very minute. Another few months and she'd no longer have to leave home at night.

Thank You, Lord. He had definitely been watching over her, answering her prayers when her father-in-law offered to foot the bill for a big portion of her new kitchen. She was truly blessed.

On the way to bed, she peeked in on the baby. Emma was on her tummy, her eyes closed as she slept soundly. Shelley tucked the little girl's favorite satin-edged pink blanket all around her, cocooning her in comfort, then leaned over and pressed a kiss to her forehead. "I love you, Emma," she whispered. "Always."

When she walked into Aiden's room, Prize looked up from her own comfy bed, placed where Aiden and Prize could see each other when they went to sleep and when they woke up. As usual, Aiden was on his back, with one arm slung over his head, sleeping just the way his dad always did, although Dan had long ago stopped kicking all the blankets off the bed. Shelley grinned. Like father, like son.

Without making a sound, and for what it was worth, she picked the blankets up from the floor and covered her little boy, tucking him in good and tight, at least temporarily. Aiden's eyelids fluttered; Prize stretched; and the boiler groaned again.

As she'd done with Emma, she pressed a kiss against Aiden's brow. "Sleep tight, little guy. I love you." She ruffled the fur on Prize's head and slipped quietly down the hall to her bedroom. Dan was on his back, one arm thrown over his head, the other stretched out across her pillow, as if he was waiting for her to crawl in beside him. He was sound asleep, a woodworking magazine lying open on his chest.

A few minutes later, face washed, teeth brushed, and clothed in her warmest flannel nightgown, with a pair of thick socks pulled on for extra comfort, she crawled into bed, her head finding its natural place on Dan's shoulder. She felt Dan's lips on the top of her head, kissing her tenderly. His arm gathered her a little closer. And seconds later, at ease now, knowing she was home and safe, his breathing deepened, and she drifted off to sleep.

Wham!

Shelley and Dan jolted up in bed. Prize barked. Both Emma and Aiden wailed.

"That stupid boiler!" Dan's exasperation echoed through the bedroom as he tossed back the blankets and bolted out of bed. "I tinkered with it all evening and—"

"Please, Dan," Shelley said, hoping to calm down her husband, "it'll be all right. I know it."

"It'll be all right when we've spent every last penny in our bank account getting it fixed."

Aiden tore into the room with Prize right behind him. Shelley could easily see the fear in his eyes when he jumped into his dad's arms. "What was that, Daddy? Did a ship hit our house? Or an airplane?"

"Nothing that bad." Dan ruffled Aiden's hair. "Just the boiler. Want to go down to the basement with me to see what's happened?"

"It won't be scary, will it?" she heard Aiden ask as she headed off to Emma's room to rescue her screaming daughter.

"No, son, it won't be scary."

And—Shelley sighed—she hoped it wouldn't cost an arm and a leg.

* * *

"Oh dear."

"What is it?" Allan asked Margaret as he poured her a cup of steaming coffee to go with the maple and pecan waffles he'd prepared for her and Adelaide.

Margaret was peering out the window. "Shelley told me yesterday that her boiler was on the fritz, and now the Don't Panic, Call Vanek plumbing van is in their drive."

Allan chuckled, not that Shelley and Dan's situation was funny, but he seemed to be remembering something, an abominable situation that was coming back to Margaret too.

"Remember when our boiler blew up? Back in 1983 or 1984, as I recall."

"It was 1986. I was pregnant with Adelaide when it happened."

"Right. How could I possibly forget? You'd gained too much weight and you were miserable."

Margaret frowned at her husband. "I did not gain too much weight. Adelaide was a big baby."

Allan laughed. "She was a big baby, all right, but that was no fault of hers. Seems to me all you wanted to eat was ice cream and lobster rolls, and I was running to the store constantly. And then your grandfather came to visit and complained that the winters were much more brutal here than in Vermont."

"And he couldn't understand how we could possibly love Marble Cove or the sound of the ocean that kept him awake all night."

"Not to mention the creaky stairs, and the boiler. We never had a bit of trouble with it until he came to stay."

Oh, Margaret remembered those days and her crotchety grandfather all too well. "Seems to me that every time Grandpa groaned, the boiler did too."

"I loved that old guy," Allan said, blowing the hot coffee in his mug. "But if that boiler hadn't blown, he might have lived with us for another ten years."

Margaret laughed. "And that could have sounded a death knell for our marriage." She wrapped an arm around her husband's waist. "We always were rather set in our ways. Adelaide fit in perfectly, but Grandpa was a definite mismatch."

"I think we've always been content with just the three of us living here." Allan kissed her cheek. "Might have been nice having more kids, but I couldn't be happier with the one we have."

Margaret thought about Allan's words as she puttered around the gallery later that morning, dusting frames and spritzing display cases with glass cleaner, then rubbing them until they were spotless. She hadn't planned to open the gallery today. Heaven knew there wouldn't be many customers, unless a stray tourist or two who didn't mind the cold and snow stopped in to have a look around. And she had shipped the few orders she'd gotten through her new Web site.

She unwrapped a piece of saltwater taffy and popped it into her mouth, chewing thoughtfully as she looked at the star she'd painted in the window. It still wasn't right; she just didn't know what it needed. With luck, she'd figure it out before the *Courier*'s Best Christmas Window contest judges came a-calling.

The jingle bells hanging on the door rang out, taking her completely by surprise. She hadn't seen anyone walk by the store or gaze through the window, and she was even more surprised when Jeff Mackenzie, Beverly's friend, and the man who'd taken the mysterious photos, walked inside.

"Remember me?" he said, pulling off a black wool cap and tucking it into the pocket of his navy blue parka.

"Of course I remember you. It's Jeff, right?"

He nodded. "And you're Margaret?"

"Yes, sir."

How could she possibly not remember this man? As Shelley had said numerous times, he was gorgeous, definitely tall, dark, and handsome, with disheveled black hair that had just a slight sprinkling of gray mixed in, and twinkling blue eyes.

"What can I help you with?" Margaret asked, trying to look like the owner of the gallery and not the cleaning lady. She glanced down at the feather duster in her hand and the splotch of Prussian blue paint on her charcoal gray slacks.

"Beverly told me you were an artist, and I saw a couple of your paintings hanging in the Quarterdeck Inn, where I'm staying." If he bought something, Margaret decided, she'd have to give Josie, the Quarterdeck's owner, a special discount on her next purchase from the gallery. "You've got a nice way with color," Jeff continued, walking about with his hands clasped behind his back, "and I thought I'd drop by to see more of your work."

"Thank you," she said. She couldn't help but wonder if he was trying to flatter her, or if he was serious. In the end she opted for serious.

"I have other artists on display here as well," Margaret said, pointing out an overlarge watercolor of a single seashell painted in soft pastels, and another of a fishing shack on the wharf that was all decked out in brightly colored Christmas lights. "I also have jewelry, if you're interested."

"It's your lighthouses I'm mainly interested in. Orlean Point Light in particular."

That certainly wasn't much of a surprise.

She folded her hands behind her back, the feather duster dangling from her fingers, as she crossed the room and showed him one of her favorites, the tall, stately white lighthouse with its red tile cupola silhouetted against an orange sunrise.

"I like the way you've captured the blue sky and painted the clouds nearly the same shade of orange as the horizon." He moved in closer, studying something on the painting. "Those bushes at the back of the lighthouse. Are those the ones hiding the secret door?"

Jeff Mackenzie had shocked her once again. "You know about that?"

He nodded. "I've done a lot of research on the place, but there's so much more I'd like to know."

"I suppose Beverly's told you about our research?"

"Briefly." He chuckled. "We were supposed to get together night before last, to talk more about the lighthouse—"

"And the pictures you took," Margaret interrupted. "The ones that show the lights."

"Those too, although I'm beginning to think there might have been a problem with my camera."

"Really?" Margaret asked. "Your camera looked rather new and very sophisticated, not like an inexpensive model that could easily act up."

"Sophisticated or not, I've spent several evenings out at the lighthouse and I've yet to see—with my own eyes—any lights beaming through the windows, and since there's no apparatus at the top of the tower to create any light, it must have been a camera problem. Or maybe a reflection hitting the lens." He shook his head. "But I don't really believe that."

Margaret had no idea how much Jeff knew about the lights or if Beverly had told him that she'd seen them before. She wasn't about to open up and talk about those sightings now. Instead she said, "There are all sorts of stories about Orlean Point Light."

"Yes, I imagine there are." Jeff moved to a watercolor she'd painted last year after Marble Cove's lobster-trap tree was up and decorated. "And what's this?"

"It's one of the highlights of our year here in town, and this year's rather special. We're hoping to erect the tallest lobster-trap tree ever seen in Maine, which will be quite a feat if we can pull it off.

"We paint buoys and wrap the whole thing up in lights and the pièce de résistance is the flashing lobster that's topped the tree since 1979."

"It's gotta be something special to see."

"It is, and if you're going to be in town tomorrow, we'll start building the thing about 8:00 AM, and we could always use another able-bodied man who's not afraid to climb twenty or thirty feet or so, carrying a trap or two along with him."

"Well, I will be in town and the tree ought to be good material for a photographer. You'll be there, won't you? And your friends?"

Margaret smiled. "Yes, I'll be there, and I'm sure Shelley, Diane, and Beverly will be there too."

Jeff smiled, looking quite contented as he walked toward another one of Margaret's paintings, this one a group of puffins she'd painted out on Seal Island. She was about to tell him the story behind that painting when she spotted a shaggy blond head peering through the gallery's front window.

It was the boy from the lighthouse.

"Excuse me a moment," Margaret said through the lump forming in her throat. Was it really him, or her imagination playing tricks on her?

She rushed to the front door, the tinkling of the bells mixing with the crunch of car tires rolling over the salt sprinkled on the cobblestone street. The boy stood there, his eyes narrowed, but not in fear this time. "Please, don't run away."

He waited, not saying a word.

"I have your picture of the lighthouse," she said, smiling down at the boy. He had freckles across his nose and cheeks and darkening circles beneath his eyes. They weren't bruises but signs that he wasn't getting much sleep. But why?

"Your sketch is beautiful. I have it at home, but if you'd like to have it back—"

"I can draw more," he said, but that was all.

"You must draw a lot," Margaret said, trying to stretch out the conversation, wanting to know more about him or if he needed help. "Are you taking lessons?"

"Not anymore." He turned his head, looking at the buildings on the other side of the street, at the Vanek Plumbing van rumbling up the road. Was her imagination running wild, or was he looking for something? Maybe trying to hide from someone?

"Would you like to come inside? I could make you some hot cocoa."

He shook his head. "I have to go."

"I have some wonderful how-to-paint and how-to-draw books if you'd like to borrow them."

"That's okay. I really have to go." He started to walk backward, keeping his doubtful gaze on Margaret.

"I'm here most every day. Please, come by whenever you want."

He frowned deeply, shaking his head, and then he started to run.

Only then did Margaret realize she hadn't asked his name. Now it was too late. When he disappeared between a couple of buildings on Main Street, she walked back into the gallery, only to find Jeff Mackenzie staring at her with an incredulous look that nearly matched the boy's.

"Everything okay?" he asked.

She nodded slowly. "Yes. Everything's fine."

Just another mystery to drive her crazy.

Chapter Seven

"Feeling any better?" Beverly asked her father Wednesday afternoon when she came downstairs from the second-story room she'd turned into an office. She'd heard him cough only a few times today, thank heaven. He wanted to spend a couple of hours watching the lobster-trap tree being built, but she wasn't about to let him go if he wasn't feeling better.

"That lemon balm concoction isn't all that tasty, but it's driving out this cold."

Beverly smiled. Her father could be stubborn when it came to taking medicine, and she'd had to convince him that this homemade remedy would actually help him.

"What would you like for dinner tonight?" Beverly leaned against the doorjamb leading into her father's library. It smelled of lemon oil and Old Spice aftershave mixed with pine and the pumpkin-spice candles that had been burning the past few hours. "If I hadn't let the morning get away from me, I would have started a pot of soup or—"

The doorbell rang, cutting off her sentence.

"I'll get it."

"It's probably Mrs. Peabody." He chuckled.

Even through the ornate glass on the front door, Beverly could see short, curly-white-haired Mrs. Peabody, who lived in the lavender Victorian across the street. The older woman—in her early eighties, if Beverly had to guess—had a widow's walk around her house, and Beverly often imagined Mrs. Peabody standing there in the spring and summer with a spyglass, watching the ships on the ocean, not to mention everything going on in and around her neighbors' homes. Not that she'd ever noticed Mrs. Peabody spying on her neighbors, but she'd heard rumors, and there were those in town who had a tendency to call her Mrs. Busybody.

"Good afternoon, Mrs. Peabody," Beverly said, opening the door wide. A gust of cold air swept in, followed by Mrs. Peabody. She breezed past Beverly and went straight into the library, knowing full well that "the mister," as she often called Beverly's father, spent the biggest part of his day holed up in that room.

"Had the feeling I'd find you here, Harold. I've brought you one of my prize-winning chocolate cream pies. Such a shame you've got that diabetes, because it isn't quite as good made with artificial sweetener, but I'm not about to feed you something that could be hazardous to your health." Mrs. Peabody handed the glass pie plate to Beverly right after thrusting it under her father's nose so he could get a whiff of the heavenly scent, which even now was making Beverly hungry.

"I know your daughter's busy with her work—goodness, I caught a glimpse of her working on her computer this morning and then again just half an hour ago—so I was certain she might not have time to fix you a proper lunch. If you've all the right ingredients in your kitchen, I could whip up an omelet or crab cakes. Whatever you'd like."

"No need to bother—"

"Oh, it's no bother, Harold. If there's one thing I like to do, it's cook."

"Father and I are helping stack lobster traps for the Marble Cove Christmas tree this afternoon," Beverly said, looking at her watch. It was nearly two o'clock and she'd told her friends she and her father would be there by three. "Would you like to join us?"

"That would be lovely, my dear, and thanks for asking." That faraway smile graced Mrs. Peabody's face again. "There was a time when I used to help decorate that tree, but I don't have the stamina that I used to have, and standing out in the cold's not all that good for these old bones. Think I'll just stay inside and watch the festivities from an upstairs window."

Or from your widow's walk through a pair of high-powered binoculars, Beverly couldn't help but muse.

"That tree's always a sight to behold," Mrs. Peabody said wistfully. Beverly agreed and began to reminisce about the Christmas season. Back when her mother was alive, all three of them would gather around the old console piano her mother had played and sing their favorite Christmas songs. Would she ever again experience a Christmas Eve like those she'd loved so much?

"Is that feller of yours," Mrs. Peabody said, clearing her throat and drawing Beverly out of her reverie, "that Jeff Mackenzie guy, going to help build the tree?"

As far as she knew, he'd gone back to Portland or on a photo-taking excursion far from Marble Cove. He'd seemed a bit miffed when she'd called Monday night to cancel their get-together, and he hadn't bothered to call and take her up on the rain check. Beverly had rather hoped he was gone for good, but once again he was back in her thoughts.

"Mr. Mackenzie is just an acquaintance," Beverly said, "and he lives in Portland. I doubt he even knows about the lobster-trap tree, and, as far as I know, he isn't in town."

"Oh, but he is." Mrs. Peabody had a gleam in her eye. "I saw him coming out of the Shearwater Gallery this morning and going into the Quarterdeck Inn just before noon today."

So he hadn't left town.

It was really none of her business what Jeff did or didn't do, where he went, whom he talked to or took out for coffee, or anything else for that matter. If Mrs. Peabody hadn't been watching her with such rapt curiosity, Beverly thought for sure she might sigh. Jeff hadn't left town but he hadn't called either.

Why, oh why, did that bother her?

Chapter Eight

Be careful," Margaret called out to Adelaide as her daughter helped a dozen or more children and a few adults carry lobster traps to the brave men—and Shelley—who stood on ladders to carefully stack the old wooden pots. They weren't all that heavy, but they were awkward, all different shapes and sizes, and the snow that had dusted the ground earlier in the day had left the cobblestoned square a bit slippery. She might be a tad overprotective—she and Allan had been from the day Adelaide was born—but she didn't want Adelaide taking a fall.

"You gotta help too, Mom. It's fun," Adelaide shouted, holding one side of a trap while Reverend Locke held the other.

Margaret much preferred painting buoys, but as Shelley had said just the other day, a girl's gotta do what a girl's gotta do.

Margaret lugged a pot up from the ground, handed it off, and went back for another. She'd never admit to a soul that she thought she might be getting a little too old for this kind of work.

Shelley, petite as she was, had helped build the tree for years now, and Dan had been stacking since he was a kid.

They knew exactly how to arrange each trap so that when they were finished, their creation would be shaped like a Christmas tree: hollow on the inside; rather intriguing on the outside, and almost perfectly symmetrical.

Five pots later, Margaret joined the spectators who kibitzed on the sidelines, completely out of breath and her hands now half-frozen.

"Does it always smell so pungent?" Diane's nose wrinkled as she handed Margaret and Allan cups of steaming coffee to help ward off the cold.

"Yep." Allan gripped his paper cup with two hands, holding it close to his mouth, the coffee's steam mixing with the fog of his breath. "Many a lobster has spent time in those traps, not to mention the herring that's used for bait. If you had lobster and herring hanging around your house day and night, not even the most ardent suitor would get close to you."

Diane smiled. "I'll remember that if I'm ever in the market for a suitor. But right now, I promised Shelley I'd pass out gingerbread cookies to the crowd."

"That woman's going to drive herself into an early grave if she doesn't slow down," Allan said. "Dan tries not to show it, but I can sense he's worried to the gills about her."

"I've scolded her and I know a good half a dozen of her friends from church have asked her to slow down," Margaret said, "but I'm afraid all our warnings fall on deaf ears. She's determined to make a success of her business."

"That's what the cookies are all about," Diane stated, holding up the basket for all to see. "Each one's individually wrapped in a cellophane bag, with her pretty pink Lighthouse Sweet Shoppe business card attached."

"'Making each day a little sweeter,' they say," Margaret told her husband, remembering the care Shelley had put into every bit of advertising she'd created for the business. She peered at the business card. "It's got her Web site address on it too."

Before long, Margaret was lugging traps again. The more the merrier, she figured, anything to get the smelly job done faster. Allan went in for a cleaner job, carrying the basket full of Shelley's cookies while Diane handed them out, letting each person who received one know where they'd come from.

"Need some help?"

Margaret spun around to see Beverly, dressed down in jeans and a nice pair of leather boots. When would the pretty professional learn that around Marble Cove, serviceable hiking boots, galoshes, or waders were proper attire, especially when working with lobster traps? Margaret herself was in her oldest pair of flannel-lined jeans and a worse-for-wear L.L. Bean parka—straight from their flagship store in Freeport, Maine.

"Looks like we're getting fairly close to the end," Margaret said to her friend, "but grab a trap or two and find someone standing on a ladder to hand them to."

"You wouldn't catch me dead standing on one of those ladders or, worse yet, near the very top of the tree. It looks like this thing could come tumbling down at any minute."

"Nope. Haven't had even one catastrophe in the three decades Allan and I have lived here; doubt we'll have one in the next." Margaret looked up to the top of tree, shading her eyes from the sun, which had shone down on them to make their work easier. "The stackers, Shelley included, know exactly what they're doing."

"Who's watching Aiden and Emma while she's working?" Beverly asked, wrinkling her nose as she grabbed a trap from a pile that was in easy reach.

"Frances Bauer, Dan's mom. She and Shelley have their moments, but she sure dotes on her grandkids. I think she's pulling Shelley's little ones around on a sled, looking at some of the decorated houses around town."

"Good for her."

"Hey, Beverly," a male voice called down from somewhere close to the top of the tree, "how 'bout climbing up on a ladder and handing me that trap you're holding."

Margaret couldn't help but notice the look of sheer surprise that crossed Beverly's face when she heard the voice. She probably should have told Beverly that Jeff Mackenzie had been helping out with the tree since early morning.

Beverly's head jerked upward, a frown on her face as she shaded her eyes for a better view.

"Come on, Beverly," Jeff hollered down. "Give it a shot."

Beverly shook her head, still looking displeased. Margaret couldn't tell if the glower was at the thought of climbing the tree or seeing Jeff Mackenzie at the top. Of course, it could have been for both. Margaret might have asked her if Beverly hadn't sized up the tree, then shouted up to Jeff, "You have to be out of your mind. I'm not about to climb up there."

"But you can see forever when you're up here on top."

Margaret nudged Beverly's arm. "Go on. I did it when I was your age."

"I need to watch Father," Beverly said, turning to look at her dad and a few older men sitting on lawn chairs watching the action.

"I'll keep an eye on him." Again Margaret nudged Beverly. "Now get on up there."

Beverly laughed, then marched forward, putting one foot and then another on the rungs of the ladder, moving cautiously until she was nearly halfway up the tree. After this, Margaret thought, Beverly might buy a sensible pair of boots, ones with heavy treads and waterproofing.

Shelley reached out and grabbed Beverly's hand as she stepped onto one of the already-stacked traps. Margaret watched, every one of Beverly's missteps helping to form a lump in Margaret's throat.

"That's the way." Margaret could hear Jeff encouraging her. "Just a few more steps. Keep on coming."

By now a crowd had gathered, all eyes turned up to the top of the tree, watching Beverly's ascent. At long last Jeff caught hold of both Beverly's hands and pulled her up beside him.

The crowd cheered.

Beverly smiled. She was almost always serious, a bit guarded, and as far as Margaret had been able to gather, Beverly didn't let anyone—except maybe Diane—get all that close to her. But at that moment, if only for the moment, she seemed to be letting down her guard.

One more miraculous—or semimiraculous—occurrence in Marble Cove.

* * *

Beverly sat next to Jeff at the very top of a lobster-trap Christmas tree, breathing in the scents of both pungent lobster and sweet ginger from the cookies that had been passed out to the workers when the massive tree was nearly complete. She folded her gloved hands in her lap. "You really can see forever from up here." She looked out across the ocean, spotting a few islands way off in the distance, and the first speck of moon cresting on the horizon. "Too bad you don't have your camera with you." Beverly's lighthearted mood dimmed in less than a heartbeat. "Then again…"

Jeff had been rubbing his hands together for warmth, waiting for the giant plastic lobster to be hauled up the tree so he and some of the other guys could fasten it into place. Now he turned to look at Beverly, a frown on his unshaven face. "Then again, what?"

It seemed like an odd place to talk about those strange photographs he'd taken, but they were together, and she wanted to know the truth.

"Well, there have been rumblings that you might have played around with those photos you took at the lighthouse Sunday night."

“Played around?” His frown deepened. “What are you talking about?”

“You know, doctored them up on your computer to make it look like angels were flying around the lighthouse.”

It didn’t seem possible for his scowl to grow any deeper or darker, but it did. His eyebrows nearly knitted together. “Why would I want to do that?”

“I didn’t say *I* think you doctored the photos.”

“I can count on two hands the number of people I’ve shown those pictures to. So which one—or more—of your friends think I’d fake those images?”

Beverly sighed, shaking her head. She wished she hadn’t said anything. “I don’t think any of my friends truly believe you’d do such a thing, it’s just that the lights are mysterious. They’re odd—”

“And they could easily be a myth. That’s what people in town have told me.” He blew on his hands for a little additional warmth, while Beverly tightly gripped the lobster trap she was sitting on, hoping and praying she wouldn’t fall or worse, that Jeff might—no, he’d never push her off. She was being ridiculous now. This wasn’t a scene from one of Diane’s books; this was real life. “Most people in town have never seen them—”

“And those who have are considered to be crackpots,” Beverly interrupted. “Which means I’m a crackpot, because I’ve seen them.”

Jeff chuckled lightly. “I don’t believe it.”

“It’s true. I have seen them, not that they looked like those swirls of light in your pictures. They’re just beams.”

She looked him in the eye. "Are you sure you didn't doctor the pictures?"

"Positive." He pointed toward the lighthouse, the last rays of sunshine casting a soft orange glow on its white walls. "I've photographed a lot of beautiful things, but I can't create that kind of beauty. I leave that up to God. There are far too many things in this world that we don't understand. And, for the record"—he turned toward her again, a smile on his face—"I don't think you're a crackpot."

Beverly smiled back, loosening her hands on the lobster trap, certain that Jeff wouldn't let her fall. "Okay then, we're even. I don't think you're a fraud."

★ ★ ★

It was well past seven o'clock when the last string of lights and the last colorfully painted buoy were hung on the tree. *Children should be getting ready for bed right about now,* Margaret thought, *but how could any parents deny their child the excitement of the day and the impending awe of the tree being lit?*

Allan swept his arm around Margaret's waist and she held on to Adelaide's hand as they stood together with their friends. Emma, bundled up in a lavender snow suit, her chubby cheeks red from the cold, rested on Shelley's hip; Dan had boosted a sleepy-eyed Aiden onto his shoulders. Beverly stood behind her father, and Jeff stood at her side.

"May I join you?" Diane asked, as she squeezed in by her friends. She might be alone, a widow whose adult children lived too far away to visit all that often, but she'd never be lonely here in Marble Cove.

"All right everyone, it's countdown time." Evelyn Waters, the only mayor most anyone living in Marble Cove could remember, stood at the base of the tree, a light switch in her hand. She was bundled up in fake fur, and just as soon as she started her countdown, a few flakes of snow began to fall.

"Three. Two. One."

"Lights! Action!" Someone in the crowd shouted, and once again, Marble Cove's lobster-trap Christmas tree came to life.

"Wow. It's beautiful," Diane murmured. "I've never seen anything quite like it."

After the applause and cheers died down, the choir from Old First, directed by Maddie Bancroft, began to hum, and then to sing. "*Silent night! Holy night! All is calm, all is bright.*"

A hush came over the gathering, and then the townspeople joined together in song. It was, as the Christmas song said, "the perfect ending of a perfect day."

Chapter Nine

"What do you think, Rocky? Am I making this book far too simplistic using curare as a poison?" Rocky sat at one end of the sofa, Diane at the other, her laptop battery getting hot since the computer had been resting on her legs for well over an hour. Rocky's ears perked up at Diane's question. He tilted his head, obviously needing more explanation in order to make an informed decision. "Maybe I'm overthinking the method of murder. After all, the killer in this book isn't all that bright."

Rocky yawned good and long, then plopped down on the sofa, his head resting on his paws.

"I'm thinking this story should take place at Christmastime, that all of my suspects should be singing carols together, acting as though they're enjoying their community. In fact, I think they should build a lobster-trap Christmas tree in the square. How does that sound?"

Rocky's brows raised; the tip of his tongue poked out of his mouth, and all of a sudden, he appeared to be smiling. Diane laughed.

"I'm so glad you like that idea. I thought about it last night when Beverly joined Jeff at the top of the lobster-trap tree. I'm sure she was scared out of her mind climbing up that thing. I know I would have been. But can't you just imagine a sinister hand jutting out from between the traps—a man's hand, the hand of a man who's crawled up inside the tree where he's hidden from view—and just sort of shoving the victim off the side? The traps are slippery, you know. No one would ever expect that the victim had been pushed. They'd just think her shoe"—Diane rolled her eyes—"her fancy boots, I should say, slipped on a slimy trap and down, down, down she fell. Dead."

Rocky's eyes were closed. He didn't even bother to look up.

"Well, Rocky, that might have sounded good in theory, but I suppose it's all rather boring. Maybe I'll stick with the—"

The phone rang, startling Rocky. He bolted off the couch and ran for the bedroom. Diane looked at the phone number, hoping it was Jessica or Justin calling to let her know they were definitely coming for Christmas, but when she answered, it turned out to be Gilda Harris from the Marble Cove library.

"I hope I haven't disturbed you," Gilda said, her voice very much that of an old-fashioned librarian, soft and just barely above a whisper.

Gilda had disturbed her, but all of the Marble Cove librarians had been more than generous with their offers to help in her research, not just details about her books, but about Orlean Point Light as well, and they were nice to boot. "Of course you didn't disturb me, Gilda. What can I do for you?"

"I know this is late notice, and I really apologize for that, but the speaker for our Christmas open house and canned food drive has canceled on us and, well, I know you're an author and I was thinking—"

Oh, please don't ask me to speak. Not in front of real live people.

"Well, we'd love to have you give a talk on writing. You know, how you got started, where you get your inspiration, how long did it take you to sell your first book. That type of thing."

"Oh, I don't know, Gilda." *Just say no,* Diane told herself, but that one simple word wouldn't come out of her mouth. "It's Christmastime and I've so much to do, what with writing and decorating and—"

"Yes, yes, I completely understand, and as I said, this is rather last minute, but we've already sent out invitations and we have notices about the open house coming out in the *Courier,* and a lot of people have already signed up. They've paid their money to come and hear a real live author."

But I haven't even had a book published yet. They'll think I'm a phony.

"I know you're busy, Diane, but this could be tremendous exposure for you. We'll put up some posters and if you already have a title for your book and a publication date—"

"I don't have the final title yet but...I suppose I could talk to my editor."

"That would be absolutely lovely, Diane. We can't pay you—"

"Of course not. I wouldn't expect that."

"Then you'll do it? Saturday, a week from tomorrow? From one until four?"

Diane felt a headache coming on, not to mention great anxiety. But she just couldn't say no. "Sure, Gilda. I'd be happy to do it."

* * *

"I've lost my mind," Diane said, walking around the Shearwater Gallery an hour after she'd gotten off the phone with Gilda, drinking a cup of Margaret's freshly made coffee and absently looking at one painting after another. "I'm not a speaker, Margaret. I'm a writer. I talk to my dog. How can I possibly speak in front of a crowd, even if that crowd only consists of ten people?"

"You know what they say," Margaret offered from a far corner in the gallery where she was wrapping a painting to send off to a customer. "Find a spot on the wall and stare at it, or single out a friend and pretend you're talking to her and her only, or—"

"Pretend they're naked!" Diane laughed. "In which case, I'd turn beet red and stammer, or burst into fits of laughter."

"Then write your speech and read it. I've read your work and I love it, especially the humorous parts. You have a knack for storytelling, Diane. Just work with that."

Diane sighed. If only Eric were here. He'd sit in the audience and smile at her. He'd be her biggest fan, would boost her courage, or give the speech for her, talking about being the poor, put-upon husband of a writer.

She was not looking forward to this Christmas without him, without her children.

The music Margaret was playing wrapped around her: "Dance of the Sugar Plum Fairy" from *The Nutcracker.* The first time she'd taken Jessica to see the ballet, her daughter had only been eleven, and she loved it. It had become a tradition, then Jessica went off to college and Jason joined the service; Eric died. Her traditions had all seemed to go up in smoke.

At least she had her memories.

"You know," Diane said, walking across the room to watch Margaret wrap the painting, "I wrote a short story for Jessica and Jason one Christmas. It was all about a Christmas present that had mysteriously disappeared. Do you think I could get by with reading that, and telling the story behind it?"

"I don't know why not."

"You're being much too easy, Margaret."

"And you're overthinking this speech. If you don't stop, you're going to worry yourself into a frazzle."

"You're right." Diane gave Margaret a friendly hug. "As usual."

Walking back into the gallery, Diane attempted to look at the newest paintings Margaret had hung, actually concentrating on them instead of allowing her mind to wander to next Saturday and her speech. She moved from one painting to another, a landscape here, a flower bursting forth from a patch of melting snow, a beach…

"Is this new?" Diane asked, staring at the painting as a feeling like warm and loving arms embraced her.

Margaret had come from the wrapping area and stood next to Diane. "It's been hanging there for a few days now. It's always been one of my favorites; I wasn't even sure I could part with it, but I decided to put it out a few days ago and a customer snatched it up immediately. Well, she put it on layaway and plans to pay in installments. That's why it's still hanging here."

"I've been to this spot before," Diane said, feeling tears forming at the corners of her eyes. If the painting were still for sale, she'd snatch it up in a heartbeat. She wondered if Margaret would have a giclée print made from it. "Eric and I used to picnic on that stretch of beach every time we came to Marble Cove. I must have a dozen photos of the two of us building sand castles there or dipping our feet in the water or of Eric lazing on a blanket."

"It's called *Dawn's Early Light*," Margaret told her. "I must have painted it five or six years ago. It's not my best, but—"

"It's beautiful. I only wish it was still for sale."

"You never know," Margaret said, linking her arm through Diane's. "People who put things on layaway often change their minds."

"You'll let me know if that happens, won't you? Or"—she stopped— "will you have a giclée print made of it?"

"Yes, I—"

If Margaret had planned to say anything more, her words were stifled. She was staring at the gallery's picture window, at the back side of her Bethlehem scene.

"That's the boy I told you about," Margaret said softly, as if speaking too loud might scare him away. "Don't leave. I'll be right back."

Diane watched as Margaret bustled toward the front door. The bells hanging on the glass front door jangled when she stepped outside into the cold. Diane couldn't read lips, but Margaret was probably inviting him in, and he was shaking his head. At last, she opened the door again, and the boy came inside. He was blond, far too thin, and had dark circles under his eyes.

Just as Margaret had said, he looked like a kid in trouble, a boy who needed help. But why?

"I've really gotta get home," he said, "but I'm doing an essay for my English class on art history—the good, the bad, and the, well, not so good." He stopped in front of one of Margaret's seascapes. He studied it for a moment, then stared up at Margaret. "Did you paint this?"

She nodded, and Diane couldn't miss the look of pride on her face.

"It's good," he said. "Kind of like Renoir—"

"You know about Renoir?"

He rolled his eyes and Diane wanted to laugh. He reminded her a lot of her son Justin at that age, a little too smart for his own good. "I've been studying art since I was a kid."

Margaret glanced back at Diane with raised eyebrows, then back at the boy. "Renoir's one of the best."

"Too boring," the boy said, scratching his head. "You should try something more avant-garde, more abstract, like Wassily Kandinsky."

"Kandinsky, huh?"

"Yeah. I've always considered him one of the greatest, and his impressionistic work was far and away better than Renoir."

"You don't say."

The boy nodded, looked out at the street where a couple of kids nearly his age were hanging out, and headed for the door. "I've gotta go, but look up Kandinsky. You'll see what I mean."

"Don't go yet," Margaret said, following him to the door. "I don't even know your—" But he was already through the door and running toward his pals.

Slowly Margaret turned toward Diane, shaking her head in absolute disappointment. "And here I thought he might need my help."

Diane laughed lightly. "It's just a phase that most boys go through. He wants to show how smart he is but comes off sounding smart-alecky. He's intelligent but immature."

"You can tell all that just by that exchange the two of us just shared?"

"Justin was that age once. His hormones were completely off balance and most of the time he didn't know his left from his right. He'd try to say something nice, but he didn't want to sound like a wimp, and his words came out all wrong. Thankfully he grew out of that stage."

"Well, for what it's worth, I'm not a Kandinsky fan, and if he ever comes back again—"

"He will, Margaret. There's something here that intrigues him. Who knows? Maybe it's you."

Margaret chuckled. "Maybe, but if he does come back, I'm going to have my argument all prepared on why Renoir is far better than Kandinsky."

The bells on the door jangled again, and the boy walked back inside once more. He walked up to Margaret again, looking a little more contrite. "You wouldn't by any chance have a job opening for a salesman, would you?"

Margaret's laugh seemed to sneak out without permission. She stifled it quickly, but she was still staring at the boy, totally perplexed. "Do you have a work permit?"

"No, but I know a lot about art."

"I've no doubt about that." Margaret scratched her head. "But I can't hire you without a permit. Why don't you talk to your parents about it—"

"Yeah, that's probably a good idea."

"You could always hang out here after school. I might be able to help you with your essay."

"Maybe," he said, looking dejected. "I'll think about it." He had his hand on the door and was pulling it open, and when he turned back to look at Margaret, Diane could see something like hurt, maybe even sadness in his eyes. "Thanks anyway."

"He does need help," Diane said when he had gone. "You were definitely right about that."

"Well, it's going to be hard to help him if he doesn't come back."

"He will." Diane smiled at Margaret and, just like the boy, headed for the door. "I hate to rush off, but I've got to get home and jot down some new plot ideas. How about *The Curious Case of the Inscrutable but Bumptious Young Upstart in the Art Gallery*?"

Margaret winked at her friend. "Don't you have a speech to work on?"

Chapter Ten

It was well past nine o'clock Monday evening when Shelley let herself into the Cove, locking the door behind her. It was almost like stepping into another world with the restaurant so dark and quiet, and the only thing moving was the reflection of the outside Christmas lights dancing over the metal and glass surfaces. It made her think of the last Christmas Eve, when Aiden and Emma were snuggled up and fast asleep in bed, and she and Dan were in the living room assembling their children's presents from Santa Claus. They kept the lights turned down low and their voices hushed, but the Christmas tree glowed, and so did they.

Growing up, her home life had been less than memorable, but that didn't matter to her any longer. She had her own family now, the loves of her life, and they were making their own memories.

After taking off her hat, coat and gloves, and slipping out of her boots and putting on a pair of comfy clogs, she headed into the kitchen, flipped on the lights, and turned one of the ovens on to 400 degrees, preheating it so she could get the shells for her cranberry cheesecake tarts baked right off the bat.

She laid her carefully planned chart for her evening's work on one of the counters and immediately set out to make her flaky dough. Without a moment to waste, Shelley took out her canister of flour and tub of shortening from the cabinet set aside strictly for her supplies. It would be so easy for one of the Cove staff to borrow from her stockpile, but the owner had put up a big and colorful sign on the outside of the cabinet door: For Lighthouse Sweet Shoppe Use Only. So far, it had worked.

The tart shells were out of the oven and cooling and so was the first batch of gingerbread men that would be sold—on consignment—at a few places in town, when she thought she heard a knock at the front door. She ignored it, thinking it might be the wind or her imagination, and continued to mix red food coloring into a portion of the icing she'd use for the gingerbread men's mouths.

Again she heard the knock and, grabbing a dish towel, wiped her hands as she peeked out of the kitchen and into the dining area, to see Margaret and Adelaide standing outside the glass front door. Rushing across the dining room, Shelley unlocked the door and let her friends in from the cold, quickly relocking the door behind them.

"I thought I saw a light on in the kitchen," Margaret said, shoving back the faux-fur-lined hood on her parka. "I'm sure we're bothering you, but I hope you have a moment."

Shelley pushed a lock of hair out of her eyes with the back of a flour-dusted hand. She definitely wasn't used to company while she worked late at night at the Cove, but Margaret and Adelaide were always welcome. "Come on back to the kitchen. I've learned to multitask, so decorating and carrying on a conversation shouldn't be a problem at all."

"Mom and I went Christmas shopping today," Adelaide said, her words slow and her eyes wide with excitement. "We got Daddy a...a..." She frowned as she looked toward her mother. "What was it?"

"A set of carving knives." Margaret chuckled. "There's a woodworking shop in Augusta and even though I'm sure Allan has every hand tool known to man, they told me the carving knives were new on the market and that they're all the rage with master furniture makers."

Shelley smiled as she filled a pastry bag with icing. "I'll have to keep the place in mind in case Dan ever gets to the point with his woodwork that he needs something like that."

"Allan tells me Dan's a natural." Margaret slipped out of her coat and helped Adelaide with hers. "He says that with a few more years of work under his belt, Dan could easily rival some of the men and women who call themselves masters."

"That would be awfully nice. Dan talks about Allan's craftsmanship all the time, and he definitely enjoys helping out with the frames."

Margaret found a chair and plopped down with a sigh. "I'm sorry that hasn't panned out quite as we expected. I mean, we've been able to give Dan *some* work, but not as much as we'd hoped."

Shelley glanced up from her work. "Margaret, please don't worry about that. Dan loves working with Allan! Even if it is a side job, it still has really helped us out."

"Thanks, Shelley. That means a lot." Margaret leaned forward. "That's not why I came by, though. Is there any chance you could bake something for me tonight? Or do you have something special already made up, something a bunch of little old ladies my age might enjoy? I should have asked you last week, but with Christmas coming, it completely slipped my mind."

Thank goodness she kept lists now, Shelley thought. As busy as life had been lately, without those lists she could easily forget her own name.

"Are you expecting company?" Shelley asked.

"A Bible study group from my church. I can't get away from the gallery on the day they meet, and since the group's rather small, they asked if we could try holding the get-togethers in the gallery. See if it works out, or if it's too disruptive. And they'd abandon me after the first meeting if I tried feeding them something I made myself."

"You could give them gingerbread men," Adelaide said. She'd picked up Shelley's rolling pin, studying the flour dusted out on the cutting board, waiting for Shelley to roll out and cut another batch of cookies.

"Have you made gingerbread men before?" Shelley asked Adelaide, watching the way Margaret's daughter handled the pin with care.

Adelaide shook her head. "Mom and I made Christmas cookies once, but they didn't taste too good."

"My fault entirely," Margaret said, a grin on her face. "I may have put in too much sugar or not enough baking powder...or something. Adelaide's being kind. They were far worse than not too good. They were horrid."

Shelley laughed as she took a ball of gingerbread dough from one of the refrigerators. "It's not that hard to make good cookies if you love what you're doing."

"I love to paint, not bake." Margaret crossed one leg and rubbed her ankle. "Though my Christmas snowballs are really good."

"I'll make up some chocolate mousse tarts for you. I've already got the shells made and it won't take all that much time to mix up the filling. I'll throw in some sugar cookies too."

"Oh, thank you, Shelley. You're a godsend."

Shelley didn't think that exactly, but He'd truly blessed her, and she liked sharing her blessings with her friends.

"Would you like to roll out some dough?" Shelley asked Adelaide after dropping the chilled dough on the floured surface.

Adelaide clapped, excited at the prospect. "Do I have to wash my hands first?"

"Yes, you do," Shelley said, turning the water on in the sink for Adelaide and setting a towel out on the counter.

When she realized she should have asked Margaret's permission first, Shelley turned to her friend. "Do you have time to let Adelaide try her hand at gingerbread cookies?"

It was late, Margaret looked exhausted, and she hoped she hadn't made a big mistake, keeping her from getting up and going straight home.

"We can stay a little longer. But I'm dying to get off my feet. I think Adelaide and I hit every store in the mall today, and, boy, were there a lot of frenzied shoppers bustling around."

They chatted away as Shelley stood behind Adelaide, arms around the young woman, and showed her how to roll out the dough. Adelaide's face beamed when she did it on her own, rolling slowly and carefully, making sure the dough was just the thickness Shelley had showed her. The young woman might not be fast, but she certainly loved what she was doing.

"What's the latest on your boiler crisis?" Margaret asked. "Allan and I noticed that you had a plumber at the house last week."

"He says if the boiler lasts the winter, he'll be shocked. Right now, thankfully, it's still working, but not up to par. I've had to put extra blankets on the beds and we're wearing long johns and sweatshirts around the house during the day."

Shelley looked up from her mixer to see Margaret yawning. Her friend was fading fast, yet Adelaide was still completely wrapped up in the process of cookie baking.

"Would you mind if Adelaide stays here with me until I'm ready to close up shop for the night?" Shelley asked Margaret. "I'll walk her home and make sure she's inside once we're all done here."

Margaret's eyes narrowed. She wasn't frowning, merely thinking, a look to which Shelley had become accustomed.

Margaret and Allan doted on their daughter and it could easily be said that they were often overprotective. Even when Adelaide helped Shelley out by watching Aiden and Emma during the day, playing on the floor with the little ones and keeping them entertained, Allan and Margaret worried. Shelley knew they loved their daughter dearly, but she had a feeling Adelaide was capable of doing more than they realized.

"Can I stay, Mom?"

At last Margaret said, "Yes, honey. Just make sure you do what Shelley tells you to do."

A few minutes later, Margaret hugged her daughter good-bye and headed through the door Shelley held open for her. "I'll send your box of goodies home with Adelaide. Sleep tight, Margaret!"

"Thanks, Shelley."

For the next two hours, Shelley showed Adelaide how to cut out gingerbread men and women and how to use a spatula to scoop them up and put them on the cookie sheet. A few ripped in half. A couple ended up on the floor. But after a while, Adelaide was working like a pro—slowly but surely, laughing and smiling with each of her successes. She was turning out to be a great helper.

Boy, what Shelley would give to have someone even half as good as Adelaide to help her around the place.

* * *

"You're up and around early this morning."

Margaret turned away from the wall of bookcases she'd been searching through when Allan stepped up beside her and brushed a kiss across her cheek. She kissed him back, a light kiss on his bearded jaw. "Somewhere around here I have some wonderful art instruction books."

"You have thousands of books, and as far as I can tell, you no longer need anything that gives you instructions on how to do anything artistic."

"They're not for me," Margaret said, continuing her search, nearly caressing the titles on each book. "They're for the young boy I told you about."

"You don't even know if you're ever going to see him again. And let's not forget that he doesn't appear to be a big fan of your work, so why on earth would you want to give him some of your books?"

Margaret sighed. How could she make Allan understand? "I might never see him again, true, but if I do, I want to give him a little something that'll show how much I care."

"That still doesn't make sense, Margaret. He was rude to you. Why should you care?"

"Because he's hurting inside. I hear it in his voice. I can see it in his eyes. I don't know what's going on in his life, but I want him to know that if he needs help, I'm here for him."

"That's what schoolteachers and guidance counselors and ministers are supposed to do."

"Allan. He might not have a minister; his teacher and guidance counselor might think everything's fine in his family."

"It just doesn't seem like something you should get involved in."

Margaret kissed her husband's cheek. "I've been involved from the moment I saw him up at the lighthouse. God drew me up to Orlean Point for a reason."

Allan smiled. "You really believe that, don't you?"

"With all my heart."

He cradled Margaret's face in his work-roughed hands. "Then you've got my support."

She always had, no matter what the situation. Margaret had learned that his questions were meant to help him understand, not to doubt her.

"So what books are we looking for?" Allan asked.

"For the life of me I can't remember the titles, but they're full of poetry and quotations and examples of painting and sketching with light and shadow. There was a time when I might have been able to recite them word for word—*Aha!* I found them."

Margaret pulled both books out of the bookcase and spun around. "You might not remember it, but you bought these for me eons ago."

Allan studied the covers good and hard. "I do remember. They were Christmas gifts, the year before our Adelaide was born." He smiled warmly, a look she'd always treasured. "You talked up a blue streak before and after we were married about how you wanted to pursue your art someday, and—"

"And you were tired of me being all words and no action."

Allan shook his head. "Not so. I merely wanted to encourage you."

"And look at me now." Margaret kissed him again. "Will you think me all kinds of awful if I give these away?"

"I'd think you all kinds of wonderful. The best gifts are the ones that are given with love."

Margaret smiled and wrapping a hand around the crook of her husband's elbow, headed to the kitchen. "Think you could make me some coffee while I dust these off and find something to wrap them in? I'm sure I have some Picasso- or Dali-inspired wrapping paper around somewhere."

Allan chuckled, obviously thinking she was going a little overboard. Maybe she was, but when the boy came in—not *if*! She needed to think positive—she wanted their visit to be something special.

Margaret took a dish towel from one of the kitchen drawers and carefully dusted each book's still-shiny jacket, remembering the Christmas morning when she'd slowly torn the wrapping away and seen the covers. It was probably silly to give away such precious gifts, but she did have the memories. And those were far more precious.

"Did you see the cookies Adelaide baked last night?" Allan asked, scooping coffee from the canister into the coffeemaker, then pointing at the plate laden with gingerbread men on the kitchen table. "Like to thought she'd never get home, but she was beaming when she came in the door and showed me what she'd made."

Margaret forgot about her books for a moment and looked at the plate full of cookies. They weren't exactly works of art. Some of the icing smiles were a bit cockeyed, a few were missing arms and legs, but they were Adelaide's masterpieces, and that made them extraspecial.

"I made them all by myself, Mom." Adelaide rubbed her pretty brown eyes when she came into the kitchen, still in her pajamas, her short, honey-colored hair all tousled. She looked at the plate of cookies, smiled brightly, then threw her arms around her mother. "Miss Shelley's the best teacher. She said I made the prettiest cookies ever."

Margaret cradled her daughter's face in her hands, tilting it up so she could see her face. "They almost look too good to eat."

Adelaide grimaced. "But you have to eat them, Mom. And Daddy too. I made them pretty, but they taste good too. I want you to see how good I am at making cookies."

"Well, I don't care if it spoils my breakfast," Allan said, picking up one of the cookies. "I'm having one right now."

"Me too," Adelaide agreed.

"Me three," Margaret chimed in.

Adelaide laughed and took a bite of gingerbread, leaving a few crumbs behind on her chin.

Margaret hated to bite off the head with the cockeyed smile, but she did. The ginger and sugar and touch of cinnamon almost melted in her mouth. "Oh my goodness, Adelaide. They're delicious."

"Wish I could be a baker like Shelley," Adelaide said. "I'd make gingerbread men all the time."

Margaret saw the passion in her daughter's face, the desire to do something meaningful in life. Maybe she shouldn't have let her stay with Shelley last night, to allow Adelaide to be filled with false hope.

Or maybe, just maybe, she and Allan had protected their daughter too much. Maybe she was capable of more than they imagined.

Chapter Eleven

The fog was so thick outside that Shelley could just barely see Prize when she let her out back at 7:00 AM, Tuesday. "Hurry it up, Prize," she called out, shivering in her nightgown, wool socks, and a zip-up sweatshirt, while she stood on the back porch waiting for Prize to do her morning duty. *This really should have been Dan's job*, she thought. He was the one who brought the dog home. She hadn't even wanted the poor thing, but that didn't mean she hadn't fallen in love with the mutt, just like everyone else in her family.

She curled her hands around a hot mug of coffee, hoping it would warm her up. It had been exceedingly cold during the night, and even though Dan had bundled Aiden and Emma up in extra warm pj's before putting them to bed, she'd found a few more warm blankets to cover them with.

At long last Prize flew up the back steps and through the kitchen door. Shelley had balked at the idea, but maybe Dan was right. They needed to put in a doggie door to avoid mornings like this. She'd hated the idea of Prize tracking in mud and snow and who knows what else, but the dog was doing it anyway. With the doggie door, maybe she could sleep in a little later, and just let Dan get his own breakfast.

Emma and Aiden were still asleep when Dan came into the kitchen in work boots, jeans, and a sweatshirt. He was fresh out of the shower, his face was cleanly shaved, and he smelled really nice. Shelley guessed that she smelled like gingerbread and cranberries, not that that was all that bad, but, oh, how she wished she'd been able to take a leisurely bath this morning. She laughed to herself as she cracked an egg into a bowl to make Dan a three-egg omelet. When the children were fully grown, or at least old enough to take care of themselves, she thought, she just might be able to take that bath and lounge all day long.

"Your thoughts seem to be a million miles away," Dan said, pouring himself a cup of coffee and doctoring it with cream and a healthy amount of sugar.

"Just dreaming of a hot bubble bath. It's been forever since I took anything more than a quick, lukewarm shower. Not that I'm complaining," she added quickly. She hated to start the mornings on a sour note. She truly wasn't dissatisfied with her life. It was really rather wonderful, all things considered.

Dan took a couple of plates down from a kitchen cabinet and set out forks and napkins. "That omelet's going to be awfully big. Do you want some?"

"Might be a good idea." Shelley laughed. "I gorged on raw cookie dough last night. I could use a bit of protein to counteract all the carbs."

"Shell," he scolded with a wry smile. "Think it was the cookie dough that kept you tossin' and turnin' all night?"

"That and the boiler." Shelley grated a handful of cheddar for the inside of the omelet, wishing she'd sautéed some mushrooms for it too, but mushrooms were on Dan's I-refuse-to-eat-it list. "If that thing doesn't give up the ghost soon so we can buy a new one, I think I'll go out of my mind."

Dan laughed. "Never in my life I thought I'd see you wanting to spend money."

"There are many things we can do without, but warmth isn't one of them. It was wicked cold during the night and—"

"Mama, Mama, Mama!"

"Oh dear," Shelley found herself uttering out loud, when Aiden burst into the kitchen. "What's wrong now?"

Aiden wrapped his arms around Shelley's legs, squeezing tight. He looked up at her with wide eyes. "I can't wait to see Santa Claus. Can we go now? Please?"

Shelley handed the spatula to Dan. "Would you finish up the omelet, please? Just flip it over once, let it cook for another minute, then it should be done."

Dan rolled his eyes—he absolutely hated to cook, even though he could grill a steak to perfection—but bumped her out from in front of the stove so he could take over. Shelley scooped Aiden up in her arms and kissed his very pink wind-chapped cheeks. "That's not until next week, honey."

"I don't want to wait till next week. I *can't* wait till next week." Shelley had never seen her little boy so adamant. "I have to give Santa my list."

Aiden couldn't write yet, but he'd prepared a list? *Hmm.* Shelley needed to know more.

"Want to share your list with me?"

"That's not the same, Mama. Santa Claus gives me toys, not you."

"Well, there are a lot of children in the world getting toys from Santa, and I imagine he's in some other countries today, tomorrow, and the next day, asking other little children what they want for Christmas. He can't be everyplace at the same time."

"God can."

Shelley laughed. "You got that right, Aiden."

Suddenly, she heard a groan from the basement. It was deep and loud, mixed with a few clanks, and then it was silent.

Shelley walked into the kitchen. Dan had a forkful of cheesy omelet halfway to his mouth. They stared at each other, and Shelley said with little remorse, "I think it just died."

"Either that, or this is the calm before the storm."

Dan was right.

All of a sudden the boiler rumbled. The wood floor beneath Shelley's feet shimmied, and then smoke oozed into the kitchen through the narrow space at the bottom of the basement door.

"Mama! Mama!" Aiden shrieked. "The house is on fire!"

"No, Aiden," Dan said, scooping up his son. "It's the boiler putting up a fuss. That's all."

Shelley opened the basement door to run downstairs, and the boiler coughed, spewing even more smoke in Shelley's direction. "Oh dear." The inevitable had finally happened.

★ ★ ★

"It was a dark and stormy night."

Heavens no! I can't start a book or even a chapter with those words. Diane chastised herself for trying to take the easy way out as she sought a vivid opening line for Chapter 10. She'd been up since five o'clock and it was now a little past nine, and somehow she'd only managed to write, well, nothing. She absolutely loved to write. There was nothing else she'd rather do for a living and felt truly blessed that she'd sold the first book she'd ever written and was now working on the second. But there were days, like today, when she just couldn't concentrate.

"Should we go into the kitchen and fix some breakfast?" she asked Rocky, who'd been lying at her feet, barely moving all morning. She felt his head jerk up and a moment later his dark brown eyes and wet black nose appeared just over her knees.

She stood at the kitchen window and looked at the mixture of sleet and snow bearing down on the trees out back. Her home, like Shelley's, sat at the very end of Newport Avenue, spitting distance from where the waves crashed onto the shore—not that she'd ever tested the distance in such a fashion.

Switching on the CD player, she sang along with "God Rest Ye Merry Gentlemen." She took out a saucepan to make herself some oatmeal with some sugar-free syrup and a spoonful of real butter. She tried to get her mind back on her book, to that chapter opener which so often hung her up.

"How does this sound?" she asked Rocky, as she waited for the water to boil. *"They found Evelyn Vandermeer's footprints in the sand. They were spotted at the back door of her cottage and tracked down to the beach, then along the shoreline, and right up to the lighthouse door. There her footsteps stopped. Disappeared. But Evelyn Vandermeer, either living or dead, was nowhere to be found."*

Rocky's tailed wagged back and forth, dusting the tile floor. He peered up at her with a "not bad" expression. He'd probably heard better lines for starting a chapter, but she'd go with those to begin with. She could always tighten it up later.

"I really have to buckle down," she said as she stirred in the oatmeal and continued to stir so it wouldn't scorch the bottom of the pan. "I have deadlines to meet and a speech to write"—although she didn't want to think about that—"and with Christmas coming and all the shopping I still have to do, plus parties to attend, not to mention my volunteer duties at church, I have to set a certain number of pages to write each day."

Rocky continued to look at her, completely devoted no matter what she had to say.

The oatmeal was on the verge of boiling over when she heard the knock at the front door. "And I really should ignore that knock, eat breakfast, and get back to work, but you know me, Rocky. I'll answer the door and get caught up in a conversation with whoever's there."

Diane turned off the burner, put a lid on her pot of oatmeal, and hoped it would still be hot when she returned. If it turned lumpy, that would be fine. She'd always liked lumpy oatmeal.

"I'm so sorry to bother you!" Diane had opened the front door to find a shivering Shelley clad in pajamas, sweatshirt, and snow boots, her face the picture of devastation. "Our boiler finally gave up the ghost and it's freezing inside. I was wondering, could I possibly borrow a little bit of your wood? We have a fireplace, and we'll just have to make do with it until the boiler's repaired, but right now, I don't have time to run out for wood."

"Come in out of the cold," Diane said.

Shelley stepped in. "But only for a second. Aiden and Emma are by themselves and I need to get back now. Just a couple of pieces will do."

Diane rushed to her fireplace, bundled up at least half a dozen logs, hoping they wouldn't be too heavy for Shelley to carry, and took them back to the door. "I can bring more over later," Diane offered.

"Dan said he'd pick some up when he takes his lunch break. This should be fine for now." Shelley turned into the flurry of snow. "Thanks a bunch," she hollered over her shoulder as she made her way back home.

A few hours later, lumpy oatmeal fully enjoyed by both Diane and Rocky, and with a cup of steaming tea sitting by her computer, Diane had completed three new pages of her book and the opening line of her speech. "Hello, my name is Diane Spencer. I'm a writer." Opening lines for a speech were every bit as hard as for a book.

Stretching, she looked out the window and noticed that the sleet and snow had finally stopped and a speck of blue sky was peering through the clouds. It might turn into a pretty day after all.

At least for her.

She heard the siren before she saw the old red fire engine careering up the street. Her street. Newport Avenue. *Please, Lord,* she prayed, *let this only be a fire drill. It's Christmastime. No one needs a fire in their home or, even worse, sickness or injury.*

The engine stopped in front of Shelley's, and Diane felt as if her heart might tear in two. Three firefighters barreled out of the fire truck and rushed to Shelley's front door. Diane could see Shelley standing inside, her face, her clothes... "Oh no!"

Diane grabbed her coat and boots from the hall closet. As quickly as she could, she shoved her feet into the boots, pulled on the parka, and zipped it up while running out the front door, leaving Rocky safely inside. One of the firefighters tried to keep her outside, but she insisted on going into Shelley's home.

"Everyone's fine inside, ma'am," a tall fireman said. His face was blackened with soot, which didn't bode well for the condition of the house.

"I'll just check it out for myself, thank you," she said, trying not to get testy with the man who was only doing his job.

She skirted around the fireman, past the hose that they'd run inside, and found Shelley covered in soot, only like the man outside.

"Where are Aiden and Emma?" were the first words out of Diane's mouth. She was sick with fear that they had been breathing in the smoke that filled the house.

"Shelley!"

Dan ran into the house. He wasn't wearing a coat or boots or a hat and he had to be somewhere close to frozen, but he grabbed Shelley and pulled her into his arms. "Are you all right? Where are the kids? Are they okay?"

"I got them bundled up and out back as soon as the fire started. They're with one of the firefighters." Shelley started to cry. "It's my fault. I put the wood in the fireplace with kindling and paper. I even remembered to open the flue, but I haven't had the chimney cleaned in years and not long after I lit the fire, the house filled with smoke and sparks started flying."

"It's not your fault," Dan said, holding Shelley tight. "As long as you and the kids are all right. That's the only thing that matters."

"You two stay here with the firefighters," Diane said, brushing a few ashes off Shelley's tear-streaked cheek. "I'll take Aiden and Emma to my place and you come over when you're finished here. I'll make some soup and sandwiches and..." Diane looked around the house, at a pair of half-burned curtains lying on the floor and walls streaked with smoke. "It may be a couple of days before you can live here without smelling smoke, so come stay at my house for a few days. Until your house is cleaned up."

"We couldn't do that, Diane." Tears still slid down Shelley's face, leaving a pale streak on her face. Her voice was choked with emotion. "There are four of us. Plus a dog. And we're noisy and—"

"I insist." Diane smiled. "Don't argue, just come on over in a little while."

Diane didn't wait for more protests. The children were outside in the snow. They were probably scared and cold and they no doubt needed a warm and comfy place to play. Shelley could have called her mother-in-law for help, but Diane could just imagine the elder Mrs. Bauer scolding Shelley for not giving the chimney a yearly cleaning. And then, even though she meant well, she'd pick on Shelley's every move if she and Dan and the kids moved in with them.

There was really no other choice, Diane decided, as she scooped Emma up and held out her hand to the little boy, telling him she was taking all of them to her house for a little while. "Prize too?" Aiden asked.

"Definitely Prize too. She and Rocky will have a great time together."

She hoped.

Her writing could wait. The speech, however, was a different matter.

Chapter Twelve

"What on earth is happening?" Margaret stood in the gallery, the phone tight against her ear. "I couldn't miss the sirens or the fire engine heading down our street. Please tell me our house is okay."

"It's Shelley's place." Allan told her about the boiler and the dirty chimney. "Diane told Shelley and Dan they could move in with her until they get the house cleaned up."

"But they're all okay? No one was hurt? There isn't any significant damage?"

"No, no. Shelley may have a sore throat from inhaling smoke, but the little ones are fine. Dan and I were in the shop when we heard the siren. Didn't take more than a few seconds for the two of us to get outside, and when Dan saw the firefighters rushing into his house, I thought he was going to have a heart attack. Never saw a man run so fast in my life. I'm just glad Adelaide was at the community center. She would have been worried sick."

"Is there anything I can do?"

"I'm whipping up a chicken casserole to take over to Diane's after I pick up Adelaide. We'll probably bake some cookies too."

"But what about me, Allan? There must be something I can do."

"Enjoy your get-together with the Bible study group, sell a painting or two, and don't worry about anything around here."

"Me worry?"

Allan chuckled, just as she'd expected. He knew that she'd always worry about her friends.

The women in her Bible study group had barely moved an inch while Margaret was on the phone, and they peppered her with questions when Margaret sat down with them, clutching her Bible tightly.

"There must be something we can do," Rita Candleford said. She took a journal from her oversized purse and began scribbling notes as Margaret filled them in on all the details.

"I'm sure the ladies from her church will pitch in to help out," Margaret said. "It would be nice to do something, but maybe it would be best if we wait a couple of days and see what Shelley needs."

"I couldn't agree more," Pamela Morgan said. "My sister had a fire in her home a few years ago and you wouldn't believe the amount of cleaning we had to do, even after the insurance company sent out a crew to deal with the damage." Pamela shook her head. "Such a shame, and so close to Christmas."

Snow was falling lightly by the time Margaret stood at the doorway and waved good-bye to her friends. She thought about closing the gallery for the rest of the day, but she'd hoped against hope that the boy from the lighthouse would drop by. Just in case he did, she'd set aside a chocolate tart and a couple of cookies.

After making a quick call to Allan, she set up an easel in the main portion of the gallery, a place where she could see anyone coming or going through the front door, or peeking through the big picture window. With a stool set close to her canvas, she settled down to paint, dabbing her brush into the various shades of green, yellow, red, and blue on her palette.

Looking through the places on the front window where she hadn't painted her mural, she could see the lobster-trap tree she'd helped to build and decorate last week. It was a perfect model and the centerpiece for her latest painting.

She'd painted the tree in short brushstrokes of bright colors that emphasized the light upon the tree. Monet and Renoir were the masters of impressionism; she was a novice, but she was giving it her all, letting her creativity flow freely, completely unhindered. With photographs of her friends scattered about a corkboard set up on another easel, she went to work painting the crowd who'd helped with the tree. She'd never been much of a portrait painter, preferring landscape and still life, but found the impressionist style made it rather easy to create the faces of friends carrying traps and hanging the colorful buoys painted with snowflakes, candy canes, and snowmen.

She rose and stood back to take a good look at her work. She smiled. But when she looked at the inlaid wood clock that Allan had designed for her, she noticed how much time had slipped by. It was nearly three o'clock. School must have gotten out at least half an hour ago. If the boy was going to stop by, no doubt he would have done so by now.

But who was she kidding? He was just a kid and she was old enough to be his grandmother, maybe even his great grandmother. When she was his age, she would never have stopped by an old lady's art gallery to sit and talk, not when she could be off playing with friends.

No doubt that's what he was doing now—sledding, ice skating, having a snowball fight.

And no doubt she was becoming a foolish old woman, thinking the boy needed her help.

When the phone rang, she raced across the gallery. A customer who had bought one of her Seal Island puffin paintings was calling to ask for something similar. "Could you e-mail me a photo of a few different paintings?" Mr. Cabot asked in his British accent. "Oil or watercolor would be fine. Something small that'll fit in a nook. Then once you've sent the pics, my wife or I will send you an order."

"I'll get them to you as soon as possible," Margaret said. "Tonight, for sure."

Something that'll fit in a nook. Margaret walked back to her studio to sort through a number of unframed puffin paintings. She found several that were perfect, but how on earth could she take pictures to send via e-mail when her digital camera was at home?

She tried calling Allan and got no answer, then decided to call Diane's, since Allan had said he was going to take her a chicken casserole to help feed her unexpected guests.

Grabbing the office phone, Margaret quickly punched in Diane's phone number. "Hope I didn't catch you in the middle of typing a pithy line of dialogue, something you'll never again be able to recapture," she said when she heard Diane's voice.

"I've given up writing for the day." Diane sounded harried.

"Everything okay?"

"You heard about the fire at Shelley's?"

"Heard about it. Saw the fire engines too. That's the last thing poor Shelley needs, considering all the other trials and tribulations she and Dan have gone through lately."

In the background, drowning out whatever it was Diane was trying to say, Margaret heard barking and a child crying. "Sorry, Margaret, this isn't a good time. I'm taking care of Aiden and Emma while Shelley and Dan do an assessment for their insurance company. And then…" Margaret heard Diane's sigh. "They're moving in with me for a couple of days."

"That's what Allan told me." She wondered how Diane could write with the added noise of a young family and an extra dog in the house. "I'm so sorry I bothered you, Diane, but I was trying to reach Allan—"

"He's in the kitchen. Hang on a second and I'll get him for you."

"No, no, don't bother. Would you just ask him to bring my digital camera to the gallery?"

"I'd be happy to."

"And while you're at it, if you have an extra spare second or two, you could put a bug in his ear that I'd absolutely love a new and ultrafancy digital camera for Christmas."

At long last Diane chuckled. "Your wish is my command."

If only it was that easy, Margaret thought, as she hung up the phone and went back to searching for just the right puffin. She found a ten-by-ten watercolor, one of her first serious attempts to paint something abstract. It wasn't exactly Kandinsky, the artist the boy from the lighthouse thought was totally awesome, so much better than Renoir or Margaret Hoskins, but it wasn't bad, even if she did say so herself.

She set the painting aside and found a few extras that would complement the puffins—a frothy wave; a starfish lazing in a tide pool; a pair of whales waltzing in a deep blue sea. Which would he like the best? Margaret smiled at the thought that popped into her head. He just might like all of them.

Lost in thoughts of getting a fairly nice order from a man she hoped would remain a good customer, she almost didn't hear the tinkling of the bells on the gallery door. She pressed her hands against the small of her back, working out the kink that had settled in while bending over the paintings, then peered around a display wall expecting to see Allan with her camera.

But it wasn't Allan; it was the boy.

The aches and pains in her back were suddenly forgotten. She even smiled.

"Hello there." Margaret walked into the main part of the gallery, watching the boy stomp his boots on the rug just inside the door, knocking off a bit of snow. "It's nice to see you again."

"I can't stay long." He looked around the gallery, his blue eyes bright in spite of the dark circles beneath them.

She welcomed him in and held out her hand. "I'm Margaret Hoskins."

He hesitated, his eyes narrowing as he gave her an appraising look. At long last he shook her hand, his chilled fingers barely touching hers for just a second before he pulled away. "I'm Caleb Wadsworth," he said finally. "Like Henry Wadsworth Longfellow. You've heard of him, haven't you?"

She had to be careful what she said. There was no doubt in her mind that Caleb Wadsworth thought she could easily be as ancient as his namesake. "As a matter of fact, I have. He's long been one of my favorite poets."

"Some people say he was a hack."

Margaret laughed. "I try not to listen to what random people have to say. I trust my own instincts. "

"Yeah, that's what I think too."

He slid out of his backpack and set it on the floor near the door. Then he tucked his hands in the pockets of his jacket and wandered around, looking at one painting after another.

"So," Margaret said, standing far enough away so he'd feel comfortable roaming, "are you related to Longfellow?"

Caleb glanced back at her and shrugged. "A great-uncle."

He must have spent a good five minutes in total silence, ignoring the glassware and jewelry in and on the display cases. If he wasn't so young, if he wasn't wearing battered boots, jeans with holes in the knees, and a bright orange parka that had seen better days, he could have passed for a New York art connoisseur, given the way he moved, the way he tilted his head one way and another, taking in the paintings from different vantages.

"Would you like some cookies?" Margaret asked. "I have some cocoa I can heat up in the microwave too."

"No..." The word drifted off, and then he tilted his head in Margaret's direction. "Well, I'd like it if it's free."

Margaret smiled, noticing that it wasn't just his parka that was worn. His knitted cap had a hole on one side. For all she knew, that could have been the current fashion, the "in" thing. Still, she imagined the awful truth was that his folks couldn't afford a new coat or even a cap each winter, that he wore hand-me-downs or thrift shop relics. Of course, what he lacked in fashion, and possibly even manners, he seemed to make up for with a good education, or at least an inherent amount of smarts.

"Would you like marshmallows in your cocoa? That's the way I make it for my daughter Adelaide."

"Yes, thank you."

Ah, so he did have manners after all. Maybe he'd been trying to hide them in an attempt to look cool.

And maybe she was trying to analyze him far too much.

There were so many questions she wanted to ask him, but she didn't. Something told her that if she tried to invade his privacy, he'd bolt.

"I'll just be back in my office for a minute or two."

He nodded, his eyes intent on the paintings.

When she came out of her office with a tray bearing a mug of cocoa with marshmallows melting on top and a plate of her Christmas snowball cookies, the gallery was empty. Had he sneaked out while she was fussing around with the microwave?

She heard a noise in the studio and found him in the nook at the back of the gallery, fingering her brushes.

"You're more than welcome to try your hand at painting with my oils or my watercolors," she said, setting the tray atop her worktable.

"That's okay. I just wanted to see if you used good ones or something cheap."

"They're not exactly the best money can buy, but they're definitely not cheap. I use top-notch canvas too."

"Do you stretch and prime it yourself?"

Margaret nodded. She picked up a cookie from the plate and nibbled at the edge, hoping Caleb would follow her lead. She wanted to ask how he knew so much about painting, but he needed to volunteer that information himself. She was a fast learner, and she now knew she had to take Caleb slow and easy.

"You have a real talent, Caleb." She hoped flattery wouldn't scare him off. "Your sketch of the lighthouse was wonderful, so much better than I could have done with pencil or charcoal."

"I like drawing. I wouldn't be any good if I didn't."

"Your parents must be so proud of you."

The frown that crossed his face told Margaret she'd said the wrong thing.

"I've gotta go." He looked longingly at the cookies, the tart, and the glass of milk.

"Hang on a minute and I'll get a bag to put the cookies in."

She forced herself not to sigh when she went into her back room. She found a plastic container for the tart and a bag to put it and the cookies in and— She heard the bells on the front door, and peered out into the gallery just in time to see Caleb and his bright orange parka outside, running past her big picture window.

Margaret blew out a puff of air. She'd managed to learn his name, but nothing else. She had such a sense that she was meant to help him. But how, if he wouldn't talk to her?

Heading back to her studio to grab another one of the cookies or maybe even that last chocolate tart, she found an empty plate and a half-full glass of milk. Poor kid must have been famished. Next time he came she'd have something a little more substantial in the fridge.

And she certainly hoped there'd be a next time.

Chapter Thirteen

Beverly stood beneath one of the immensely tall archways inside her Augusta home, taking a good long look at a few of the paintings her late husband had commissioned and had hung here, there, and everywhere. Had she ever liked the style that he'd loved so much? What had he called it? Metaphysical art? Most of it was dreamlike paintings of visionary worlds that left her cold. Give her one of Margaret's country sunflowers or seascapes any day.

Why am I keeping this house or the paintings? It had never really felt like a home, not when it was always kept so immaculate—no shoes kicked off inside the front door, no hat rack in the entry or a table where she could drop her keys, purse, and the mail. Will may have designed and built it for them before their wedding, but it had been his design, not hers. It was a showplace where they'd entertained his clients. Now it was merely a place to spend the night when she wasn't telecommuting from Marble Cove.

She should sell it. Get out from under the mortgage payments and the need to pay for a gardener in spring, summer, and fall. The expensive custom furniture still filled the space, but Will's presence and his pride in his home was just a memory. And now, the traces of perfume she noticed in the kitchen and downstairs guest bath belonged to one of her co-workers who'd been living here, keeping an eye on the place until she decided what she wanted to do next.

This house had never felt like home. Home had become Marble Cove. Home was her newfound friends.

Beverly lifted the box filled with some of the Christmas ornaments she and Will had collected during their marriage—the only reason she'd stopped by the house—locked up tight, climbed into her car, and started the engine. Then she turned her mind to a man she'd thought about on her hour-long drive to Augusta this morning: Edward Maker.

The Edward Maker. The man who'd carved "I'm sorry. E.M." into the concrete base of Orlean Point Light.

She drove through Augusta, heading for the older neighborhood where Edward Maker lived. She, Diane, Margaret, and Shelley had learned so much about Edward Maker in the past few months, but there was still so much she wanted to know, especially why he had carved "I'm sorry" into the lighthouse, and what he was sorry about.

The sun was just a sliver of orange on the horizon when she pulled her car to a stop in front of Edward Maker's home. The yard that had been so beautifully landscaped when she and her friends were here before was now blanketed in white. He had a simple wreath on the door and an electric candle graced each window—festive but not fussy.

Bundled up in her best camel-colored wool coat and knee-high boots in almost the same color, Beverly tugged the hood over her head and strolled up the flagstone walkway that appeared to have recently been shoveled free of snow. She still found it hard to believe that her own father had grown up in this house, and that he and Edward Maker had known each other when they were kids.

The coincidence was amazing.

She and her father had taken a trip to Augusta together after Mr. Maker had refused to let Beverly and her friends into the house. It was her father who'd gotten Edward Maker to open his front door to Beverly, a woman he'd decided was a busybody, a woman who, he'd said, wanted nothing more than to dig into long-ago and should-be-forgotten history.

He'd been reluctant to let her and her father into his home, but he'd finally given in. They'd even managed to wheedle some information out of him, learning that he'd lived in the lighthouse for a couple of years when he was a kid. It was Edward who'd told Beverly about the secret door at the back of the lighthouse. It was a way for people to go in and out without being seen, but she'd wondered why that was necessary. He hadn't explained, in spite of her prodding. She hoped this visit with Mr. Maker would provide answers to some of the many questions she had.

Beverly pushed back her hood before knocking on the front door. Inside she could hear music playing faintly. It sounded like Mozart. It seemed forever before she heard footsteps on the hardwood floor and she nearly jumped back in shock when the door flew open.

"I thought you'd never get here and I've been worried half out of my—" Mr. Maker frowned. "Oh, sorry. I was expecting someone else."

She smiled slowly at the elderly man with a full head of salt-and-pepper hair. "Hello, Mr. Maker. Remember me? Beverly Wheeland-Parker. Harold Wheeland's daughter?"

He nodded.

"I had to come into Augusta for a meeting today and thought I'd stop by to say hello."

His thick white brows nearly knitted together as he stared at her as if she were the Creature from the Black Lagoon, or worse, someone trying to butt into his business. Fortunately his demeanor softened. "Yes, I remember you." He sighed. "Come in. Please."

"I brought you some cookies from my friend's bakery. You remember Shelley Bauer, don't you? She was with me and two of my other friends the first time I dropped by."

He grinned slightly. "Was she the older one, the younger one, or the one in the middle?"

"The young one. Pretty and petite with long blonde hair."

"I remember her." He looked down at the pink box Beverly was holding. "Cookies, huh?"

Diane nodded. "Shelley makes the best cookies ever. I've brought you a variety—oatmeal raisin, white chocolate macadamia nut, triple chocolate, and a few of her special gingerbread men."

"I would have invited you in even without the cookies, but thank you." He opened the door wide, letting her in to the hundred-plus-year-old two-story house. The honey-colored hardwood floors and the scent of lemon oil and what had to be freshly perked coffee were inviting, and the moment he closed the door behind her she was enveloped by the warmth she could feel coming from the fire burning in the hearth.

Mr. Maker took the pink Lighthouse Sweet Shoppe box from Beverly, opened the top, and inhaled the multitude of scents. Beverly could smell cinnamon, chocolate, and cloves, and her stomach growled.

"You go have a seat in the living room and I'll get you a cup of coffee and put these cookies on a plate. You're so darn skinny you'll blow away with the first wind if I don't get some food into you."

"Want some help?"

"Nah, you just make yourself comfortable. I'll be right back."

Beverly smiled as she tucked her gloves in her coat pocket, took it off, and hung it on the old coat stand, then wandered into the immaculate living room, admiring the simplicity of the built-in hutch and furniture.

"Cream and sugar?" she heard Mr. Maker holler from the kitchen.

"Just black, please."

He chuckled. "Should have known you wouldn't put anything fattening in your coffee."

The music on the radio shifted to a Bach fugue, and she wandered about the room, looking at beautiful photos that had been enlarged, placed behind black or white mats, and elegantly framed. They were everywhere, on walls and tabletops and the fireplace mantle, tucked into a garland of fresh, fragrant evergreens and pinecones. How odd that she hadn't noticed them the last time she was here. Of course, Edward Maker had seemed far more leery then; he hadn't left her and her dad alone for more than a moment.

She lifted one of the frames and studied the image of the bright orange sun sinking behind the Egyptian sphinx, which stood all powerful and magnificent, casting its shadow over a lone camel and its rider.

"My grandson took that." Mr. Maker set the cookies on the coffee table and placed a mug of coffee on an occasional table between two brown leather armchairs. "Travels the world taking pictures. Not a bad job, if you ask me. Sure is a lot better than working in a cannery."

"You worked in a cannery?"

"Yep," he laughed, his pale blue eyes twinkling, "for one day, until the big boss found out a nine-year-old was unloading boats. My mother, on the other hand, put up with the stench of packing sardines for a couple of years."

"Brave woman."

"She would have done anything to keep a roof over our heads and food in my belly." He put a few cookies on a napkin for himself and lowered himself into one of the sturdy chairs. "Those were tough years. I knew she hated it, but she never complained. Went to work every day with a smile on her face. When the war started and guys were heading overseas, she went to work building ships. She was a swell mechanic—a lot of women were—and that's the job she loved. In fact, she—"

A knock sounded at the door.

"That must be my grandson now. He was supposed to be here an hour ago."

Mr. Maker pushed out of the chair. He moved like a man half his age. "Like to think you'd never get here," he muttered, the same phrase he'd used when he opened the door to Beverly.

"My stop at the camera store took longer than I imagined—"

Beverly could barely comprehend anything else the man said, not when she recognized the voice. It was Jeff Mackenzie! She looked at the framed photographs that surrounded her, and the connection was made.

"Beverly?"

She spun around in her chair and couldn't miss Jeff's look of surprise that slowly morphed into pleasure.

Her own surprise became a soft yet hesitant smile. "Hello." One secret was revealed. Jeff was Mr. Maker's grandson. That was the reason for his interest in the lighthouse.

"You two know each other?" Mr. Maker asked, the sound of his shoes heavy on the beautifully polished hardwood floor as he made his way back to his chair.

Jeff nodded. "We met a long time ago, and ran into each other again a couple of months back in Marble Cove."

Mr. Maker grinned as he looked from Jeff to Beverly then back to Jeff again. "You don't say."

Beverly wasn't about to touch that comment. There was nothing between her and Jeff; there never would be. They were becoming friends, maybe, but that was it.

Jeff shrugged out of his parka and hung it on the coat rack. He wore a pair of dark blue jeans, lace-up hiking boots, and a navy blue and forest green plaid flannel shirt over a white turtleneck.

He reached for one of Shelley's deep and dark chocolate cookies, broke off an edge, and popped it into his mouth. "Did you make these?"

"They're Shelley's." She laughed lightly. "Mine would be made with wheat flour and sugar substitute..."

"And no doubt taste like cardboard." Mr. Maker chuckled. "My doctor tells me I should cut back on sweets and fat, eat more fiber and lean meat, but I'm in perfect health and my blood tests prove it. At my age, I'm not about to change my habits."

Jeff sat in an antique rocker, pulling it up close to the coffee table and the plate of cookies. He looked from Beverly, to his grandfather, then back to Beverly, curiosity written clearly on his face. "So how do the two of you know each other?"

"It's a long story," Beverly said.

"Not that long," Mr. Maker corrected. "She and her friends and even her dad, who I knew when I lived in Marble Cove back in the dark ages, have been hounding me for information about Orlean Point Light."

"If we've been hounding you," Beverly said, "I'm truly sorry."

"*Hounding* is a favorite word of his." Jeff picked up an oatmeal cookie this time. "When I was a kid, I was always hounding or badgering him, but truth be told, I think he rather liked it."

"He was a good kid, but a nuisance at times." Mr. Maker laughed, and she could easily hear and see the love he had for his grandson. "Jeff's been hounding me a lot lately too. For the life of me, I don't know why that lighthouse is so fascinating all of a sudden. It was decommissioned half a century ago. As for all those reports of lights shining down from the tower—they're nothing but bunk. There are no lights—"

"There *are* lights, Grandpa. I showed you the pictures I took. I told you that I didn't see the lights myself, but they appeared in the photographs."

"I've seen the lights too, Mr. Maker, not just in Jeff's photos, but with my own eyes," Beverly said, amazed that she'd so easily admitted the truth in front of Jeff and his grandfather. "As much as I've wanted to believe they're nothing more than a figment of my imagination, I'm sure they're real."

"Impossible." Mr. Maker was adamant. "Those strange lights are nothing more than a legend. I wouldn't be surprised if someone made them the focus of a horror movie one of these days."

"It's not just the lights that are strange," Beverly said, "but the lighthouse itself. I never thought I'd get caught up in trying to solve a mystery, but there's so much my friends and I would like to know."

"It's history." He made a gesture as if pushing away the thought. The easy demeanor she'd seen earlier was fading, and Beverly wondered how much longer she—and Jeff—could keep up the questions before he got up and walked out of the room.

"It might be history, Grandpa, but it's history that you've kept bottled up inside." Jeff balanced his elbows on his knees, leaning forward, giving his grandfather a deep, curiosity-filled stare. "My mom told me she was sure something bad happened to you when you were a kid. She tried talking to Grandma about it, but either Grandma didn't know what secrets you were hiding, or she wouldn't talk about it."

"I'm not hiding anything."

"Yet you carved the words *I'm sorry* into the lighthouse." There. Beverly had put that card on the table. Maybe now she could find out what a very young Edward Maker had been sorry about.

Jeff glanced at Beverly. "'I'm sorry'? I thought I'd inspected every square inch of the lighthouse. I've seen other things scribbled there, but—"

"It's there," Beverly said. "'I'm sorry. E.M.' That's what led me—and Margaret, Shelley, and Diane—to your grandfather."

Jeff faced his grandfather again. "Did you carve that into the lighthouse?"

Mr. Maker pushed out of his chair. He crossed the room, opened the bottom drawer in an old rolltop desk, and pulled out what looked like a photo album. He sat back down in the middle of the sofa and asked Jeff and Beverly to join him. When they were settled on either side of him, he opened the album.

He tapped a finger on the first picture. "That's me and my dad at the lighthouse back in 1933. That's the year he got hired as the light keeper. I'd just turned five when we moved in, and thought I'd died and gone to heaven. There were a lot of things for a kid to do around that place, running up and down the stairs, staying up late at night helping to make sure the light didn't burn out."

"How long were you there?" Jeff asked.

"Two years. Could have been longer, but..."

"But what, Grandpa?"

He flipped the page in the photo album. "That's my mom. Bless her heart, I don't know how she put up with my antics."

"You were a bundle of trouble?" Beverly asked, not finding that all that difficult to believe.

"Not as much as my dad. He'd get drunk, and when he drank he got angry, never at my mom, but at me."

"He hit you?" Jeff asked, frowning.

Mr. Maker shook his head. "Nah, nothing like that, but when he lost his temper the words would fly, and I'd hide, or head into town and fall asleep in one of the churches, Old First usually, since their doors were always unlocked. There are a lot of caves in the cliffs beneath the lighthouse too. They could be cold and damp and scary, but not as scary as my dad."

"How'd he get the liquor?" Jeff asked. "Wasn't Prohibition going on?"

"Yes, but where there's a will there's a way, and Dad always found a way to get his hands on booze, usually bootlegged. If he hadn't been drinking, he wouldn't have lost his job, and if he hadn't lost his job, we wouldn't have had to leave Marble Cove. My mom might not have ended up working in the canneries, either. But like I said, that's history."

Mr. Maker closed the photo album and set it on the coffee table. He rose and stretched the kinks out of his back. "I've talked more tonight than I have in ages and now—I'm heading to bed."

"It's early, Grandpa. Why don't I take the three of us out to dinner?"

"It might be early, but I'm getting old and right now I'm tired. You two can look at that album all you want, go out to dinner, or raid my fridge. But I'm bushed."

He didn't shake Beverly's hand, say good night, or even look her way before climbing the stairs and disappearing from sight. They'd asked too many questions. They should have let him reveal more in his own good time. But they wouldn't learn anything more tonight.

"Want to have dinner with me?" Jeff asked. "There's a good Italian place a few blocks from here."

She did. They could talk about all that his grandfather had told them. They could talk about the lights and Jeff's photography, but she looked at her watch and then out the window, where fat snowflakes were falling. "I really need to get back to Marble Cove. Father's expecting me home tonight and with the snow coming down and—"

Jeff laughed. "You know, you could just say no."

She smiled. "Could I have a rain check?"

"Definitely. That's a lot better than no."

Beverly went to the entryway and took her coat from the rack. "There's still a lot your grandfather's holding back."

"At least we managed to put a small crack in that wall he's built up around himself. A little more prodding might do the trick." He held Beverly's coat for her as she slipped her arms into the sleeves. "I'll be back in Marble Cove next week. I'm not sure when, but I'll call you. We could go to that lobster place for dinner."

"Or you could come by the house and join Father and me. I'm sure he'd like to hear about your travels and photography."

Jeff looked a touch downcast, but that couldn't be helped. She hadn't known him all that long. She felt anxious when she was alone with him. Uncomfortable. And she didn't want him expecting more from her than she wanted to give.

Chapter Fourteen

"What are you looking for?" Allan asked, leaning over Margaret as she sat at the computer, still wearing her flannel pajamas, with her first cup of morning coffee sitting beside her. She stared at a photograph of the artist Longfellow Wadsworth, a square-jawed man with piercing blue eyes and shaggy blond hair, who seemed to be looking through her, even in a two-dimensional photograph.

"Just trying to find any information I can on Caleb Wadsworth's family, and I ran across this artist—Longfellow Wadsworth. I'm not sure if he's any relation, but I wouldn't be surprised. They have the same look about them, plus the blue eyes and blond hair. This man's the right age and, well, I wouldn't be at all surprised if Caleb got his artistic talent from one of his parents, or both."

"You could ask Caleb."

"Easier said than done. He's not all that forthcoming about anything in his life and I'm sure he's trying to cover something up. Maybe something about his family."

"Why do you say that?"

"I made one simple statement about his parents when he showed up at the gallery yesterday, said they must be so proud of him, and he clammed up and said he had to leave."

"Maybe you're reading too much into all of this. He's a young kid; he probably has to be home at a certain time to keep his folks from worrying. Or, let's face it, he might have had something far more exciting to do than hang around the gallery."

"You could be right." She took a sip of her coffee. "But you know my instincts are usually spot-on. And if I don't keep digging but then find out that he's being abused, or he and his family are homeless, or something bad, I'll never forgive myself."

Allan kissed the top of her head. "What's with you and all the sleuthing? First the lighthouse, then the lights, and now a little boy. And I don't recall you ever reading mysteries before, but lately you've put your nose in one every night when we go to bed."

"I'm expanding my horizons where reading's concerned. And I have to admit that having a mystery writer living next door makes me see a mystery in nearly everything I look at."

"Have you found anything mysterious or odd about this man you think might be Caleb's dad?"

"Well, he was quite a hit in New York art circles for a year or two. And not that it's the least bit odd, but he was born and raised in Maine, and his age seems around right to have a child Caleb's age."

Allan chuckled, the sound filling the room. "I hate to remind you of this, my dear, but even *I* could have a child Caleb's age."

"Oh, Allan!" Margaret fussed at her husband. "Humor me a little, won't you? I don't know for sure that this man is Caleb's dad, but he certainly could be. He has that same scruffy look about him and"—she tapped the monitor with the tip of her fingernail—"I can just imagine this man having freckles, just like Caleb, when he was younger. But I haven't told you the most intriguing part."

"Which is?"

"He disappeared."

"Ah, I see. The Invisible Man."

Husbands! They could be so exasperating at times.

"I seriously doubt he concocted some magic elixir in a secret laboratory, but it does appear he dropped off the face of the earth."

"No one knows why?" Allan asked, somewhat serious at last. "No one knows where he went?"

"I haven't found any whys or wherefores yet, but I've read the reviews on one of his showings, and he must have been very good. Manhattan galleries were clamoring for his work—oh, if only I could be so fortunate."

"Maybe he 'disappeared' for the publicity. A little notoriety never hurt an artist of any kind. Fewer paintings for sale could drive up the price of an original."

Margaret looked up at her husband. She grinned. "Maybe I should disappear for a while."

Allan laughed. "I'd miss you something awful."

The ringing phone drew Margaret away from the computer. When she heard Shelley's voice on the other end, a heaviness wrapped around her heart. "I was so, so sorry to hear about the fire. I hope there wasn't a lot of damage."

"The curtains are history, and the place smells like smoke, but thank God, no one was hurt and we came out of it pretty much unscathed."

"Is there anything I can do to help?"

"I think Dan and I have it under control, thanks, and already so many friends—like Allan and people from church—have stopped by Diane's with casseroles and desserts." She laughed lightly. "Tell Allan that we feasted on his chicken casserole last night, and it was absolutely delicious. He offered to bring even more, bless his heart, but please tell him we already have more than we could eat in a month of Sundays, so we've decided to donate some to the food pantry."

"What about your insurance company? Will an adjuster be out soon?"

"Around noon. Dan's at the dock working today, of all days. It's been days since they've needed him to work, and of course today, when I really could have used his help at the house…" Margaret heard Shelley sigh. "I don't mean to complain. The fire could have been so much worse. Someone could have gotten hurt. But right now, I feel completely overwhelmed with all the Christmas orders that have come in and the baking I have to do for the Cove on top of it."

"I'd offer to help you out, but people'd end up canceling orders right and left."

"That's sweet of you, Margaret, but please don't think I'm asking for help, not from you, or anyone. The fire's completely my fault—"

"Allan told me about the creosote in the chimney and, believe you me, what happened to you could have happened to anyone. And I wasn't thinking you called to ask me for help, but I'm here for you if you need anything, even if you just want to talk."

"Actually, I'd planned to call you yesterday before everything went up in smoke." Shelley laughed a bit cynically. "I didn't even get around to telling Allan this last night, but Adelaide was such a wonderful help, careful with all of my equipment, and did a great job rolling dough and cutting out cookies."

"You know, Shelley, if you don't think Adelaide would get in your way, she could help you out a few hours each week."

"Of course she wouldn't be in the way!" Shelley exclaimed. "And, oh my gosh, I'd love to have her help."

"I'd have to talk to her about it, of course, but I know she'd love to do it. She won't accept any payment, though. It's strictly a friend-helping-a-friend kind of thing."

"I couldn't possibly let her do it for nothing. That wouldn't be fair, and I wouldn't feel right."

"Then what if we consider your baking and decorating instructions payment enough?"

"Are you sure? You don't think Allan would mind?"

"He's standing right here. Let me ask him."

Allan was leaning against the door leading into the dining room. He must have heard every word of the conversation, and the grin he wore on his whiskered face was a sure sign that he wouldn't mind at all. "We should ask Adelaide—"

"Ask me what, Daddy?"

Adelaide stood next to Allan. Oreo curled up in her arms, her fingers softly digging through the feline's black-and-white fur.

"You enjoyed working with Shelley at the bakery the other night, right?" Allan asked their daughter.

Adelaide nodded dramatically, her broad smile brightening her face. "It was great!"

"Would you like to work with Shelley again?" Margaret asked. "A few nights a week from now until Christmas?"

Adelaide's eyes widened. "Could I? Really?"

Allan wrapped an arm around Adelaide's shoulders. "Yes, sweetheart. Really."

A moment later Margaret removed her hand from the phone's speaker. "Allan's definitely okay with it and Adelaide's over the moon."

"That's the best news I've had in weeks," Shelley said, happiness ringing in her voice. "It might just be the best Christmas present I ever could have wished for."

⋆ ⋆ ⋆

With instrumental Christmas carols echoing through the earphones clasped against her ears, Diane stared at the very first revision letter she'd ever received. Book number one in her series was finished—at least that's what she'd thought, until the e-mail arrived late yesterday afternoon.

"You have such a keen sense of humor, which is going to send your readers into fits of laughter," her editor had written. "And I absolutely love the way our heroine runs her theories by her dog. But..."

Why did there have to be a *but* in the letter? And not just one *but*, but five or six.

Diane's head hurt and she wanted some aspirin, but she didn't dare leave her office, not with Emma toddling around the living room, Aiden turning her small dining room table into a race track for his cars, Dan tracking slushy snow into the house on the many trips he and Shelley made to and from their home last night, Prize barking every time one of Aiden's cars sailed off the table, and Shelley humming Christmas tunes all morning, ever since she learned Adelaide would be helping her with her baking a few nights a week. Diane marveled at how oblivious to the chaos her young friend seemed.

Had the home she'd shared with Eric been this frenzied when Jessica and Justin were little? Had she simply forgotten the madness, remembering only the good times?

Rocky peered up at her from his hiding place beneath the desk. "It's okay, Rocky. They really did need a place to stay, and I'm glad that they're here, but it shouldn't be much more than another day or two before they head home. Before my speech at the library on Saturday, I hope."

Rocky stared at her, looking a tad confused, and then let out a long doggy sigh. Diane wanted to sigh too. She had so much to do on her book—an awful lot of unexpected writing and revising—and couldn't concentrate. The music piping through her headphones masked the bustle outside her office but added its own distraction.

And her speech was barely half written. She didn't dare try talking from only an outline. She was taking Margaret's suggestion and writing it out word for word, although right now it was still only handwritten notes, buried beneath the manuscript she was revising.

Why, oh why, had she agreed to give the speech? With book two's first deadline looming and book one's revisions due all too soon, she was starting to stress. Was this what the remainder of her life would be like? One deadline after another?

Her office door flew open, banging against the wall, and Aiden and Prize bounded into the room. "You about done in here, Miss Diane?" Aiden asked, crawling onto her lap after she spun around in her chair. "I want you to play Legos with me."

Prize nosed around Diane's feet, trying to figure out how to get under the desk to be with Rocky, but that wasn't necessary. Rocky squeezed out, and with one long, low, menacing growl, chased Aiden's dog out of the office.

How much longer could she take this insanity?

"I wish I could play with you, Aiden," Diane said softly, in spite of the headache that was growing worse by the minute. "But I have so much work to do and I'll probably be busy until late tonight."

Aiden pouted, his sweet brown eyes filling with tears. "But I'm bored. All my toys are at my house and Mama says it's too stinky over there for me and Emma to play in our own rooms."

"Your mother's right. All that smoke could make you sick, and that's the last thing you want, especially with Christmas coming."

His eyes widened. "Is next week the week when we get to see Santa Claus?"

"Yes—he's coming to Marble Cove's Christmas Stroll, you know, the big party where we go from one shop to another having cookies and cocoa."

"Santa Claus too?"

"Most definitely. Santa Claus loves cocoa and cookies."

"'Specially Mama's cookies. They're the best!"

Aiden scooted off her lap and jumped onto the floor, taking with him at least two-thirds of the manuscript she'd printed out and already scribbled notes on in bright red ink, changes she needed to incorporate into the manuscript within the next few days. "Before I take off for the Christmas holidays, if at all possible," her editor Jane had said.

Right now, of course, the pages were scattered across the office floor, Aiden's somewhat muddy shoes making tracks on the sheets—and right in the middle of the mess, she saw the handwritten notes for her speech.

Aiden looked up at her with wide, apologetic eyes. His lip quivered. "Sorry, Miss Diane." He knelt down and starting picking up the scattered papers.

"No, honey, I can get it."

And she would have gotten most all of it if Prize hadn't run back into the room, with Emma toddling in after her. Prize chomped a handful of paper between his jaws—oh no! the speech!—and Rocky, not wanting an intruder to mess with his owner's belongings, tried to get them back, his powerful teeth poking holes in manuscript pages and ripping some in half.

"Prize! Aiden!" Shelley shouted at her son and her dog, raced across the room, scooped a squirming Aiden up in one arm, and grabbed Prize's collar with the other. "I'm so, so sorry, Diane."

Could the day possibly get any worse?

Chapter Fifteen

Margaret breezed into the Cove at a little past one on Thursday, glad to have a respite from the gallery, which had been rife with energy since ten o'clock, thanks, no doubt, to her buy-one-get-one-for-half-price three-hour saleathon.

"Didn't think I was going to make it," Margaret said, ordering a sandwich at the counter, grabbing a cup of coffee, then sitting down at the table where Shelley, Diane, and Beverly were already drinking coffee and gabbing. "Once the gallery started to quiet down, Allan and Adelaide, bless their hearts, urged me to go have lunch and said they'd keep an eye on things for an hour or so."

"I haven't done a lick of Christmas shopping," Shelley said, holding a sleeping Emma. "Aiden's at Maddie Bancroft's this afternoon, so I'm taking advantage of the peace and quiet to unwind a bit from the craziness of the last couple of days. And thankfully Dan's mom has offered to watch the kids one day next week so I can head into Augusta and do some marathon Christmas shopping."

"You're all still planning to come to our place Christmas night, aren't you?" Beverly clasped her cup of steaming coffee. "Father's so looking forward to having everyone there."

"I've already told Justin and Jessica to plan on it," Diane said. "That is, if they can get away."

"You mean they might not be coming?" Margaret asked. "That would be terrible."

Diane took a quick sip of her coffee. "Jessica, my lawyer extraordinaire, is in the middle of a big case and the courts don't close down for the holidays. She's trying to arrange her schedule so she can get away for three days, but she's just not sure yet. As for Justin, he's at the mercy of the US Army." She laughed lightly. "I'm still making all my plans as if they'll be here, and I've done a heavy dose of praying that nothing keeps them away."

"Diane had the cottage decorated so lovely, but she's had to put some of her prettier decorations away to keep them from getting...well, destroyed." Shelley gave her friends a knowing smile. "She's been such a peach, taking us in like she did, and we've made a total mess of her entire house. I never realized how noisy my family is or just how rambunctious Aiden—and Dan—can be. Oh my gosh, I've tried desperately to hush everyone up so Diane's not disturbed while she's writing, but it's useless."

Shelley picked at her muffin, looking from one friend to another. "Aiden scattered her manuscript all over the floor, and then on top of it, the dogs shredded a few pieces of paper."

"A good fifty or more pieces of paper—plus the notes for my speech." Diane laughed, patting Shelley's hand. "That's when my laptop and I retreated to the library until closing time. Unfortunately, all those stories about public libraries being bastions of peace and quiet, places to read and reflect, are totally and completely false. There were toddlers roaming around with their moms, all of them searching for just the right book to read, and, and…" She laughed again. "Trust me, it wasn't the least bit tranquil."

"When do you think you'll be able to move back home?" Margaret asked Shelley, sure that Diane wished she could have an answer to that question too.

"Well…" Shelley rolled her eyes. "The plumber promised to have the new boiler installed today, but when I called this morning, he told me it hadn't come in yet. 'Maybe tomorrow, if you're lucky,' he said, and then he had the nerve to say, 'but the way things have been lately—it gets wicked busy around here in the wintertime—it'll probably be sometime next week.'" Shelley sighed. "Dan was supposed to call yesterday, but you know how men can be—he got busy at work and forgot. If it's not installed by Monday, I'll…well, I guess I'll just have to have a heart-to-heart talk with the owner of Vanek Plumbing."

"Will you have to get a new Christmas tree? What about decorations?" Beverly asked.

"The tree is long gone but what few decorations we'd had a chance to put up were salvageable. The cleaners were in yesterday. Can you believe that? I'm shocked at how fast our insurance company has worked to get all of this done. There's still a bit of the smoky smell, but if I keep the windows open when the weather allows it, that should go away soon. And, of course, I have to get a new sofa and chairs and drapes."

"You keep saying there's nothing we can help you with," Beverly said, "but there must be something."

"Maybe some prayers for patience for me, and sanity for Diane?"

The friends laughed and promised to pray.

Margaret was just taking a bite of the chicken salad on her croissant when Evelyn Waters, Marble Cove's mayor, and Charlotte Vincent, chairwoman of the Marble Cove Chamber of Commerce and the Christmas Stroll committee, stopped at their table. "Hello, ladies," Evelyn said.

Hellos were offered all around the table, then Evelyn looked directly at Margaret. "Love your holiday window, Margaret. I'm one of the judges for the *Courier*'s Best Christmas Window contest, so I can't say much more than that, but you did a wonderful job."

"I couldn't agree more," Charlotte said. "I haven't had a chance yet to stop by the gallery to see how you've decorated the inside, but I look forward to seeing it during the Stroll. You and the other downtown businesses are going to make this year's Stroll even better than last year's."

"And Diane," Charlotte added, before Margaret could issue her thank-yous, "I can't wait to hear your talk at the library this Saturday. It's a shame the other speaker had to cancel, but what a godsend you are, stepping up at the last minute to help out."

"We have such a wonderful library," Evelyn said. "If it weren't for volunteers, we'd have a difficult time keeping it open, and this fund-raiser will be such a big help in providing money for next year's summer reading programs."

"What will you be talking about?" Charlotte asked. "There are so many would-be writers in town—myself included—and your talk has gotten quite the buzz, you know. Everyone's hoping you'll share the secret on how to get published."

"I'm learning quite rapidly that Thomas Edison was right: it's ten percent inspiration and ninety percent perspiration," Diane told her. "Unfortunately, there are no magic words and there isn't a secret handshake."

Charlotte looked crestfallen. "Oh well, that's rather depressing. I hope you won't say that during your talk. It's Christmastime after all—a time for joy."

Evelyn placed her hand on Diane's shoulder. "I'm sure it'll be wonderful, and I'll be in the front row, cheering you on."

"Thank you so much," Diane said. She waited until Charlotte and Evelyn were out of earshot and whispered to her friends. "That's exactly what I'd planned to say. I have it all sketched out—the difficulty of revisions, sitting at your computer and writing when you'd rather be outside building a snowman with the neighbor kids or watching Cary Grant romancing Grace Kelly on TV. Or," she chuckled, "being asked to give a speech, when you shake in your boots and get totally nauseated just thinking about it."

Margaret patted Diane's hand. "We'll be there to support you."

"And you should talk about whatever you want to talk about," Shelley added. "Even if you want to talk about the chaos of having a family of four and their dog move in with you."

"That's right," Beverly said. "It's your speech. You graciously offered to give even though you were asked at the last moment. And let's face it, Diane, in most people's eyes you're a star. You've accomplished something most of them dream about but will never achieve, and they're going to hang on your every word."

"You think so?" Diane asked.

"I know so," Beverly stated firmly.

"By the way, Margaret," Diane asked, after taking a sip of coffee, "have you seen that young boy again—the one who drew the picture of the lighthouse?"

"What picture?" Beverly and Shelley asked in unison, and Margaret quickly explained before addressing Diane's question.

"He came by the gallery a couple of days ago. His name's Caleb Wadsworth, and before you ask, yes, Henry Wadsworth Longfellow is one of his ancestors. In fact, I think Caleb's father's name is Longfellow Wadsworth."

"The artist?" Beverly asked, her eyes narrowing.

"You've heard of him?" Margaret asked. She took a quick bite of her sandwich before the conversation came back to her.

"I went to one of his showings a few years back. I'd read a lot of positive reviews about his work and wanted to see if it was as good as everyone said."

Margaret swallowed. "And?"

Beverly shrugged. "Not my style and I didn't buy anything, but that doesn't mean it wasn't good."

"He's dropped completely off the art scene," Margaret said, "and I'm sure that's part of the reason young Caleb is so secretive. If he comes by again, I hope to learn more. I'm certain he needs help of some kind, and I want to be there for him."

"Speaking of secrets," Beverly said, "I dropped in on Edward Maker night before last."

Shelley's spoon clanked loudly against the side of her cup and her jaw dropped. "And you're just now telling us this? Something like that couldn't possibly have slipped your mind."

"I spent all day yesterday working on a PowerPoint presentation for work." Beverly shook her head. "But... you'll never believe this: Jeff Mackenzie is Edward Maker's grandson."

"What?" Shelley said, staring at Beverly. "How'd you find that out?"

"Jeff dropped in on Mr. Maker while I was there. Took me totally by surprise."

"Is his grandfather the reason he's been snooping around Marble Cove, doing research on the lighthouse?" Margaret asked, and took a sip of coffee to wash down the last of her sandwich.

"I didn't ask," Beverly said, "but that would be my guess. He said his grandfather never talked about his childhood and whenever the subject came up, he'd ignore it or change the subject. I imagine Jeff's been trying to find out why Marble Cove is such a touchy topic."

"Has he learned anything?" Margaret asked, looking at her watch. She had to get back to the gallery, but she couldn't leave until she knew all the details about Beverly's visit with Mr. Maker.

"Mr. Maker was awfully quiet at first, but he finally dragged out an old photo album. He showed us pictures of him, his mother, and his father, taken at the lighthouse back in the thirties, and he opened up a bit. It turns out his father lost his job as light keeper because he had a problem with alcohol."

"Interesting," Margaret said. "You didn't by any chance ask him why he carved 'I'm sorry' into the lighthouse, did you?"

"I did. That's what led to the discussion of his father's drinking problem. He even told Jeff and me about his father having a temper, and he talked about hiding out from his dad so he wouldn't have to listen to him yell. But he clammed up before divulging any information about that carving."

"So we're still in the dark," Diane said.

"Afraid so, but I'm having Jeff over to dinner next time he's in town. Maybe I'll learn something more."

One could hope, Margaret thought. There were suddenly one too many mysteries in her life, and she wanted to learn the truth about all of them.

Chapter Sixteen

"See you later," Margaret said, kissing Adelaide and Allan when they left the gallery at three that afternoon. From where she stood in the doorway, she could hear Adelaide chatting a mile a minute to her dad, telling him all about the tarts she'd helped Shelley make the night before.

As their voices faded, Margaret stepped back into the gallery. All the shoppers had gone, leaving in their wake several empty spaces where paintings had hung. The CD player was silent for a moment between songs, and Margaret thought about Diane, longing for Jessica and Justin to find a way to join her for the holiday. She offered a quick and silent prayer for schedules to open and travel plans to be smooth.

She had gone into her studio, looking for just the right paintings to take the place of those that had been sold, when the jangle of the door bells startled her. Caleb stomped his feet on the rug just inside the door and sauntered across the gallery's main floor when he saw her peeking out of her studio.

"Hi there," Margaret said.

"Hey." He dropped his backpack beside her worktable, making himself at home. "I had some time to kill. You don't mind me hanging out here for a while, do you?"

"Not at all. Why don't I show you where the refrigerator is and you can help yourself to whatever you find inside." He frowned, and Margaret hoped she hadn't sounded a bit too accommodating.

"You know, if I had grandchildren your age, I'd love having them stop by here on the way home from school. I almost always have cookies or some other goodie in the fridge, and milk, and I'd hope they'd make themselves at home."

"You're sure?"

"Positive."

She led him to the office, which held the coffeemaker and a dorm-sized refrigerator. "Help yourself."

Caleb was hesitant at first, but he opened the refrigerator and grabbed a soda. He spied the bowl of mixed nuts on the counter, and he dug into them, popping a handful into his mouth.

"My dad always kept peanuts next to his easel, but most of the time he was too caught up in his work to eat them or anything else."

Finally, Margaret thought, he'd opened up about something.

"Your dad's an artist?" she asked, not wanting to mention Longfellow Wadsworth, the artist whose picture and biography she'd found on the Internet.

"Used to be." He looked at Margaret with pride shining in his eyes; yet she saw something more. Was it sadness? She wanted to ask why his father had stopped painting, why he'd completely disappeared from the New York art scene, but she couldn't. She knew that would be too intrusive, that she'd surely run him off.

"Did you father sketch, like you?"

"He did it all." Caleb grabbed more nuts, chewed them slowly, then took a sip of his soda. "He didn't paint the stuff like you sell here."

I'm sure he doesn't meant to be rude, Margaret told herself.

Caleb sauntered into the main gallery, still wearing his coat, munching on nuts, and drinking his soda. He looked cocky, but Margaret felt sure it masked something. Maybe he needed to talk to someone, to share his troubles.

"Like, if my dad had painted this picture," he said, stopping in front of an oil painting Margaret had done of Orlean Point Light, "he might have given it one long arm pointing toward the ocean, with a giant hand, and an index finger curled upward, beckoning a ship toward the shore, instead of warning the captain to turn away from the rocks."

"Sounds rather macabre."

Caleb shrugged. "He was a surrealist. That's the way they see things."

"So he painted like Dali?"

Caleb shook his head, a twist of disdain in his mouth. "More like Max Ernst."

"Do you want to paint like Max Ernst?"

Again he shrugged. "Haven't decided yet."

Did she dare ask about his family again? "I imagine your dad has taught you a lot about painting."

"He used to teach me, but he had to get a real job, so he doesn't paint anymore."

"I'm sorry to hear that."

"Me too, but...well, life's tough sometimes."

"Do you have any brothers or sisters?"

He paused. "Used to."

Without saying another word, he headed into the studio and grabbed his backpack. "Gotta go. My mom'll flip out if I'm not home by four."

Margaret shook her head and watched as he scurried away into the winter gloom. Closing the door and walking to her desk at the back of the gallery, she forced herself to turn her mind away from Caleb for now, yet it frustrated her, knowing something had to be wrong in his family, and that she couldn't help.

Margaret noticed a light flashing on the answering machine and realized she must have missed a call earlier in the day when she was so busy. She listened to the voice mail and was positive she was dreaming when she hung up the phone. Mr. Cabot had called to order all four paintings she had shown him. It was like an early Christmas present to the Shearwater Gallery. With the money from a sale like that, she could go out and buy one of the best digital cameras on the market, if Allan didn't wrap one up for her and tuck it under the Christmas tree.

God was surely smiling down on her.

The jingle bells at the front door jangled. Another customer, she hoped.

Margaret ran her hands down her navy blue slacks, smoothing wrinkles out of the fabric, and stepped into the gallery. Jeff Mackenzie strolled around the room, dressed in a charcoal turtleneck under a steel blue flannel shirt and jeans. He looked very handsome. Why Beverly was afraid to spend more time with this man was beyond her.

"Hello, Jeff. May I help you?"

He turned slowly, his eyes brightened by one of the spotlights beaming down on a grouping of pictures. "It's nice to see you again, Margaret. Thought I'd drop by and see anything new you might have."

"I have some handblown glass by a local woman whose work hasn't been shown anywhere else. A few new pieces of pottery. You told me before that you're not all that interested in jewelry, but in case you've changed your mind"—she was thinking of a possible Christmas gift for Beverly—"I can show you some stunning pieces carved from shells from our own Marble Cove beaches."

"Actually, I was hoping to look at more of *your* paintings. Ones you've done of Orlean Point Light."

"With or without the mysterious lights shining down?"

One of his eyebrows rose. "I take it you're the one who thinks I touched up my photographs. That I used computer software to add those lights, to make it seem as if angels were flying around the lighthouse late at night."

She wasn't about to tell him it was Shelley who thought that might have been possible. Margaret had done some Internet research and saw just how easy it was to touch up digital photos. She didn't want to believe Beverly's friend could do such a thing. Still, she asked, "Did you?"

"No." He turned away from Margaret and walked toward a watercolor from another local artist. It was a field of daisies, the only ode to springtime that she currently had hanging in the gallery. He seemed to study it for a moment, thinking about her question.

"I suppose it's rather rude of some of us to think that you might have done such a thing," Margaret said, "but we hardly know you from Adam. And, in case Beverly hasn't told you, there are a lot of people in town who think that anyone claiming to have seen those lights is a crackpot."

"Have you seen them?" Jeff asked, without looking back at Margaret.

"Of course."

"I don't think you're a crackpot." He turned slowly, smiling back at her. "I don't know if I'll ever see the lights for real. Having them show up in some of my photographs may be the only way I'll ever see them. But I truly believe what Beverly told me is true, even though she's hesitant to believe it herself."

"What has she told you?"

"She thinks the lights could be a beacon of hope, a light shining down on someone in need."

Margaret frowned. "You're not making fun of us?"

He shook his head. "My faith is strong, Margaret. I believe that God works miracles in ways we don't always understand."

Margaret smiled. "I'm so glad you feel that way. If you didn't, well, I'd have to tell Beverly to steer clear of you."

He grinned and looked at his watch. "Wish I had more time to talk and look at more of your paintings, but I have an appointment with Reverend Locke at Old First Church."

"Did you know that's the oldest church in town? Built in the late eighteenth century."

"So I've heard."

"Thinking of joining Old First?"

"Not today."

Did that mean he might be thinking of moving to Marble Cove? To be closer to Beverly, perhaps? Or maybe he'd fallen in love with her much beloved little town.

Goodness, there were just so many questions.

"Why don't you tell me what you're going to do at Old First—if you don't mind, that is—while I show you some of my lighthouse paintings."

"Are you always this curious, Margaret?"

"Not usually, but I was telling the truth when I said that I don't know you from Adam, and I like to know my customers. It helps me help them choose the perfect piece of artwork."

He chuckled. "Well, if you must know, I'm going to photograph some of the interiors in Old First for a book I'm thinking of putting together on New England's historic churches."

"Oh, you'll find endless things to photograph in Old First. I don't go there myself, but the stained glass is wonderful. And the woodwork is—"

"To die for, at least that's what my grandfather told me." Jeff looked at her and winked. "I'm guessing Beverly told you that Edward Maker is my grandfather."

Margaret nodded, stopping before a watercolor of Orlean Point Light decked out for Christmas. "It did come up in conversation." She smiled.

"Well, now you and Beverly know nearly as much about my grandfather as I do, at least the part about his life here in Marble Cove when he was a boy."

Jeff studied the lighthouse painting, a contemplative gaze on his face. "This is nice, but I have something else in mind, something you might not even have."

"Which is?"

"I want a painting that makes you believe you can step out of the present and into the past, right through the lighthouse's front door."

Jeff Mackenzie definitely had good taste. That's the kind of painting she liked too.

"How about one where the lighthouse is shrouded in fog," she asked, "with a hint of moonlight shining behind?"

Jeff smiled. "You have something like that?"

"In my studio. It's one of my favorites, one I wasn't sure I wanted to part with."

"Mind if I take a look?"

"Not at all." She led Jeff back to her studio, to half a dozen paintings leaning together against a wall. She sorted through them and at last handed Jeff a painting that wasn't much bigger than a folded-in-half newspaper. "What do you think?"

He looked at it for the longest time, studying the softness of the blues and grays, with the lighthouse and the moon and even the beacon of light muted by the fog. “It’s perfect. I’m not sure how my grandfather will react when I give it to him, but—”

“If he doesn’t like it, bring it back and pick out another.”

“That’s if he doesn’t toss it in the trash.” Jeff chuckled. “And chuck me out of the house right along with it.”

What an odd thing to say, but that was par for the course. Most everyone she came in contact with lately left her wondering what was going on in their life.

★ ★ ★

Beverly hadn’t expected to hear from Jeff so soon. It had been only two days since she’d seen him, and now his name showed up on her ringing cell phone. She thought about ignoring it, continuing to work in her upstairs office, making up for the time she’d lost while having lunch with her friends a few hours ago, but the phone continued to ring. Five times. Six.

How annoying.

She sighed, punched the talk button, and said “Hello.”

“How would you like to go to Abenaki Isle tomorrow?”

He hadn’t bothered to say hello, how are you, or anything like that. He’d just hit her with a question, one she hadn’t been at all prepared for.

“Thanks for the invitation, but I’m in the middle of a project for work.” She stared at the PowerPoint presentation on her computer, one that was giving her fits. She didn't want to analyze these budgeting inconsistencies, not tonight. But she didn't have to make the presentation until next Wednesday, so… "What's on Abenaki Isle?"

"Great photo opportunities," Jeff answered, his voice full of enthusiasm, something she seemed to be losing for her own work. "Lobster boats, lobsters, islanders who rarely come to the mainland and have a lot of old folktales to tell. I'm going over on the mail boat tomorrow and I've hired someone to bring me—or us—back tomorrow evening. Sound like fun?"

It did. Great fun. But…

"You're hesitating, Beverly," Jeff said, a hint of laughter in his voice. "Am I so frightening?"

"No. Not at all." Not frightening, just daunting. "I just have so much work to do and—"

"Play hooky."

That wasn't her style. She'd never ditched a class, not even in high school when so many of her friends were doing it. She'd never been late for work. She didn't call in sick when she had a headache or just wanted a day off. "I shouldn't."

"You told me before that you work a good sixty hours a week. Surely you can take one day off."

She hesitated.

"We'll eat fresh lobster and wild mushroom bisque."

Beverly found herself smiling at the way he was tempting her. "You've already checked out the restaurant menus?"

"Only one restaurant on the island and other than lobster, they have one soup and one dessert per day. Tomorrow's the bisque and chocolate and coconut cream pie. If my company doesn't sound all that interesting, at least the food must."

"Well...I shouldn't, but—"

"I'll take that as a yes, which means I'll pick you up at seven in the morning. Bring a change of clothes in case you get wet."

Beverly found herself laughing. "You don't plan on throwing me into the drink, do you?"

Silence. A great, near-deafening silence.

It took a moment before she realized what she'd said. The words had come so easily, and now they settled heavily in the pit of her stomach. They must have hit Jeff hard too. She wasn't the only one who'd suffered after Will drowned. Jeff had too. Even though they'd talked about it, she knew that a sense of guilt must still be hanging over Jeff, just as it hung over her. If they hadn't been teasing each other while sailing with Will, if they hadn't been caught up in each other's company, they might have prevented Will from drowning.

"I'm sorry, Jeff," she said slowly. "That was insensitive. I wasn't thinking and it just came out."

"I could have said something just as insensitive." The line was silent for a moment. "But we can't continue to torture ourselves, Beverly. Will's been gone for five years. We didn't cause his death, and we couldn't have prevented it."

"If we'd been in the water with him instead of on the boat... If we'd been watching him—"

"We were talking, Beverly, nothing more. And Will had a seizure. The doctors said they doubted we could have done anything to save him."

"But I don't know for sure. I'll never know."

"Neither will I. But I want to go on, Beverly. I have to go on."

She knew that she did too. Beverly sighed, wishing she could turn back time at least five minutes and not utter that careless comment. "Let's just try to have a good time tomorrow and not think about the past."

"Can you do that?" Jeff asked softly.

"I can try."

Chapter Seventeen

"I can't believe you've never been here before," Jeff said, as he and Beverly strolled along the wharf on Abenaki Isle, looking at the colorful Christmas lights decorating the fishing shacks and boats, the screeching seagulls diving down toward the water, looking for scraps.

"I guess we always just went other places around Marble Cove when we visited every summer. Every once in awhile we'd take the Penobscot Ferry out to Matinicus, North Haven, and Vinalhaven." Beverly laughed as fond memories came back to her. "Mother and Father thought vacations should be a chance to learn about your surroundings. Mostly social studies, since that's what Father taught, although I'd get a few botany lessons along the way."

She picked up what looked like part of a lobster claw and tossed it out onto the water. The seagulls swooped down as if she'd just thrown them a banquet.

"My father loves everything about New England, especially the coast. I can still hear the history lessons he dished out when we hiked the beaches and rocks. 'Many famous buildings in Washington, DC, Boston, Philadelphia, and New York City were constructed out of Vinalhaven granite,' he'd tell us." Beverly laughed. "While my friends were playing on the beach, building sandcastles and body surfing, I was learning every minute detail about our Founding Fathers, the seventeenth-century settlements in this part of the country, and that the worst disaster in American naval history, up until Pearl Harbor, happened right here in Penobscot Bay during the Revolution."

Jeff leaned against one of the shacks, listening intently, even though most of the time he had his eye on his camera's viewfinder, snapping one photo after another.

"You know," he said, "you might be trying to sound as if none of that interested you, but you're failing miserably."

"Really? How can you tell?"

"Your eyes light up. Your face is animated in a way I've never seen before."

"You haven't seen me all that often."

"But you do love the history of this place, don't you?"

"I love history, period." Beverly jumped the short distance down from the wharf onto the beach, and Jeff followed right behind. "Mother taught history and Father taught social studies—history being his favorite topic—and I rebelled against both of them. Deep inside I wanted to follow their lead, but I studied statistics and math instead. Fortunately, I loved that too."

"Now there I can easily relate to you and your dad. It's not only photography that has taken me all over the world, it's the people and their stories and the history behind everything that has led up to today—rebellions, peace talks, war."

They continued to chat as they walked along the rocky beach, keeping their conversation light. At the moment Beverly felt far away from the memories they shared of Will's death.

Most of the boats in the harbor were used by lobstermen. They had names like *Foggy Lady, Run Aground Sue, Davy Jones's Lobster,* and *Willit Float,* and Jeff snapped their photos as they bobbed on the water and seagulls circled overhead. He snapped pictures of their captains too, and together they listened to the men tell tall tales about their exploits out on the water.

The cold wind blew in off the ocean, and she should have been chilled to the bone, but in spite of the three or four inches of snow on the ground, the sky was blue, the sun was high, the air was calm, and she was sure she hadn't enjoyed herself this much in years.

Ever since they got on the boat that morning, Jeff had explained the workings of the camera to her, talking about shutter speed and how to take pictures in slow motion, something he often did when photographing waterfalls, he'd said, creating a soft, flowing effect of the water, while keeping the rocks and everything else in the background looking sharp.

He made it all sound so easy. And she was glad she'd played hooky; she'd buried herself so deep in work that she rarely came up for air. This breather was nice, but not something she'd allow herself to do too often.

"I don't know about you," Beverly said, "but that wild mushroom bisque and freshly caught lobster is starting to sound awfully good."

"Come on then, let's find the restaurant and hope and pray that they're open, since it doesn't appear anything else around here is."

"What did you expect in December? Marble Cove's on the mainland, but even we don't get all that many tourists or that much traffic passing through in the dead of winter."

"But this is when life is at its best. Slow and peaceful."

They gazed through the windows of shops that had closed for the winter, admiring an albatross sculpted out of metal, seals and puffins carved out of dark and shimmering granite, and beaded jewelry. "Margaret needs to get hold of some of these artists," Beverly said, jotting down names in a notebook she'd tucked away in the leather tote slung over her shoulder. "Their work is beautiful."

"I bought one of Margaret's paintings yesterday." Jeff snapped several photos of the wind-roughened storefronts on the town's only street. "I'm giving it to my grandfather as an early Christmas present. Want to join me when I go to Augusta to see him on Wednesday?"

"Actually, I'll already be in Augusta that day. This time of year, in spite of the holidays, I have an endless stream of meetings to attend. I just don't know if I can make the time."

"Well," he sounded a touch defeated, "I've got your cell phone number. I can give you a call and let you know what I'm up to."

"That would be nice. Thank you."

He tucked his arm through hers, no more than a friendly gesture, thank goodness, and at last they ducked into the one and only restaurant in town, which was little more than a shack.

It was warm inside, a cozy place full of atmosphere, where coffee cups with names handwritten on them in indelible ink hung over the back counter and souvenir lobsters in all shapes and sizes, some stuffed, some plastic, were on display alongside *The Lobster Shack Cookbook*.

"Take a seat wherever you want," a woman shouted from the kitchen. "As you can see, we're not all that crowded."

That was an understatement. They were the only patrons in the place. They sat next to the window, which was spotlessly clean and overlooked the wharf, where a couple of men were just climbing off a boat.

"That's my husband and son out there," the woman said. She'd walked into the dining room wearing knee-high rubber Wellingtons, tan corduroy pants, a black turtleneck, and a red apron that said Lobster Shack on the front. "Lobsterin's been good this year, and the weather like it is today makes it a perfect time to check the pots. If you're here for lobster, you might be able to pick yours out from whatever they've just hauled in."

"That would be lovely," Beverly said. "I'm falling in love with your island."

"Most people do," the woman said. Her hair was red but salted with gray and white, piled on top of her head Gibson girl style. "'Course, we get a few people who come over to the island, buy an old cottage, determined to fix it up, then leave when the first snow falls, never to come back. Don't bother me much. I don't need the tourist trade to make a living, not when the locals tend to come here a couple times a week for lunch or dinner."

The woman stuck out her hand. "I'm Cass MacDuffie, former mayor and owner of this fine establishment."

Beverly and Jeff introduced themselves, shaking Cass's warm, wind- and cold-chapped hand.

"Not many sightseers around this time of year," Cass said. "I seen you out there taking pictures. You a professional?"

Jeff nodded. "I'd heard the sunsets here were some of the prettiest on earth, and I thought I might try to catch a few shots in wintertime."

"Ayuh, sunsets don't get much prettier than what you can see from out there on the end of the wharf, but if you're looking for something different, there's a trail out back that leads about half a mile inland. You just might like what you see."

"Can you give us a hint?" Beverly asked.

"It's what's left of the first church on the island. Built from the wood of wrecked ships, and believe you me, there were a lot of wrecks back in the day. But I don't want to talk your ears off. My guess is, you came in here for lobster. Not much on the menu besides that today."

Jeff frowned. "I saw wild mushroom bisque on your Web site."

Cass chuckled. "That thing hasn't been updated in a dog's age. Only get wild mushrooms around here in summer, but I've got some good thick clam chowder, chock-full of potatoes and carrots, not to mention the best clams in New England, simmering on the stove. Want to try a cup or bowl?"

"We'll both have a bowl. And bring out your biggest and best-looking lobsters, one for each of us."

"Not a problem. Be right back with the chowder. You want bread or oyster crackers?"

"Neither," Beverly said. "The chowder's bound to be more than enough carbs."

Jeff laughed. "We'll take the bread. And lots of butter."

"I can't possibly eat a whole bowl of chowder and a whole lobster," Beverly said, folding her arms atop the blue and white checked tablecloth.

"I'll eat what you don't."

They dug into the thick and steaming clam chowder just moments after Cass set the big stoneware bowls on the table in front of them. Beverly allowed herself to sigh after her first bite, feeling as if she'd died and gone to heaven. She took another bite, sighed again, then looked up at Jeff, who was watching her every move. "My apologies for the sound effects. I'm not much of one to sigh over anything, but this is good."

"Mind if I take your picture?"

His question brought a grimace. "Please don't. I'm a mess. My hair's windblown and I'm sure most of my makeup was washed away by this morning's fog. Besides, there are far more interesting things around here to take pictures of."

Thankfully he didn't argue and he didn't try to snap her photo.

When Cass brought the lobster, Beverly found herself eating with abandon, a luxury she rarely allowed herself. Her fingers were coated with drawn butter, and she tried to lick them clean, all to no avail. She actually laughed at herself, and that rare moment felt good. She was relaxing, and she was glad she'd come today.

Outside she heard the clang of a boat's bell, and she looked through the window to see yet another vessel come into the quaint harbor. Off in the distance, she thought for sure she could see the mainland. "Look. Way out there," she said, and Jeff turned toward the window. "Is that Orlean Point Light?"

"Could be. I would have thought we were too far away, but—"

"Did you just mention Orlean Point Light?" Cass asked, standing beside the table, refilling their mugs with dark, rich coffee.

"Yes," Beverly said. "It's in Marble Cove, where I live. Have you seen it before?"

"Yes." Cass uttered the word through nearly gritted teeth. "The mere mention of that lighthouse makes my heart shudder."

Jeff looked at her curiously. "Why's that?"

"My grandmother and grandfather, not to mention two of my uncles, and an aunt died when the sailing ship *Newcastle* crashed on the rocks off Orlean Point back in 1935, all because the light in the lighthouse failed to work. At least that's the excuse the authorities offered my mother. *Failed.* Can you believe that?"

"It does happen," Beverly said, no longer hungry, not with Cass's anger putting a chill on the room.

"It never happened before the wreck of 1935. Orlean Point Light was as reliable as they come, until then. In fact, it was supposed to be one of the most reliable lighthouses on the New England coast. It had been operating since the eighteenth century and it had never failed. So why did the light not work that night? Why were so many people—*my* people—killed?"

"Surely the government looked into the accident," Jeff said.

"They said they did." Cass laughed cynically. "But who knows how good an investigation they did. People were paid off all the time in the thirties, just to keep things secret. I know deep down in my heart that something more happened, that the true reason the *Newcastle* sank was covered up."

Was that truth the reason Edward Maker had carved 'I'm sorry' into the lighthouse? Was the wreck of the *Newcastle* and the failure of Orlean Point Light the reason Edward Maker refused to talk about his past?

Cass walked back into the kitchen, shoving the swinging door open and letting it slam behind her.

Beverly looked at Jeff, whose eyes were now filled with questions. "I've changed my mind. I'll find a way to join you on Wednesday when you go to see your grandfather."

Chapter Eighteen

Saturday at five minutes until noon, Diane stood in a far corner of the library with Beverly, Margaret, and Shelley, butterflies flitting about wildly in her stomach, trying to figure out why she was there. Surely she wasn't really giving a speech in five minutes.

She dragged in a deep breath.

"It'll go great," Beverly said, picking a piece of lint off of Diane's jacket. Thank goodness her friend wasn't cleaning dog drool or something worse—like Emma's breakfast—off the forest green fabric. "Just remember to say hello at the beginning, thank your library hosts and everyone who's come to listen to you. And be sure at the end you ask if anyone has any questions."

"Are you sure you can't hold up cue cards for me to read?" Diane quipped.

"No, dear," Margaret said, giving Diane's arm a maternal squeeze. "But we promise to catch you should you faint dead away."

Diane chuckled. "I knew I could count on all of you for support."

"It's time, Diane," one of the Friends of the Library, Sara Silverthorn, said. "Your notes are on the podium already, along with a bottle of water, and the seats are full, except for the four in front which are reserved for your friends. At least ten additional people are standing, and everyone's clamoring to hear your talk."

Diane looked from Beverly to Shelley to Margaret. "Wish me luck."

"Always," Beverly said. "Now go up there and knock 'em dead." Shelley put her hands together and looked up, a sign that she'd be praying for Diane.

Diane thought her legs would collapse beneath her as she walked through the library stacks and past the folding chairs filled with men and women. Beverly, Shelley, and Margaret took their seats, the head of the library introduced her—Marble Cove's very own published novelist!—and moments later, her stomach churning, her head throbbing, she thanked the librarians, the Friends of the Library, and everyone who'd come today, to learn the secret of getting published.

"It's all about passion," she told them, looking down at her speech, printed in big letters so she could easily read it. She had a slight catch in her throat after two paragraphs and took a drink of water. She looked about the room at all the people who shared the same dream she'd once had, of selling that first book. Gerald Kimball, from the *Courier*, sat near the front. Diane hoped he was there for his own enjoyment rather than writing a review of the lecture for the paper.

"I was once like you. Hopeful. Filled with anticipation. Sure that someone—somewhere—would eventually want to buy my book. After all, I'd poured my heart and my soul into it."

She was absolutely certain her voice droned on, that she had to be putting people to sleep, but she didn't see anyone yawning, only eyes focused on her face, everyone carefully listening to her each and every word.

She read a few passages from her first book—ones her editor had praised, not the parts that needed revision. She could tell them from now until doomsday about the headaches that came after selling a book, but more than likely they wouldn't believe her. Let them believe the fantasy, she thought as she talked. She'd had pie-in-the-sky ideas about it too, that an editor would want to buy her book and within a couple of months it would be on a bookshelf, with the perfect cover, and she'd make a million dollars right off the bat.

No need to crush their dreams.

"Be yourself," she told them. "Let your passion shine through in every word you write. It's your special voice that editors are looking for. And whatever you do, don't let anyone quash that passion. Believe in yourself. Always. Thank you."

Diane took a deep breath to speak, and a wave of applause filled the room. Diane thanked everyone again and asked for questions. She spent the next twenty minutes answering some of the simplest things, like how to format a manuscript, do you create your own covers, and where do you get your ideas. When it was all over, she was exhausted, but her headache had gone away and her knees felt sturdier than they had in a week.

The library filled with applause again, and she found herself grinning. It was over, or maybe, just maybe, her speaking career as a real, honest to goodness author had just begun.

* * *

"I have to get back to the gallery. We were really busy early this morning, and poor Allan and Adelaide—if they had to keep up the pace without me being there, they're probably pulling their hair out right about now," Margaret said, a good half hour after Diane finished her talk.

"Are you sure you can't go to the Cove with Diane, Shelley, and me?" Beverly asked. "I have so much to tell you about the trip Jeff and I took to Abenaki Isle yesterday."

Diane's eyes lit up. "What trip?"

"Margaret, could you join us at the Cove or, could we join you at the gallery?"

"If you could all come to the gallery, that would be wonderful. I'll put on a fresh pot of coffee if Allan doesn't already have some brewing, and I'm sure I have some cookies—Adelaide's handiwork from the Lighthouse Sweet Shoppe, of course."

Shelley looked at her watch. "I promised Dan I'd be home—or at Diane's home, I should say—by 2:30, so I can't stay all that long. But I'm dying to hear whatever news you have to share, Beverly."

"Does going to the gallery work for you, Diane?" Beverly asked.

"As long as I can sit down and put my feet up for a bit, I'm fine. I had no idea speaking would wear me out like that."

A few moments later, Adelaide poured coffee for everyone and had put the cookies on a plate for Margaret and her friends, while Allan stayed out in the main gallery to greet customers.

"Okay, Beverly," Margaret said, "spill. What's this about you going to Abenaki Isle with Jeff yesterday?" She raised her eyebrows.

"It wasn't a date, if that's what you're thinking."

"All right," Margaret said. "But, of course, we can't wait to hear about it."

Beverly took a sip of coffee. "I didn't see a word of this is any of the research we did on Orlean Point Light, but did you know that the light failed back in 1935?"

"That's when Edward Maker's father was light keeper," Diane said. "But I didn't think the light had ever failed. Not once in the two hundred or so years it was in operation."

"But it did," Beverly continued, "causing a ship named *Newcastle* to crash on the rocks, and five people that I'm aware of died. For all I know, there could have been more fatalities."

"Why would Edward Maker hide something like that?" Shelley asked. "Why would it be covered up?"

"Maybe Mr. Maker accidentally broke the light while fooling around. After all, he was just a little boy. Or maybe he did it on purpose to get back at his dad for getting drunk and yelling so much," Diane said. "That would be a really good reason to carve 'I'm sorry' in the lighthouse wall."

"Or maybe his father fell asleep or was drunk or out at a bar getting drunk the night of the wreck," Margaret said. "There's no end to the possibilities."

"I agree, but I plan to find out the truth."

"How?" Margaret asked.

"I'm going to come right out and ask him next week. Jeff's taking an early Christmas present to him—your lighthouse painting, Margaret—and since I'll already be in Augusta, I'm going to join him."

"You'll have to call us afterward," Diane said. "I'll be on pins and needles, anxious to learn what you've found out."

"Me too," Margaret said, "but I can't understand why we didn't find any references to the beacon on the lighthouse not working."

"Maybe we just overlooked something or looked in the wrong place," Diane said. "We're not real sleuths, after all."

"Possibly." Shelley looked at her watch again. "I hate to eat and dash, but I really do need to get back to Diane's house. We've promised Dan's folks we'd come for dinner tonight, and the kids'll need baths and we'll all have to get dressed up in our Sunday-go-to-meetin' clothes." Shelley sighed. "All of this would be so much easier if we were back in our own home."

"But the boiler hasn't been replaced yet," Diane said, "and I'm not letting you go home until it is."

"Well, I've waited patiently all week, calling every day, being as nice as I could possibly be, and I still get the same response. 'We're trying as hard as we can to get that boiler, but it hasn't come into the shop yet.' But I'll tell you, if it's not there by Monday, I'm paying Vanek Plumbing an in-person call."

Chapter Nineteen

It was just after 10:00 AM, Monday, only thirteen days before Christmas, when Shelley walked into the small and dingy office at the front of Vanek Plumbing's big metal warehouse. After a week of living and causing chaos in Diane's house, she desperately wanted to go home. But the boiler had yet to show up in the warehouse—at least that's what she'd been told when she called an hour ago.

Emma was bundled up in her stroller, happily occupied pretending to read one of her favorite books. Aiden skipped along at Shelley's side, and Shelley's hand—that one holding a big basket of Lighthouse Sweet Shoppe cookies and muffins—was shaking like a lobster before being dropped in boiling water. Did she honestly think she could sweet-talk them into taking action?

She didn't know, but she had to try.

"Mornin'." A man with at least three or four day's worth of stubble on his plump and ruddy face sat behind the desk. Shelley stood there a moment before he finally looked up. "What can I do for you?"

"You don't remember me?" Shelley asked, hoping he'd notice the basket, maybe get a whiff of the sweets. "I'm Shelley Bauer. I live down at the end of Newport Avenue."

"Oh yeah. The boiler."

He couldn't have sounded any less interested. As much as she wanted to lose her cool, she didn't.

She set the basket of goodies on his desktop, beside an old gray stapler and a thick stack of dog-eared invoices. "If you're the one I talked with this morning—"

"Yeah, that would be me. Ernie."

"Pleased to meet you, Ernie." Shelley stuck out her hand, as nice and as polite as she could, even though she wasn't feeling all that nice and polite.

He looked up at last and grabbed hold of her hand with his fairly grimy one. He looked from Shelley then down at the basket. "What have we here?"

"Muffins and cookies." She offered Ernie her biggest smile. "You've sounded so overworked the last few times I called, and I couldn't help but wonder if people have been a tad obnoxious in their dealings with you, you know, complaining about work taking too long, orders not being processed, that kind of thing."

"Like I told you last week, things get hectic this time of year, what with the snow and wind and ice. It's hard to keep up with all the work."

"Then you must need a little something sweet to help you get through the days." She peeled back the red and white checkered cloth she'd tucked into the basket to cover up the goodies. "I've made you some banana nut and pumpkin muffins, some macadamia and chocolate chip cookies, and a few cranberry tarts, just to show you that I understand what it's like to be harried and have too much work to do."

He frowned at her, a look of sheer skepticism on his grizzled face. "How much is this basket of goodies going to cost me?"

"Nothing, of course. It's Christmastime, after all. It's just my gift to you."

"There's gotta be a catch."

Shelley shook her head. "No catch, unless—"

"Unless what?" his voice suddenly seemed louder. Aiden stopped jumping up and down. Emma let out a little wail, and Shelley scooped her up in her arms. "I just thought you might find a moment to check and see if the order for my new boiler could have been misplaced. You see, my children and I, not to mention my husband and our dog, are having to live with a neighbor while the boiler's out. And, of course, you might have heard we had a fire in our house, one that destroyed everything in the living room, including our Christmas tree."

His scowl softened. "Yeah, I heard."

"Well, there's only thirteen days left until Christmas, and my entire family—not to mention the neighbor we're living with—have been hoping and praying—praying with all our might—that the new boiler's installed soon so we can get back into our house, put up another tree, get it decorated, and be able to celebrate Christmas the way it ought to be celebrated."

"Yeah, it's tough not getting to celebrate Christmas at home." A wistful look crossed his face. "I remember one year when I was a kid and we—"

"So...do you think you could find the invoice for our boiler and double-check, just to make sure it's been ordered? Please?"

"I suppose, but I'm sure it hasn't arrived. If it had, we would have installed it right away." Ernie put his head down and thumbed through one of the stacks of paper on his desk, stopping when he came close to the last invoice in the second pile. "Well, what do you know."

"You found it?"

"Yeah, and it appears it was misfiled. In fact, there's a Received stamp right in the middle, and it looks like it arrived the day after it was ordered, and that was last Tuesday."

Ernie looked terribly contrite. His face might have turned red if you could see the parts that weren't covered with whiskers. "You know, Miz Bauer, we make a point of installing boilers as soon as they arrive. We know how difficult it can be, especially this time of year, to keep a house warm with an old or out-of-order boiler."

Shelley nodded. "Yes, it is rather difficult." She looked at her watch, then wanting to make an even bigger statement, she stared at the big clock on the wall. "I'll tell you what. I'll be home by 10:30, 10:35 at the very latest." She smiled sweetly. "Think you or one of your men could load up the boiler and meet me at the house by 10:40? That would give all of you time for at least one cookie or muffin. And there's more where these came from."

He swallowed hard. "I've got customers coming out of my ears, but— Yeah, I'll make sure your boiler's delivered before noon. Installation, well, that'll take some time. But we'll get it done."

"Thank you so very much, Ernie. I'll be sure to have a fresh pot of coffee perking away for you when you arrive."

Shelley tucked Emma back into the stroller, took hold of Aiden's hand, and offered Ernie a big smile. "See you in a few minutes."

He managed to smile back. "Yeah, just a few."

* * *

"Hi there!"

Margaret spun around. She'd been so caught up in her thoughts and in the soft music playing throughout the gallery that she hadn't heard Caleb come inside.

"Hi there!" she said in return, smiling as the boy dropped his backpack on the floor inside her studio, then shrugged out of his coat. "I have some cookies on my desk, ones my friend Shelley and my daughter Adelaide made. There's milk in the fridge too. Why don't you help yourself?"

"My grandma used to bake me cookies, but I haven't seen her in a long time," he said, heading for the desk, cheerful for a change, not the least bit shy. "You kinda remind me of her."

"I do, huh?" She didn't dare ask why he hadn't seen his grandmother in a long time.

"Yeah," he said, grabbing a cookie and hopping up on the edge of the desk, looking more comfortable than he had the last times he'd been in the gallery. "She had gray hair like you, but she couldn't paint or draw."

"Well, I can't cook, so I guess that makes your grandma and me kind of even."

"Kinda." He hopped off the desk and headed for her studio, with Margaret following. Thank heavens it had been quiet in the gallery all day. Right now she wanted to visit with Caleb, not try to play art salesperson.

He dropped down on her stool and spun around. "I got to thinking about the question you asked me the other day. About what kind of painter I'd like to be."

"Did you now?"

"Yeah, I want to be an illustrator. Like N. C. Wyeth and Howard Pyle. Do you like their work?"

Margaret nodded, thinking of the drama and adventure in both illustrators' works.

"I think surrealism, like my dad paints, is cool, but I want to paint swashbuckling pirates and knights on charging steeds."

"What about illustrating home and family, like Norman Rockwell?"

Caleb's shrug was pronounced.

Once again he didn't want to talk about family. So she wouldn't either. As long as they stayed away from talk of his family, he seemed to be happy.

Margaret retreated to the counter where she'd tucked away her art books. When she handed them to him, his brows furrowed. "What's this?"

"Oh, just something I thought you might enjoy as much as I did."

He peeled off the wrapping paper, revealing the books. He touched them with the same wonder and awe she had when she'd found them under the Christmas tree twenty-six years ago.

"Thank you." His eyes shone.

"Here." He pulled a handful of papers out of his backpack and showed her even more of his sketches, each as well done as the one of the lighthouse.

"You know, Caleb," Margaret said, "as beautiful as your pencil sketches are, you should really give painting a try. Your dad may not be painting any longer, but surely he still has his brushes and—"

"Nope, he got rid of them."

Why? Margaret felt a frown forming on her face. Once an artist, always an artist. You just didn't get rid of your paints or brushes. Never.

What on earth was wrong with Caleb's family? Somehow she'd have to find out. But for now, she said, "Well, you're more than welcome to use mine, and I have plenty of canvas if you want to try your hand at something different."

"Can I do it now?"

"Sure."

"I already know how to set up the easel and put paint on my palette. My dad showed me all that stuff," Caleb said, while Margaret helped him find just the right canvas. "If he wasn't working in Portland, I might see him more often."

He sighed and Margaret immediately changed the subject, wanting him to be comfortable in his surroundings.

"Have you ever tried drawing pirates or knights in shining armor?"

"I kind of got stuck drawing the lighthouse. I can see it from my bedroom window, so it's kind of embedded in my brain."

"That sketch of yours that I found was awfully good."

"Yeah, but it was kind of make-believe. The lighthouse doesn't work anymore, so I had to sketch what I thought the lights would look like."

Well, that answered her question. He hadn't seen the light that day.

"Can I use your big brush?" he asked. "The one that looks like a paintbrush."

"Help yourself." Margaret sat back in a chair and watched him pull the cobalt blue paint, spreading it out, thinning it here and there, adding a touch of black, a bit of white, turning the bottom third of the canvas into a storm-tossed ocean.

"My dad doesn't get to come home all that much," Caleb said, concentrating on his paints and the canvas. "I tried to talk him into coming in here to look around a few months ago, but he wouldn't, so we just hung around at the house, cutting wood and stuff like that."

"Couldn't you and your mom go to live with him in Portland?" Margaret was uncomfortable asking the question, but he was actually opening up, and she hoped that one simple question wouldn't make him run away again.

"Can't. My mom doesn't want to leave our house."

The bells on the front door jangled, startling both of them. "Mom! Look what I made."

Adelaide bounded into the studio with Allan following right behind.

"What is it, honey?"

"A Christmas ornament to hang on our tree."

Adelaide thrust the glitter and bead-decorated Styrofoam ball into Margaret's hands. "I used your favorite colors. Blue and green and pink."

"It's beautiful, Adelaide. And I know just where we'll put it on the tree. Right in the very front so everyone can see it."

Adelaide's smile drifted away when she saw Caleb sitting on the floor. "Hi. I'm Adelaide."

"This is my friend Caleb Wadsworth," Margaret said. Caleb stood, a touch of shyness returning to him when he looked from Adelaide to Allan, then back to Adelaide again. He held out his hand. Someone had taught him manners after all. "This is my daughter Adelaide and my husband Allan."

Allan captured Caleb's hand in both of his. "Margaret's told me all about you." He tilted his face toward Adelaide. "Caleb's an artist like your mom."

"Do you paint lighthouses and boats too?" Adelaide asked Caleb. "My mom paints really pretty lighthouses and boats."

Caleb shook his head. "I mostly sketch."

"Didn't mean to interrupt the two of you," Allan said, looking at the canvas and palette Caleb was holding. "We drove out to Willow's Corner to get Christmas wrapping paper after I picked Adelaide up from the community center, and thought we'd drop by to see if there's anything special you'd like us to bring you for dinner tonight. You are staying open until nine, aren't you?"

"Every night until Christmas Eve." Margaret laughed. "Such is the glamorous life of a gallery owner."

"Let's make a surprise for Mom!" Adelaide said to Allan.

"As long as it doesn't contain anchovies or liver, I'm open for any surprise."

"Well, then, we'll come back around six, and we'll all eat together, if you can clear off space on your worktable." Allan glanced at Caleb. "Would you like to join us? You could call your mom and see if it's okay, then I can drive you home afterward."

"I can't." Caleb shook his head. "I'm sure my mom will have a big dinner waiting for me, and she doesn't really like eating alone."

"Some other time then."

Allan kissed Margaret on the forehead, then stuck his hand out to Caleb. "Nice meeting you, Caleb."

"You too, sir." Caleb shook Allan's hand and watched Adelaide and Allan walk out of the gallery hand in hand. When they were gone, he turned back to his painting, looking at the canvas thoughtfully.

"Is something wrong with Adelaide?"

He wasn't the first person to ask her that question, but he asked with a sense of curiosity, not pity.

"She has Down syndrome. Do you know what that is?"

"I've heard of it, but that's it."

"People with Down syndrome are born with an extra chromosome. No one knows why it happens, but scientists are doing a lot of research, so maybe someday the condition can be prevented."

Caleb looked at Margaret at last. "Does the extra chromosome cause Down syndrome people to be slow?"

Margaret nodded. "People with Down syndrome perform at all different levels, but usually their muscle tone isn't as good as yours or mine, so they often move and talk slower than we do. But Adelaide and other Down syndrome children and adults go to school and can hold jobs and do all manner of things. They just need to be given the opportunity."

"Does Adelaide have a job?"

Margaret smiled, proud of Adelaide's accomplishments. "She babysits, and right now she's helping my friend in her bakery. And if I'd let her"—Margaret laughed—"she'd take in every stray cat in Marble Cove."

"She seems nice," Caleb said softly.

"She is."

He stared at his canvas again, silent for the longest time. "I had a little sister...but she died."

Margaret was caught up short, saddened by Caleb's words and the hurt in his voice. "I'm so sorry."

"Her name was Chloe." There was a catch in his voice, a lump in his throat that made the name difficult to get out. Suddenly he spun around on the stool, set his palette and brushes on the worktable, and grabbed his coat and backpack. "I'd better get home. My mom hasn't been feeling good and she might need me."

"Can I do anything? Give you a lift home?"

"Nope. I'd just better go before it gets any darker out."

He slipped into his worn coat on the way to the door.

"Will you come tomorrow? I'll look for some books at the library on Howard Pyle and N. C. Wyeth and maybe some illustrators you and I aren't familiar with."

"I'll try," he said, rushing through the door.

If only Margaret could help him. She just didn't know how.

Chapter Twenty

Diane wandered about her cottage Tuesday morning feeling free and relaxed at last. She'd slept like a baby all night in her own bed, peace and quiet surrounding her.

"Yes, Rocky, we have the house to ourselves again." Diane smiled. "Just you and me. We can write today without any interference. I can even stay in my pj's because there's no one I have to get dressed up for."

Leaning against the counter, Diane surveyed her surroundings. Everything was back in place. A trio of tall nutcrackers were lined up on a window sill, sitting in a bed of sweetly scented pine that she'd gathered in the forest not far from the lighthouse. They were special nutcrackers, ones she and Eric had found in Hamburg, Germany, when they'd splurged on a fairy-tale tour a few years back, where they'd haunted the Christmas markets in Dresden and Frankfurt, and the medieval market square in Goslar.

Once again the crystal angels that Jessica had given to her the year she'd actually been hired as a full-fledged attorney were on the bookcase, next to a few hundred-plus-year-old Bibles she and Eric had found in antiquarian bookstores.

So many things in the cottage brought back memories. If only the bearers of those memories were with her now, especially Eric.

Curling up on the sofa, with Rocky warming her feet, she picked up one of the old photo albums she'd taken out of their storage boxes the day after Thanksgiving, which she'd carefully packed away when Shelley and her gang moved in. She opened the album now, seeing Eric's face smiling up at her from where he sat at the base of their Christmas tree the first year they were married. She'd gotten him a silly tie that year; he'd gotten her a Kenny Rogers Christmas album, and both items had cost them precious money that they'd had very little of. She still had the tie and the album. This Christmas they'd both find their way under the tree, whether she was here by herself or Jessica and Justin joined her.

She reached for Rocky, combing her fingers through his fur, and said a little prayer, asking God to smile down on her and her children. She needed them this Christmas so very much.

Her cell phone rang and she ran for the kitchen to grab it. Jessica's name appeared on the screen. Had God heard her prayer and answered her already?

"Hey there! I was just thinking about you."

"Great minds think alike," Jessica responded, laughter filling her voice. She'd been such a sweet child, so shy. How she had ever become a top-notch attorney was anyone's guess, but she'd done it, and Diane and Eric couldn't have been prouder. "I wanted to wish you happy birthday a day early, Mom."

Diane groaned. "I thought we agreed to ignore my birthdays. Please just tell me you're coming for Christmas." She hadn't wanted to ask that right off the bat, not wanting to hear a negative answer and be depressed through the rest of their conversation, but she couldn't help herself.

"Actually, I was going to ask how your speech went on Saturday, but since you've asked about Christmas..."

Oh no. Here it comes. The answer.

"I've managed to clear a few days on my calendar. Justin's getting a few days off too. We don't have airline reservations yet and I'm not sure when we'll be able to get in, but we will be there, Mom. We promise. Even if we have to drive."

Diane's throat was so thick with emotion that she could barely swallow, but she didn't have to talk. Jessica was already telling her all about her latest court case, about the coolest purse she'd found at a vintage boutique. "It was originally sold way back in 1974. Can you believe that, Mom? 1974! That's eons ago."

Diane laughed at her daughter. "I graduated from high school in 1974. That's also the year I met your dad, so I remember every second of it."

"Do you still have any of your old stuff?" Jessica asked. "If you do, let's go through it while Justin and I are there. Who knows, I might find some cool clothes that you'd be willing to give me. After all, we're pretty much the same size."

Diane grinned as Jessica went on and on. Eric would be here in memory only this Christmas, but the rest of the holiday was going to be absolutely perfect.

* * *

"You don't by any chance have any books on N. C. Wyeth or Howard Pyle, do you?" Margaret asked, standing at the library's checkout desk. "Perhaps a book on American illustrators."

Gilda Harris looked up at Margaret over the reading glasses perched on the end of her nose. "You're the second person today to ask me about famous illustrators. Unfortunately, we don't have any in this library. I can order them for you from Augusta or Portland, if you'd like."

Hmm, that was a bit of a coincidence.

"The other person wouldn't have been Caleb Wadsworth?"

Gilda's lips pursed. "Now, Margaret. You should know better than to ask me a question like that. You know I can't give out personal information."

She did know that, but Gilda was an old friend. She'd lived in Marble Cove even longer than Margaret. "Could you just tell me if the other person asking about them was a young boy who's probably eleven years old, with blond hair and freckles?"

"Good try, Margaret, but I just can't divulge that kind of information." Gilda winked.

"But what if I told you he and his family might be in trouble and we could help them if only I knew where he lived?" Margaret pressed.

"What kind of trouble?" Gilda asked.

"Well, I don't want to get into it now, but I do believe that there's a reason he's been coming into my gallery and I just want to help him and his family, that's all," Margaret insisted. All night last night and all day today she'd thought about what Caleb had told her—that his little sister Chloe had died. How? Margaret wondered. Did Chloe's death have anything to do with what—if anything—was going on in the family?

Gilda didn't seem to be moved by her plea, so she continued.

"He was supposed to stop by the gallery after school today. I waited and waited, but he didn't show up. Yesterday he told me his mother is ill, and I'm worried about them. They live alone and..." Margaret sighed, wondering what all she should say. "I'm worried that they might not have enough food to eat, and I want to take a casserole or something to his house."

"Well, he looked fine when he was in here." Gilda clapped a hand over her mouth. "Oh dear, I shouldn't have said that, but the boy did look fine, Margaret. So I don't see any need to worry, not now anyway."

Gilda was probably right. She was overreacting.

"All right, I'll try not to worry. But if he doesn't show up, I'll need to go to his house. Unfortunately I don't have his address. I'm hoping you can help me, Gilda. You know you can trust me."

Gilda frowned for the longest time. Finally she typed something into her computer and scribbled some information on a piece of paper. "I do trust you, Margaret. But please, don't tell anyone where you got that information. It could mean my job. And if you give it to anyone else—"

"I won't, Gilda. Not to worry." Margaret smiled. "I owe you one."

Now, if she could just be patient for another twenty-four hours.

* * *

Margaret strolled along the boardwalk early Wednesday morning, listening to the splash of salt water against the pilings, the constant screech of gulls circling overhead, and a couple of lobster boats chugging out of the cove. It was peaceful this morning, and Margaret watched the puffs of mist rising as she breathed in the calm but frigid air. The roofs of every home, every business, from fishing shacks to towering churches, were covered in a pristine blanket of white.

With her hands tucked into the pockets of her parka and the hood pulled over the knitted wool cap she was wearing, she headed toward Main Street, her thoughts caught up in Christmas: the cards she'd just half an hour ago dropped off in the mail chute at the post office and the presents she'd ordered online late last night, because time was running out and there were a few items she wouldn't be able to get locally.

And, of course, Caleb.

Would he or wouldn't he show up this afternoon? That young boy had wiggled his way into her heart, and the compulsion, the sense of urgency she felt toward him, had not diminished.

It was nearly ten o'clock when she passed the lobster-trap Christmas tree, the midmorning sunshine pouring down on worn wood frames and wire, and on brightly painted buoys, making bits and pieces sparkle. She crossed the square to Main Street, taking it slow and easy, admiring window displays and painted glass storefronts.

Santa Claus and his elves were hard at work inside Santa's North Pole workshop, hammering and sawing on toys, the cartoonlike painting in the hardware store's front window so bright and cheery she decided if she were a judge, she just might have to award it first prize in the *Marble Cove Courier* Best Christmas Window contest.

Then again, the Crow's Nest, her favorite bookstore, had gone all out, decorating their porthole windows and rounded glass door with mermaids and Neptune reading copies of *A Christmas Carol,* "The Night Before Christmas," and *How the Grinch Stole Christmas.* The Crow's Nest could also capture that first prize award.

Margaret laughed at herself. What did it matter? She loved her window. She would have painted it the way she did whether there was a prize waiting at the other end or not.

The only thing still not quite right about it was the star. She'd nearly forgotten that it wasn't quite as perfect as the rest of the painting. Caleb, in one of his offhand comments, had said he could fix it, but he hadn't. And she didn't know if he'd ever again come to the gallery.

At long last she slipped her key into the lock on the gallery door, stepped inside, and switched on the lights. The phone started to ring immediately. She flipped the sign in the door from Closed to Open and ran to her office. "Shearwater Gallery. May I help you?"

"Hello, Margaret!" A hearty voice boomed in her ear.

"Justin! It's so nice to hear from you."

"Thanks. I've only got a couple of minutes before I have to get back to work, but my mom was raving about a painting of yours when I called her this morning. She said it was on layaway—?"

"I know exactly which painting you're talking about. It's called *Dawn's Early Light.* It was on layaway, but that was canceled just yesterday, and I'm afraid I've been so busy that I forgot to let your mother know."

"Then don't tell her. Please," Justin said. "Jessica and I would like to buy it for her Christmas present."

"She'll love it, Justin."

They discussed price, with Margaret giving Jessica and Justin a discount and throwing in the frame at cost.

"Any chance you can wrap it up for us too?" Justin asked. "We couldn't get flights until Christmas morning, so we'll be running to get to Mom's in time for the brunch she always loves to make."

"I'll take care of it, Justin, and I'll take it home with me, ready for you to pick up when you arrive."

As soon as Justin hung up, Margaret took down the painting, wrapped it securely so the frame wouldn't get any nicks or scratches, then picked out her favorite Christmas wrapping paper and made the package look beautiful, with curly ribbon and all.

The rest of the day was filled with customers and lookie-loos, just as she'd hoped it would be at this time of year. It hadn't slowed down much at all when two o'clock rolled around, and if Caleb showed up, she'd have to call Allan and ask him to lend her a hand.

But Caleb didn't show up. Not at two. Not at three. Not by four.

At four fifteen she called Allan.

"What's for dinner tonight?" she asked, peering around the office wall when she heard the jingle bells on the front door ring. Detective Fred Little came in and immediately walked toward the jewelry. She knew the perfect piece he should get for his wife, if that's who he was buying for, and she'd point it out to him as soon as she finished her conversation with Allan.

"I've got a casserole in the oven. Alfredo chicken and biscuits. Why?"

"Because I want to take it to Caleb's house."

She could hear Allan sigh, not out of frustration, but because he knew she was worried. "I take it he didn't show up again."

"I haven't heard from him. I haven't seen him, and I've watched every group of kids walking by since school let out.

I can't go another day without knowing what's wrong. For all I know, he may have gotten hurt or be sick or maybe he ran off to Portland to be with his dad."

"Don't let your imagination carry you away."

The only thing that ended up carrying her away was her van, which she climbed into after selling Fred Little a handcrafted sterling silver bracelet, and putting Allan's yummy chicken casserole and a plate of brownies on the front seat. She'd checked out Caleb's address on one of the Internet mapping sites and knew exactly where he lived, in an old farmhouse on the outskirts of town. After turning down Allan's plea to go with her, she was off.

It was dark when she turned onto the dirt road, which was crusted over with ice. The branches of the fir trees lining both sides were heavy with snow. They hung down and occasionally brushed the sides and roof of the van, the snow splatting on her windshield.

The house was nearly half a mile back, in an area that had been cleared by farmers a hundred or more years ago. Caleb's home was probably built back then too. She'd expected to see a dilapidated place, the paint on the once-white wood peeling away, a window screen or two missing, or lying on the ground beneath the window, the front porch sagging. But the house, while not perfect, was neat and well kept.

A string of multicolored lights had been strung around the front door and Margaret could see a decorated tree through one of the windows.

Margaret climbed out of the van, turned and grabbed the casserole and brownies from the passenger side, then made her way through the unshoveled snow to the porch. The door opened the moment she knocked.

Caleb stood there, shock written all over his face.

"What are you doing here?" He didn't sound perturbed or upset, only surprised.

"I've been worried about you, and your mom too. You told me she'd been sick and I thought you might have come down with something."

"I'm fine. My mom's asleep."

He didn't want Margaret here; that much was obvious.

Margaret held out the casserole. "Allan made one of my favorite dishes for you. It's Alfredo chicken and biscuits. He made brownies too." Margaret smiled. "The box is rather hot. Mind if I bring it in and put it in the kitchen for you?"

"Thanks, but I can do it."

"Won't take me but a second, and then I'll get out of your hair. Like I said, I just wanted to make sure you were okay."

"I'm fine."

So he'd said already.

"I could see your Christmas tree from the drive. It looks awfully pretty."

"Thanks. My mom and I decorated it."

"I bet you have a lot of special ornaments on it. Ones you made when you were little?"

"Some, yeah."

"Can I look? Just a quick peek after I put this box in the kitchen."

Caleb shrugged. He opened the door just wide enough for Margaret to walk in, closed it behind her, then led her to the kitchen. Even though it wasn't filled with the most up-to-date appliances, it was spotlessly clean. A mural had been painted on one wall—an English garden, splashed with roses, periwinkle, and lavender.

"Did your dad paint this?" Margaret asked, after setting the box on a counter.

"Yeah, a long time ago, when I was a baby. My mom's from England, and Dad said it made her feel at home."

"Can I help you?"

Margaret spun around at the sound of the woman's voice—the English accent quite pronounced, even though her words were barely a whisper. She was blonde, like Caleb, but her hair was disheveled, her eyes were red, the dark circles beneath them making her face look hollow. She was thin, too thin.

How could her husband leave her like this?

"I'm Margaret Hoskins." Margaret held out her hand and the woman took it. Her hands were icy cold. There was wariness in her eyes along with the redness. "I own the Shearwater Gallery."

Caleb's mother frowned. "Is that in Marble Cove? I don't remember ever seeing a gallery by that name."

"I opened the gallery in May. It's on Main Street."

Caleb looked from his mother to Margaret, clearly

uncomfortable. "I told you about Mrs. Hoskins, Mom. She's letting me use her paints and canvas."

Mrs. Wadsworth looked worried. "Are you sure, Caleb? I don't remember us talking about painting in a long time."

"I did, Mom. Honest."

She tried to smile, but it never quite made it to her eyes. It would be easy to think she was on drugs, but Margaret was sure it was something else. Grief? The loss of her daughter? Maybe abandonment by her husband? Both, more than likely.

"Caleb told me you weren't feeling well, so I brought you a casserole and some brownies. My husband's the cook, not me." Margaret laughed lightly, trying to ease the tension in the room. "Heaven forbid that I should try to feed anyone something I made."

"Thank you so much," Caleb's mother said softly. "I'm Ellie. I'm not much of a hostess, but I could fix some coffee."

"No, no, that's fine. I don't want to keep you, but I do want to tell you what a wonderful artist Caleb is. I've seen his sketches and even though he hasn't painted much—yet—he has an innate skill."

Ellie smiled softly. "You're an artist too?"

Margaret nodded. "I started painting when I was about Caleb's age, but he's so much better than I was back then. I hope you'll let him continue coming to the gallery after school. He can come during Christmas vacation too. I'll have shortened hours until spring when the tourists return."

"If he wants to, that's fine with me," she said, although there was some hesitancy in her voice. "His father's an artist." She sighed. "Caleb takes after him."

"Maybe you'll come by the gallery one day. Saturday night is the Christmas Stroll, when all the stores on Main Street will be open. We're going to sing carols and drink hot cider and cocoa, and I'll be serving goodies made by a friend of mine."

"Oh, I don't know. I don't get out much anymore, but we'll see."

Caleb slipped his hand into his mom's. "We'd have a great time. Maybe Dad could go too."

"We'll see," Ellie repeated.

Margaret said her good-byes, thankful that Caleb was fine. Now, of course, she was worried about Ellie. If only there was something she could do to really help them.

Chapter Twenty-One

The stars were brightly shining, twinkling away in the midnight blue sky, when Beverly pulled up in front of Mr. Maker's bungalow on Wednesday evening. She was tired after making a long and controversial budget presentation, but she wouldn't miss this chance to see Mr. Maker, not for the world.

Jeff pulled his Jeep into the driveway just moments after she arrived. She'd told him she was always on time, that you could almost set your watching by her comings and goings. Either he'd listened or he was punctual too. It was exactly six o'clock.

Jeff was out of the Jeep in an instant and trudged across the icy street, holding the door open for her when she climbed out. "How'd your presentation go?"

"I don't think I won many friends."

"Does that bother you?"

She shrugged. "It never used to; today it did, but I'll get over it."

"Well, you've won Grandpa over. He's far more excited about seeing you than me."

"He may change his mind about both of us when we ask him about the wreck of the *Newcastle.*"

"Well, the way I see it, the sooner he gets whatever it is that's been bothering him for nearly eighty years off his chest, the better off he'll be. He might even thank us."

"One can hope."

Beverly carried a pink box full of goodies from the Lighthouse Sweet Shoppe and Jeff the Christmas-wrapped painting of Orlean Point Light. Mr. Maker opened the door for them before they were all the way up the stairs. He must have been watching through the window, eager for their company. That, at least, was a good sign.

"Glad you could join us," Mr. Maker said. He helped Beverly out of her coat once they were all inside and hung it on the rack.

"I've brought you more of the cookies my friend Shelley makes, but this time she threw in a few cranberry-walnut bars and a loaf of her melt-in-your-mouth cranberry bread."

"And I have an early Christmas gift for you that you have to open tonight."

Mr. Maker eyed Jeff and Beverly suspiciously. "You two trying to butter me up?"

"Is that possible?" Jeff asked, winking at his grandfather.

"Depends on what you want out of me." Mr. Maker grinned at Beverly. "Depends on how good those cranberry-walnut bars are too."

Beverly had to smile. She could see why Mr. Maker and her father had gotten along so well when they were both boys.

"I'll get some napkins out of the kitchen—"

"No, you won't," Mr. Maker interrupted, before Beverly could take two steps toward the kitchen. "I may be old, but I still take care of my guests. Now get in the other room and sit yourself down."

Once they were alone, Beverly asked, "Should we ask him about the *Newcastle* right away, or wait a bit? Maybe give him the gift first?"

"The gift's going to tick him off, but—"

"What's going to tick me off?" Mr. Maker asked, setting a tray of napkins, coffee mugs, and a carafe of coffee on the coffee table. He lowered himself into his easy chair, his knees creaking.

"You told me you don't like presents," Jeff said, "that you're tired of collecting things that you'll have to add to your will—not that you're going to be leaving this world anytime soon. But"—he held the gift out to his grandfather—"I hope you'll like this."

Mr. Maker frowned as he weighed the heft of the wrapped gift. "What is it?"

"You'll find out when you open it."

"I'd complain some more about you giving me a gift, but it wouldn't do much good."

Beneath his somewhat crusty exterior, Beverly thought she saw the face of a little boy, excited to receive a Christmas gift.

Just as Beverly always did, hoping to save the paper for another year and another present, Mr. Maker took his time removing the paper. Slowly but surely, he uncovered the framed painting.

The gleam of excitement that had been in his eyes faded fast. His head jerked up, looking at Beverly and then at Jeff. "What's the meaning of this?"

"It's Orlean Point Light," Jeff said, keeping a smile on his face. "I thought it might bring back memories."

"It does. Bad ones. Ones that were buried nearly eighty years ago, and here you are, trying to dig them up and bring them back to life."

Jeff breathed deeply; Beverly did too. Oh, how she wished she could walk outside and come back in again without the painting. They'd probably get nothing out of him now, not one shred of information.

"If you don't like it, Grandpa, I'll keep it for myself," Jeff said, taking the painting out of his grandfather's lap. "Of course, since I'm living in between here, there, and everywhere else at the present time, I don't have a permanent place to keep it. So if you don't mind"—Jeff propped the painting up on the fireplace mantle, shifting a few pinecones out of the way—"I'll keep it here for the time being."

Mr. Maker grunted. "If I told you no, you'd ignore me, so suit yourself." He grabbed a cranberry-walnut bar and bit off a third, chewing it slowly. He turned toward Beverly. "Tell your friend Shelley that these are good. If she wants to send me a box, I'll buy a couple dozen."

"She'd like that," Beverly said, surprised his ire had dissipated so quickly. Either that or he was holding it back, preparing to explode the next time they presented him with something else—like questions about the *Newcastle* disaster.

"I brought fresh lobster for dinner, Grandpa. Plus a loaf of crusty French bread and real butter. Thought I'd treat you and Beverly to a little home cooking."

"I haven't had lobster in a blue moon. You shouldn't have gone to all the trouble though. I've got a lot of frozen dinners in the freezer."

"Eat too many of those and your blood pressure will go sky high," Beverly said. "On top of that, you're liable to get skinny." She grinned. "Want to look like me?"

Mr. Maker hit her with a lopsided grin. "You're not so bad."

"Then show me where you keep the biggest pot you've got and I'll get the water boiling while Jeff brings in the groceries."

* * *

Less than two hours later, their bellies were full, and Beverly complained to Jeff and Mr. Maker that she'd end up fat and sassy if she kept on eating lobster and drawn butter.

Jeff leaned back in his chair, getting comfortable. Beverly imagined he was going to now bring up the subject of the shipwreck. If she had her druthers, she would rather be anywhere but here. Still, she steeled herself for a thick dose of Edward's fury.

"Beverly and I took the mail boat out to one of the islands off Marble Cove last Friday. Ever been to Abenaki Isle?"

Mr. Maker's eyes narrowed. "Can't say that I have."

"It's pretty," Beverly said. "We hiked all over the island, in spite of the snow and the wind, and Jeff took some photos of the oldest building on the island—a church—built out of wood from a few old shipwrecks."

"You don't say."

"Guess there were a lot of freighters and schooners that went down off Abenaki in the eighteenth and nineteenth centuries," Jeff added. "Probably before that too."

"What's up with all this newfound interest in shipwrecks?" Mr. Maker asked. "People ended up dead when ships crashed. Cargo got lost. None of it was a pretty sight."

"That's true, but it was fascinating to see how the people on Abenaki Isle put the wood to good use," Beverly said, unable to think of anything brilliant to add to what Jeff had been telling his grandfather. "The church we saw must have been beautiful in its day. It's a shame no one bothered to preserve it."

"If you're thinking you might talk me into going out to that island, you're dead wrong. I spent my fair share of time on board ship during the war—that's the Korean War, in case you're wondering. Don't have any mind to get back on one again."

"Actually, Grandpa, we were wondering if you knew anything about a shipwreck that occurred in the 1930s."

"God only knows how many ships wrecked back then. Could have been hundreds."

"Not off Orlean Point," Jeff added, taking the conversation where it was bound to be too close for anyone's comfort.

Beverly brought it even closer to home. "The ship we're mostly interested in was the *Newcastle*."

"Never heard of it."

Beverly had watched Mr. Maker's face. She was sure his eyes had twitched when she mentioned the name of the ship. He knew a lot; he just didn't want to talk about it.

But would he?

"I couldn't find anything in the Marble Cove library or anywhere else about the ship," Jeff said. "For all I know, it might never have existed. But when Beverly and I were on the island, we met a woman who told us all about the wreck. She said it went down off Marble Cove, because the light in Orlean Point Light had failed to work. At least that's what the officials told her."

"No one in her family believed that story," Beverly said. "She's sure the truth was covered up."

Edward laughed. "It if happened nearly eighty years ago, what's she so upset about? Shouldn't she have forgotten all about it by now?"

"Her grandmother and grandfather died in the wreck. And not only them," Jeff continued, "but a couple of uncles and an aunt."

Mr. Maker shook his head, staring down at the floor. "What makes you think I'd know about this shipwreck?"

"Because your father must have been the light keeper at Orlean Point when it happened."

"It's a sad story," Beverly added, sensing that Jeff had hit a dead end in his questions. "Both Jeff and I have been doing a lot of research, trying to learn true stories about the lighthouse, not just the myths. We were both shocked to hear about the shipwreck, and even more shocked to find that the incident might have been covered up. If something like that had happened to anyone in my family, I'd want an apology, at the very least."

"Like I said, I don't know anything."

Mr. Maker pushed up out of his chair and threw his napkin down on the table. Not looking at either Jeff or Beverly, he trudged out of the kitchen and back into the living room, with Beverly and Jeff following. When he reached his chair, he shoved his hands through his hair. He closed his eyes and sat silently for quite a long time, with Beverly standing near the fireplace, Jeff beside a bookcase, neither one making a sound, waiting for Mr. Maker to talk.

"My father wasn't just a drunk," Edward said at last, his tone no longer filled with irritation, but with anguish. "And he wasn't just a lighthouse keeper, either. He was a bootlegger as well as a smuggler."

Beverly leaned forward in the leather easy chair. She'd never expected to hear those words. It didn't appear that Jeff had expected them, either. "You're sure about that?" Jeff asked, sitting down across from his grandfather.

"Of course I'm sure." He ran a hand through his thick hair. "Orlean Point Light worked perfectly. It never failed, not once in all the years the lighthouse was in operation."

"But the officials told the families of the people who died in the shipwreck that it failed," Beverly protested. "Why would they lie? Was the ship carrying some big government secrets, something that had to be covered up?"

Edward leaned his head against the back of the chair and stared up at the ceiling. "It was all my fault."

"Don't say that, Grandpa. You were just a kid."

Edward directed his irritated stare at Jeff. "You've been badgering me to tell you what happened back in 1935, so I'm telling you. It was all my fault. I might as well have killed all those people with my bare hands."

Jeff moved his chair closer to his grandfather and put a hand on his arm. "What happened?"

Edward closed his eyes for a moment and said nothing. He rubbed his temples, then slowly leaned back in the chair. He didn't look at either Jeff or Beverly as he spoke; his eyes seemed glazed over, as if he was seeing only the past.

"I was only seven, but I'd been watching the light since I was five. Somebody had to do it, especially on those nights when my father was out smuggling booze or getting drunk."

"You learned how to do it on your own?" Jeff asked.

Edward shook his head. "Dad taught me. He called me his little man. Said I had all the makings of a great light keeper—I just needed more practice." He laughed cynically. "I was so proud of myself. But one night, Dad had some smuggling to do. He told me the government was corrupt and people were starving because there weren't any jobs, and that he had to bootleg liquor and smuggle it too, just to keep a roof over our heads."

"Those were hard times," Beverly noted.

Edward tilted his head to look at her. "Yes, they were. I was only seven and he was my dad and back then I would have believed anything he told me. That night, though, when he left me all alone to do his real job, I fell asleep. I messed up."

"You were a *kid,*" Jeff said adamantly.

"That doesn't matter a hill of beans. I fell asleep when I had a job to do. My dad told me to keep an eye on the light, to make sure it didn't go out. If I hadn't fallen asleep, I would have been able to fix the light. The *Newcastle* wouldn't have crashed against the shore, and none of those people would have died. I was sorry then; I'm sorry now. I've carried the guilt with me for nearly eighty years. That's why I don't like looking at the lighthouse; that's why I never wanted to talk about it or my life in Marble Cove."

All three of them were silent for the longest time, then Beverly cleared her throat. "Would anyone like some coffee? I can make some."

"No, thanks," Mr. Maker said. "I've told you that much of the story, I might as well tell you the rest."

Beverly leaned forward in her chair, just as Jeff had done. Her arms rested on her knees, listening intently, while the elder man spoke.

"I thought my father would go out of his mind after the accident. He yelled at my mom; he yelled at me. I remember him banging his fists against the lighthouse, cursing himself and me and God."

"He had no business cursing you *or* God," Jeff said. "He was the one at fault for leaving you there to do his job while he went off to do something illegal."

Edward shrugged. "I don't think he saw it that way. He always felt he'd gotten a short shrift in life. That he deserved more than he'd ever received. In the end, he took the blame for the accident."

"That was big of him," Jeff muttered.

"He told his boss that he'd been sick, that he hadn't slept in days, and that even though he'd tried to keep his eyes open that night, he'd fallen asleep."

Beverly and Jeff sat quietly, letting Edward Maker tell the story of that terrible event.

"After dad took the blame, he was fired, which meant our family not only lost income, but we also lost our home."

"What about the bootlegging money? Couldn't that see you through till he got another job?"

"It might have if he hadn't left us. He just disappeared with whatever money he might have had. That's when my mother started working in the canneries. Long hours, lousy pay. But it was honest."

"And the cover-up?" Beverly asked. "What was that all about?"

"The light had failed. That wasn't a lie. The officials—the government, really, since that's who owned the lighthouse—just left out the rest of the details when they told the victims. They might have assumed the government would be sued, and it would look better, and end up costing less, if no mention was made of the light keeper falling asleep. I don't know why there's no documentation. It could have been lost in a fire. Who knows. Maybe someone on the investigating committee was part of the bootlegging operation. Maybe something really big happened at the same time that overshadowed the shipwreck. But the official statement was that the light failed and the light keeper—my dad—wasn't able to get it working, try as he might. As far as I know there was never any mention of him being fired; all anyone seemed to know was that my dad had quit his job after the accident, because he felt too much guilt and anguish over what happened. End of story. Now you know why I carved 'I'm sorry' into the lighthouse wall."

"I'm sorry too, Grandpa."

"It's history. Not something you should be sorry about." He moved away, headed for the stairs. "And now that I've told you the story, I don't want to speak about it ever again."

Chapter Twenty-Two

Margaret had far too much to do to get ready for the Christmas Stroll Saturday night. Everything needed to be dusted and polished. She needed to clean up her studio and office to make everything look presentable.

Tables needed to be set up for the food, and she had at least a dozen festive trays to wash and dry, along with her best lace tablecloths. She'd hired Shelley to cater cookies and tarts, she'd ordered a new batch of business cards and flyers, and—

She gave a weary sigh and pushed open the door to the Cove. She needed the break and had hung up the Closed sign so she could get away for half an hour. She couldn't ask Allan to watch the shop. Not again. Besides, she'd already sent him and Adelaide off to Willow's Corner to pick up Christmassy napkins and cups.

She ordered a cup of coffee, and when she had the steaming brew in hand, she joined Diane, Shelley, and Beverly at their regular table.

Beverly yawned. So did Shelley, and Margaret did too.

Diane laughed when she also succumbed. "My excuse is that I was too happy to go to sleep last night. When

Justin called for my birthday, he said he's going to fly in on Christmas morning with Jessica. I was so thrilled! But what about you three?"

"Your birthday?" Shelley cried. "Why didn't you say something, Diane? We would have thrown you a party!"

"Or had Shelley bake you a cake," Beverly added.

Margaret was about to add that Justin had mentioned he'd called when she remembered she was supposed to be keeping the painting they were giving her for Christmas a secret.

"A party is exactly what I was hoping to avoid," Diane told her friends. "I prefer to keep my birthdays low-key these days—or better yet, pretend they don't happen! So thank you for your kind intentions, but please, let's forget about it, and just tell me why *you* all are so tired."

"I have absolutely no excuse," Margaret said, "except that I'm much older than the rest of you and I'm plumb tuckered out. Getting ready for the Christmas Stroll is no easy task."

"But the gallery's going to look wonderful Saturday night," Shelley said, a twinkle in her eye. "And the desserts you'll be serving will be the best anyone has to offer."

"What are you serving?" Beverly asked. "I've never been to the Christmas Stroll and have absolutely no idea what to expect."

"I'll be serving tasty treats from the Lighthouse Sweet Shoppe." Margaret smiled at Shelley and chuckled. "Plus hot cocoa and mulled apple cider."

"And the same kind of fare will be offered in every shop in town?" Beverly asked.

"Every shop on Main Street," Diane added, "or so I've been told."

"And Santa will be coming." Shelley smiled. "That's all Aiden has talked about for weeks. I just hope he can stay awake long enough to see him."

"And what about you?" Diane asked, looking at Beverly. "What's your excuse for the big yawn? I know you were in Augusta yesterday, but—"

"I was in Augusta. I had a splitting headache during a simply awful budget presentation, and afterward, I had a lobster dinner with Jeff and his grandfather."

"Was this the dinner when you and Jeff planned to ask Mr. Maker about the shipwreck," Margaret asked, "and the lights failing to work on the lighthouse?"

"One and the same." Beverly took a sip of her coffee. "I wish you all could have heard his story." She spent the next ten minutes sharing everything she'd heard last night.

"So his father really was a bootlegger?" Shelley asked, sitting on the far side of the table, Aiden in her lap, Emma in a high chair, both of them extraquiet. "And a smuggler too?"

Beverly nodded. "Great fodder for a mystery, if it wasn't all so sad."

Diane scribbled notes on a napkin. "It is sad for Edward Maker, and his mother too. As for his father—words fail me at the moment, but when he makes his way into one of my books as a dastardly villain, and I daresay he will, watch out. There are any number of ways to do away with a man of that sort."

"I only wish there was some way of telling Cass MacDuffie the truth," Beverly said. "She wasn't alive when the shipwreck happened, but she still lost family members and she's still angry. If only I could tell her what really happened that night, maybe she'd find a way to move on."

"Why do you think Cass is so angry about the shipwreck?" Diane asked Beverly.

Beverly hesitated. She'd wondered the same thing. "I think Cass grew up feeling cheated out of knowing her grandparents." She paused. "But I also think sometimes hurt and anger can be passed from generation to generation, especially if there's no healing or opportunity for apologies or forgiveness."

"Good points, Beverly." Margaret stirred her coffee. "It wouldn't be right for you or Jeff to tell her. Mr. Maker should do it. And then maybe there'll be that opportunity for healing."

"He won't, though," Beverly said. "He told Jeff and me that he would never again talk about that night."

"Well, he certainly shouldn't feel guilty for what happened," Shelley said. "He was only seven, just a child. It's so terribly sad that he's spent nearly eighty years feeling he was responsible for the shipwreck, but it seems to me that the only way he'll ever be able to let go of those feelings, to forgive himself, is to talk to Cass. To tell her the truth."

"We might not be able to tell Cass anything," Diane said, "but why don't we do this. After church on Sunday, why don't we go up to Orlean Point and say a prayer for her and for the people who lost their lives?"

"That's a great idea," Shelley said, "and we should pray for Edward Maker too. After all, he never should have been allowed to shoulder this guilt."

"Just remember to bundle up good and warm that day," Margaret added. "I hear another storm's blowing in next weekend."

* * *

Caleb was quiet when he showed up at the gallery after school Thursday afternoon. His shoulders were hunched over and he wouldn't look directly at Margaret.

"Bad day at school?" she asked, trying to break the ice.

Caleb shook his head, and as he usually did, he dropped his backpack on the floor inside the studio, tossed his parka on top of it. "Mind if I paint a bit today?"

"I told you, Caleb, you can use whatever paints and brushes I have, and you can come in here and paint any time you want."

"Thanks."

He loaded his palette with oils, put the canvas he'd been painting on the easel, and sat on the stool in front of it. He stared at the cobalt blue sea for the longest time, then dabbed his brush in white, then emerald green, mixed the two together, then put brush to canvas.

"Would you like some hot cocoa?" Margaret asked. "You already know I'm not a good cook, not at all like your grandmother, but I can make cocoa."

"Yes. Please."

Margaret tried not to imagine what was going through Caleb's mind right now. He wasn't his usual self. He was polite, which really didn't surprise her. She'd sensed that underneath the bravado he'd shown, there was a child who'd been raised right. No, something was definitely bothering him.

She went into the kitchenette and microwaved two cups of milk, then spooned in a few heaping teaspoons of rich, dark chocolate instant cocoa, a special brand that she paid good money for because it tasted so much like the real thing. She added marshmallows and carried the mugs into the studio, listening to Bing singing, "*If you're worried and you can't sleep, just count your blessings instead of sheep...*"

"Here you go," Margaret said, setting Caleb's mug on the worktable. She sat in a chair not too far from his easel and watched him work, not sure just yet what he was painting.

He took in a deep breath and released it slowly, whatever torment was going through his mind causing him extra pain. He turned to Margaret at last, his eyes red. "I'm sorry you saw my mom like that last night."

"She wasn't feeling well. I knew that when I went to your home, Caleb. You've no need to apologize."

"She's not always like that."

"I'm sure she's not." Margaret smiled. "Why don't you drink your cocoa before it gets cold?"

He got up from his stool, lifted the mug, and typical eleven-year-old that he was, he scooped the marshmallows up with his tongue, swallowed, then slurped up a healthy mouthful of hot chocolate. "This isn't bad," he said, some of his usual cool coming back. "Not exactly homemade, but good just the same." He took another swallow. "My mom used to be a good cook."

"Used to be?"

Caleb nodded, his eyes thoughtful. "She hasn't cooked much since Chloe died." He sighed, shrugging his shoulders. "She hasn't done much at all since Chloe died."

Margaret took a sip of her cocoa. "Want to tell me what happened?"

Caleb wiped his mouth with the back of his hand. He'd been looking at Margaret, but now stared into his cup. "She didn't wake up one morning. No one knows why." He looked up slowly. "It's called SIDS."

"Sudden Infant Death Syndrome." Margaret felt an almost unbearable sadness catch at her heart, but for Caleb's sake, she tried not to let it show. "And you're right, no one really knows why it happens. A baby's healthy one day, gone the next." She shook her head. "I can't even imagine what a mother or father, or even a brother, must feel when something terrible like that happens."

"I cried a lot, but it was the toughest on my mom and dad, especially my mom. She still cries, and it's been two years."

"There's no time frame for grieving," Margaret told him, her voice soft. "We all do it in our own way, in our own time."

Caleb looked up at Margaret with reddened eyes. "Do you think she'll ever stop? The grieving?"

Margaret didn't have an answer. Still, she said, "Someday. Sooner than later, we can hope. And we can pray about it too."

He nodded.

Margaret wasn't sure she should ask the next question, but she did. "Why is your dad really in Portland?"

Caleb frowned, and Margaret hoped she hadn't asked one question too many. "He had to get a real job. I told you that." He turned back toward his painting, but he didn't pick up his brush, just stared at the swirls he'd painted. "He couldn't find one here in Marble Cove and he had to make money."

"But people were buying his paintings. He could have made money without leaving you and your mom."

Confusion flashed across Caleb's face. "How do you know that?"

Margaret felt her face flush. "I don't, for sure," Margaret said. "I'm sorry, Caleb. After you told me about your dad, I looked him up on the Internet. I-I didn't mean to pry. I just want to know what I can do to help."

"No one can help."

"How will you know if no one tries?"

"You think you can get them back together again?"

"That's a tall order, but I'll pray about it."

"I pray all the time, or at least I used to…but I don't think God hears me."

"He's heard you, Caleb. We just have to put our faith in Him, knowing He'll do what's best for us."

"I try to have faith, but—" He swallowed hard. "It's taking too long."

"The things we want the most rarely come fast," Margaret said. "Sometimes it seems we wait forever."

"All I want is for my dad to come home. For things to be the way they used to be."

"You mean when your dad was painting?"

Caleb nodded. "He was good. Really good. The critics said so, but he changed after Chloe died. He said his imagination dried up, but I think it was more than that."

"What do you think it was?"

"My mom. She wouldn't stop crying. She wouldn't eat and she couldn't sleep. My dad was sad too, but my mom made him even sadder. She wouldn't talk to him; she wouldn't go see a counselor. They'd argue at night and she'd cry even more." Caleb shrugged. "One night I heard Dad say he couldn't take it anymore. He told my mom he loved her, but he had to leave. He said it was too hard to live in a house with a woman who didn't have any desire to live."

"Oh, Caleb, I'm so sorry."

"Me too." He sighed. "I want things to be normal again. I pray for that all the time, but I don't think it's going to happen."

Unless his prayers had already been answered. Margaret was sure God had sent her to help Caleb. She just needed to figure out exactly how He wanted her to do that.

* * *

Not long after Caleb left the gallery, Margaret hung her Closed sign—even though the Christmas rush was on—and climbed into her van and headed to church.

Not so long ago she hadn't really believed there was a God. Not that she'd disbelieved, exactly. She just hadn't known in her heart if He was real. All of that changed when she'd nearly drowned, when God sent someone to save her.

That had been a miracle.

Walking into Our Savior's Sanctuary now, the church she, Allan, and Adelaide had attended since "the miracle," she sat in one of the pews at the back of the sanctuary, folded her hands and closed her eyes. "Dear Lord, I'm pretty sure you sent me to help Caleb Wadsworth and his family, but I'm at a loss for what to do. He wants so much for his mother and father to get back together, for their family to be whole once more. Please, Lord. Guide me in the right direction. Show me the way to help them."

Her prayer was short, not the long chat she'd planned, but there didn't seem to be all that much more to say. She just had to give her problem up to Him, and let Him lead the way.

Half an hour later, Margaret stopped at the post office to pick up the gallery's mail, then headed back to Main Street, unlocked her shop, flipped the Closed sign to Open, and went into the back to put on a pot of coffee. She sat down at her desk, sliced open over half a dozen envelopes, and pulled out the contents.

She scanned each piece of mail, tossing some, filing others away in the folders in her desk drawer, and then... The crisp linen announcement did more than just catch her attention. It appeared to be an answer to her prayers.

Gallery Opening
Be the first to experience the
power and beauty
of
artist David Julius
whose oils and watercolors will transport you
into realms of sheer happiness…

She didn't need to read any more. Suddenly she knew what she had to do.

Caleb Wadsworth needed a showing. His artwork needed to be displayed for all to see—especially his parents.

And she had to do it soon. But when? And then it hit her.

The Christmas Stroll! It was Saturday night, which left her just forty-eight hours to prepare, but she could do it. She had to.

What paintings by Caleb Wadsworth could she show?

She rushed into her studio and looked at the two canvases he'd hastily painted this afternoon. They were similar—both bearing the single word *family*, yet both were so different. In one the word floated on a cloud. In the second, the letters were scattered about that stormy cobalt blue sea he'd painted, disjointed, completely broken apart. The colors were bright and vivid in one; dark and depressing in the other.

They were perfect.

On her drafting table sat Caleb's sketchbook. He'd left it behind that first time he'd trusted her enough to show off some of his sketches. He'd told her it was full of his dreams, all sorts of imaginative things. Margaret touched it; she wanted to flip over the cover and look inside, but she sensed it was private. She couldn't look, not unless Caleb said it was okay.

He hadn't hid the paintings though. He'd told her she could have them, and without a doubt, Margaret would hang them in her gallery for all to see—especially, she prayed earnestly, the two most important people in his life.

* * *

Friday afternoon Margaret stood at her easel, and Caleb stood at his. She looked at him out of the corner of her eye, watching the way he dipped his brush into the oil colors on his palette and how he stood back and contemplated nearly every stroke of paint he applied to the canvas.

Yesterday she'd been sure of her plan. She'd wanted to hang Caleb's paintings whether he approved or not. But she couldn't do that to him. He trusted her, which meant she had to ask first.

"Remember when I told you your paintings might hang in this gallery sooner than you ever imagined possible?"

Caleb peered around the side of his canvas. "Yeah. I'm guessing it'll be at least five or six more years."

Margaret shook her head. "I was thinking more like tomorrow night."

Caleb's eyes widened. "That's impossible. I don't have a style. I don't have a perspective. I still know next to nothing about light and shadow."

"Stop being so unsure of yourself."

Margaret went to the back of the studio and picked up Caleb's completed canvases. "Take a look at these, Caleb. They're very good. They have far more than style and perspective—they express emotion. Intense emotion. And passion. Didn't I tell you how important that is? That without it, a painting is nothing?"

He shrugged. "I suppose so."

Margaret laughed. "We're definitely going to have to work on your confidence."

Caleb touched the tip of his brush's handle against his chin, deep in thought as he looked at Margaret. "Do you really want to hang those two paintings here?"

Margaret nodded. "I want people to see them when they drop by during the Christmas Stroll."

"Really?"

"Really. And if you had some extraspecial sketches that you wouldn't mind sharing, I might frame them too. The more the merrier, I always say."

He frowned. "You haven't looked in my sketchbook, have you?"

"No, Caleb. That's yours, and I've always believed that sketchbooks are private. Sometimes they contain nothing more than ideas, plans that you're not ready for the world to see."

"I've already shown you some, but I suppose I could show you one or two more, if you're interested."

Margaret smiled. "You know I'm interested."

Caleb put his brush down, picked up his sketchbook, and opened the cover. He thumbed through the pages, stopping at last halfway through the book. He looked at the page long and hard, then passed the book over to Margaret.

Her breath caught in her throat. It was a young boy standing at an easel, painting a picture of an artist. Could that really be his father? The artist, like the boy, was standing at an easel.

"This is you painting your father, isn't it?" Margaret asked, touched by the picture.

Caleb nodded. "That's how I see him. Always painting. That's when he was happy. When we were all happy."

"Would you like to show this sketch? I could have Allan frame it."

"I don't know." He sighed. "You understand it, but that doesn't mean everyone else will."

"That doesn't matter."

"Well, if you want to hang it, okay."

"What should we call it?"

Caleb thought about the question for a long moment, and finally answered. "*When We Were Happy.*"

Chapter Twenty-Three

"Mama! Daddy! Can we see Santa Claus now?" Aiden shouted, skipping alongside his mom and dad through the hustle and bustle on Main Street.

"I'm not sure he's made it into town yet, but he should be arriving any minute now." Dan boosted Aiden up on his shoulders while Shelley pushed Emma's stroller over the cobblestones on Main Street, the bumps making the little girl laugh as they went from store to store.

Marble Cove's evening Christmas Stroll had turned out to be absolutely beautiful, with the temperature just a few degrees below freezing, the wind calm, the sky clear, and stars shining brightly above. Shelley was taking a much-needed break, though she had worked fiendishly earlier to finish her orders so she could spend this time with her husband and children. It was the kind of evening she'd thought she'd never again enjoy. Work was keeping her busy beyond compare, but she loved it. Having Adelaide helping her out the last couple of weeks, and having all the extra money coming in, had eased her stress.

Thank You, Lo—

"Mama! Mama!" Aiden's voice cut through her thoughts. "There he is, Mama. I can see him. He's here! He's here!"

Shelley looked up into her little boy's eyes and saw all the wonder of Christmas. She was sure Dan and her friends could see the same wonder in hers. Tonight she felt like a little girl again, giddy and happy, anxious to see Santa, even more anxious for Christmas morning to arrive.

The lobster boat carrying Santa chugged to a halt along the wharf and after it was tied up, a couple of brawny elves—some of the guys Dan often worked with on the docks, if Shelley wasn't mistaken—helped the man in red alight. A massive sack of wrapped boxes, with a few dolls and stuffed animals hanging over the side, was slung over Santa's shoulder, and he lumbered along the wharf, his belly shaking like the proverbial bowl full of jelly when he laughed.

"Merry Christmas!" Santa shouted. "Merry Christmas!"

Dan, Shelley, Aiden, and Emma followed after him, as if Santa were the Pied Piper, and stood in line with friends, acquaintances, and strangers. At long last Santa took a seat on the lofty hand-painted wood and velvet throne he'd used every season as long as anyone could remember. The throne, the elves, the whole Santa's toy shop scene was truly a sight to behold.

Several other couples and a whole lot of kids stood in front of Shelley's family. Aiden tugged on Dan's sleeve. "What if Santa has to leave before I get to talk to him?" Aiden said. "I have to give him my list."

"Oh, honey," Shelley said, cradling Aiden's cheek in the palm of her hand, "Santa knows you've been waiting for weeks and weeks to see him. He's not going to leave until you've climbed on his lap and told him everything you want."

Aiden eyed his mother suspiciously. "Okay. But I'm not going to take my eyes off of him."

They inched up the line slowly, one child climbing onto Santa's lap after another, anticipation building with each step forward.

"Hi there!"

Shelley spun around to see Beverly and her father—even Jeff Mackenzie, who, she had decided, might not be a con artist after all—all bundled up good and warm. Their noses were Christmas red, and every breath they took fogged around them.

"Having a good time?" Shelley asked.

"Father's talked about the Christmas Stroll for years, but this is the first time I've ever been," Beverly said.

"And she bought something in nearly every store," Mr. Wheeland added. "Even picked up a little something for Rocky and Prize at the Pet Place."

Beverly nudged her father. "That was supposed to be a secret, Father." She shook her head, but laughed. "He was never very good at keeping secrets, especially at Christmastime."

"My dad was just the opposite," Jeff said. "He made sure the presents—every single one of them—were hidden away and not put under the Christmas tree until I was sound asleep. I plan on doing the same thing when and if

I ever have kids. I like the surprise of waking up Christmas morning, and I want them to experience that too."

"Me too!" Aiden chimed in. Everyone laughed.

"Have you stopped by Margaret's gallery yet?" Beverly asked, tucking a gloved hand around her dad's arm.

"That's the last stop on tonight's agenda," Shelley said, "right after Aiden talks to Santa. How about you?"

"We spent more time there than anywhere else," Jeff said.

"Her young protégé Caleb Longfellow is quite a hit, standing by his paintings and talking to anyone and everyone," Beverly added. "You'd think he was an old pro at working an art show."

"What about his mom and dad?" Shelley asked. "Did they come?"

Beverly shook her head. "Not yet, and Margaret's beside herself, wondering if she should call his mother again to remind her, or to leave well enough alone. She wants desperately to keep it a secret that she invited his parents. I just hope it all works out."

"If it's meant to be, they'll show up," Shelley said, and after Beverly, her father, and Jeff headed off to another shop, she closed her eyes and said a little prayer.

"My turn! My turn!"

Shelley's eyes popped open to see Aiden squirming out of Dan's arms.

"Don't run, Aiden," Shelley called after her little boy, but he was off and running, his long-awaited visit with Santa about to begin.

"Santa! I've got a really humongous list," Aiden hollered, before one of the elves could latch on to him and boost him up on Santa's lap. "And my mama's gonna have the best cookies in the whole wide world waiting for you at our house—it's on Newport Avenue, right close to the ocean."

Santa's deep belly laugh rang through the crowd. "I've heard tales about your mama's cookies. In fact, I've been told they're the best in all of Maine."

"They are, Santa." Aiden's eyes were shining.

"You'll leave me a big glass of milk too, I hope."

Aiden nodded fast and furious. "Do you want to hear my list now?"

Santa cleared his throat. "Now, you know, Aiden, humongous lists are awfully nice, but I've got a lot of kids to visit on Christmas Eve, and if every good little boy and girl had a humongous list, and I gave them everything they wanted, why, my sleigh would be so heavy that Rudolph and Dasher and Dancer and all my other reindeer would never be able to fly."

Aiden looked up at him in desperation. "Can I tell you my favorite things on the list?"

"Sure, Aiden, as long as it's only a few."

Shelley nudged Dan. "I'm listening to this list, but you listen too, since I have absolutely no idea what he hopes to find under the Christmas tree."

"Well," Aiden said, "first, I'd like a big dump truck that burps. I saw it on TV and it's really funny. Mama says I should ask for pajamas, but I know she'll get me some and so will Grandma, so you don't have to get those for me. And I'd kind of like a bicycle. It doesn't have to have training wheels, but they might be a good idea 'cause I'm still kind of little. And, well, I'd also kind of like another puppy or maybe a kitty, but what I'd really like is a baby brother. Emma's okay, but she's a girl..."

Dan slung an arm around Shelley's shoulders and kissed the top of her head. "Did you put that idea into his head?"

"No. Did you?"

Dan shook his head, but he grinned all the same.

* * *

Margaret walked around the gallery carrying a tray full of cookies and nut breads, delicacies that Shelley and Adelaide had made over the last couple of nights. A steady swarm of people had buzzed around the gallery, looking at paintings and jewelry, glassware and pottery, a few buying, most just looking.

"Having a good time?" Allan asked, walking up behind her and kissing her cheek.

"I miss the three of us strolling up and down Main Street, but it's also nice to stay in one place—our place—especially since we're out of the cold and I can show off all the artwork that I love so much. The only thing that could make the evening better—"

"You're wondering if Caleb's parents are going to show up."

Margaret sighed. "Everyone else I've invited has come by." She'd managed to find out from Caleb where his father was working and called him at four thirty last night. He didn't answer the phone so she'd had to leave a voice mail message, and she had no way of knowing whether or not he'd actually received it.

She'd been able to reach Caleb's mother, but she'd sounded so tired when Margaret called her, weary and defeated. She'd said she'd try to make it if she felt better.

"The night isn't over yet," Allan said. "Have faith, Margaret."

"I'm trying." She looked across the gallery at Caleb, whose blond hair was shaggier than ever. But he had a smile on his face and he was talking up a storm with Pastor Carl from Marble Cove Community Church. "I've prayed too, Allan. A lot, but I didn't get very good vibes from either one of Caleb's parents. I don't know what I'll do if they don't show up."

"You know, you'd battle with the devil if he stood between you and Adelaide. Caleb's parents have a devil to fight too, and grief can be a miserable thing to go up against. But you've told me what a good kid Caleb is, and that means his parents raised him right." He gave her a hug. "I'm praying too."

People who had never before come to her gallery, as well as some of her regulars, stopped her to say how much they liked her gallery and all of the artwork. She wanted so much to revel in their words, but she couldn't help but worry about Caleb.

"Hello, Mrs. Hoskins."

Margaret recognized the English accent before she spun around. She was overwhelmed with happiness when she saw Caleb's mom.

"Hello, Ellie." Margaret smiled brightly. The dark circles beneath Ellie's eyes had been camouflaged with makeup, and her long blonde hair was washed and pulled back in a French braid, showing off the beautiful contours of her face. Her clothes were a bit bohemian, but they suited her perfectly. She was absolutely beautiful. "I'm so glad you could make it."

"I wanted to come with Caleb, but—"

"Mom! You're here." Caleb threw his arms around his mother. "I was afraid you wouldn't come."

Ellie smiled softly. "I wouldn't have missed this for the world."

"Does Dad know about this? Is he coming?"

Ellie looked in her son's eager eyes. "I don't know, Caleb. I hope so."

Margaret knew he wanted to cry, knew with all her heart that Caleb's evening wouldn't be complete without his father. Still, he took hold of his mother's hand. "Come on, Mom. Let me show you my paintings."

Margaret stood back, delighting in the joy on Caleb's face as he showed his mother his work, not just his paintings, but the sketch he'd made of himself and his dad. A partial reunion was better, Margaret told herself, than no reunion at all.

"You look sad," Adelaide said, linking her arm through Margaret's. "Are you sad?"

"No, honey, I'm not sad." Margaret kissed her daughter's brow. "It's a beautiful night, isn't it?"

Adelaide nodded. "They're going to announce the winner of the window contest soon. You're gonna win, Mom. I know it."

She'd nearly forgotten about the contest, and she'd definitely forgotten about her unfinished star. There had been too much going on.

The jingle bells on the front door jangled, and as Margaret had been doing all evening, she spun around to see who was coming inside. A man walked in. He was tall and blond. His hair was disheveled, looking so much like Caleb's that Margaret recognized him in an instant. Her eyes filled.

Longfellow Wadsworth made his way across the room. He'd caught his wife's eye, and Margaret couldn't help but notice the longing they had for each other. He took his wife's hand when she extended it and kissed the back, his lips lingering on her skin. Caleb turned slowly, and when he saw his dad, wrapped his arms around his waist and hugged him tight.

Margaret wanted so much to meet Caleb's dad, but a lump the size of Maine stuck in her throat.

"Everything okay?" Diane asked, walking up to Margaret with a tray of cookies in her hands. She'd been helping with the hostess duties, doing a far better job than Margaret could do herself.

"Margaret?" Allan stood by her too, wiping a tear from her eye with his thumb. "What's wrong?"

"Absolutely nothing. In fact, everything's right with the world." She glanced over to Caleb and his family.

"Mom! Mom!" Adelaide ran up to her, tugging on her hand. "Come on, Mom. The mayor's gonna announce the winner of the best window contest."

Adelaide pulled Margaret through the gallery, anxious to get outside for the big announcement. Most everyone in the gallery was filing out too, ready to hear Mayor Waters give her Christmas Stroll speech and, most importantly, hand out the Best Christmas Window award.

"Marble Cove couldn't have asked for a more spectacular night to hold its annual Christmas Stroll, and what a night it has been..."

Standing arm in arm with her daughter and husband, who'd linked his arm through Diane's too, Margaret listened to Evelyn Waters talk about the special people of Marble Cove, the camaraderie, the sense of caring and sharing, which was all so important this time of year. The speech went on for long, long minutes, and Margaret took a moment to look back at her gallery, at her dream come to life. Its window glowed warmth into the cold night.

Outside, silhouetted in the light of the big window, where she'd painted the little town of Bethlehem, stood Caleb, his mom and his dad. Caleb held a palette in one hand and a brush in the other, and even though Margaret couldn't hear a word, she sensed Caleb was telling his dad about the star, how something about it just wasn't right.

Caleb held the brush out to his dad, but Longfellow shook his head. He stepped back for a moment, as if the brush were poison. Margaret could almost hear him telling Caleb to fix the star himself, but Caleb was adamant. *You can do it, Dad.* Margaret was certain those were the words she'd seen on Caleb's lips. *You're the best, Dad. You can make it perfect. You can make it shine better than anyone else.*

Longfellow Wadsworth ran his hands through his hair and at long last took the brush from his son. He took the palette in his left hand, studied the star Margaret had painted, the star that wasn't quite right, then dipped his brush into the paint. He reached up high and dabbed on a little silver, the brush moving over the glass as if it had been touched by magic.

Less than a minute passed by. Mayor Waters's speech was a blur behind her. Margaret heard nothing but noise—she was too busy concentrating on the Wadsworth family and her holiday window. Another minute or so went by, and Caleb, Longfellow, and Ellie stepped out onto the cobblestone street to look at the window.

"And the winner of the *Marble Cove Courier* Best Christmas Window contest is..."

Margaret looked at the window too. Not just at the star, but the whole picture. She wasn't sure just what Longfellow Wadsworth had done, but whatever touches he'd added had definitely transformed the scene. It was perfect now. The star literally glowed.

"...the Crow's Nest!"

Margaret clapped along with everyone else. The Crow's Nest's window had been creative. A stroke of genius. Her favorite bookstore deserved the award.

Besides, she'd received far, far more tonight than a plaque to hang on her wall. She'd watched a family reunite.

Chapter Twenty-Four

Beverly stood in the foyer with her father, helping him into his Sunday best overcoat. He had no business going out in this weather, not when he'd just gotten over a miserable cold. He seemed just as determined that she should go along with him, and going to church just wasn't her thing.

"You haven't been to church in ages, Father—"

"Which makes it perfectly reasonable for me to want to go today. Now please, Beverly, put on your coat and galoshes, and let's get going."

Beverly curled a lock of hair behind her ear. "I'm not dressed for church; I'm dressed to spend the morning working on a personnel budget proposal for a meeting tomorrow afternoon. On top of that, I have Christmas presents to wrap—"

Her father's brow rose. When was the last time she'd seen that? When she was thirteen and told him and her mother that she wanted to wear a spaghetti-strap dress to middle school graduation instead of the old lady lace-sleeved dress her mother had bought without consulting her.

Father was definitely a man to be reckoned with this morning.

"I suppose you'd have me walk to Old First on my own? Or worse yet, drive? On icy roads, no less?" He shook his head. "You know my hip's been giving me fits. What if it should give out? What if I should fall on a slippery sidewalk or while I'm crossing the street?"

"All right. All right." Beverly threw up her hands. "I'll take you to church."

"No, dear, I'd like you to attend with me, not just take me there. Now get your coat on."

Beverly looked at the delicate gold watch on her wrist. "Give me a moment to put on a dress. From what I hear, everyone at Old First dresses up on Sunday morning."

"That's because a lot of them are out to impress each other. God doesn't give a fig how you dress."

"I care, Father."

Half an hour later Beverly pulled into the parking lot adjacent to Old First. Old was definitely right. Old, but beautiful. Wearing her best dark scarlet wool dress, a black coat, and a pair of knee-high black leather boots, she climbed out of the car and rushed around to the passenger side to help her dad out. She definitely didn't want him falling on the ice. The last thing either one of them needed was for him to end up with a broken hip.

"Here, let me help you."

Jeff Mackenzie seemed to materialize from nowhere. Or had his presence been planned, a scheme cooked up by her dear old dad? She had to admit it was rather nice to see him this morning, and he looked decidedly handsome in a dark green pullover sweater, a black turtleneck and black slacks. She'd grown accustomed to seeing him in jeans; he looked casual, full of fun, yet warm. Now he looked like a million bucks.

"Glad you could make it," her father said to Jeff when he climbed out of the car. "Reverend Locke puts on quite a sermon, if I remember correctly. Of course"—he slammed the car door behind him—"I've often found it hard to concentrate on the sermon when there's so much to see inside Old First."

"Reverend Locke showed me around the other day," Jeff said. "I must have snapped fifty or sixty pictures just of the rose window, and caught the tower from a lot of different angles."

"Going for the best shade and light, right?"

"That's right," Jeff said. He was carrying on such a nice conversation with her father, Beverly thought she might as well have stayed at home.

As they walked toward the church, the two men continued to talk, and Beverly found herself caught up in their discussion of eighteenth-century churches, like Old First, that had been designed in the gothic style. She'd attended Old First a time or two, mostly when her mother was still alive, but she'd always been so busy, her mind on work. But today she saw it differently. The stone exterior was well over two hundred years old, and its crenellated tower looked like a castle battlement from days of yore.

Jeff opened the heavy wooden doors for Beverly and her father, and she stepped inside to find prisms of colored light radiating off one of dozens of old stained glass windows and sparkling over the whitewashed stone walls. There had to be a lot of history here. Her father, and more than likely Reverend Locke, could probably relate a lot of tales about Old First. Tales like that hadn't interested her in the past; suddenly she thought she might like to know more.

"This pew looks good," her father said. "Not too close to the front; not too far back."

Beverly slipped into the pew, her father on one side, Jeff on the other. The wood was cold and hard, polished thousands of times over by parishioners sliding in and out of the seats. But as Beverly sat back, she found it quite comfortable.

Christmas was only days away. The pulpit was surrounded by lush red poinsettias and the organist was playing a beautiful variation on "O Come, O Come, Emmanuel." It was all so beautiful and inspiring. But it felt new and a little foreign to her.

Jeff, on the other hand, seemed comfortable here, his face almost like a child's, filled with wonder and awe as Reverend Locke delivered his sermon. It was hard to ignore, though. The pastor's voice was confident and intense; not exactly stern, but definitely not touchy-feely. It was almost like listening to a favorite college professor, and Beverly liked that about him—his intelligence along with his faith. He was a thinking person's preacher, and Beverly found herself drawn into the thoughtful words he presented to the congregation.

"Many of us suffer not only physically, but emotionally. From guilt. Regret. Remorse. From countless transgressions.

Yet the prophet Isaiah looked far into the future, and what did he see? 'The people who walked in darkness have seen a great light,' he said. 'Those who dwelt in the land of the shadow of death, upon them a light has shined.' It was Jesus that Isaiah saw. Emmanuel, God With Us, who came to bring a great light into our lives. He came to dispel the darkness of guilt and replace it with the light of joy and the radiance of His everlasting peace."

If only Edward Maker could see that light, Beverly found herself thinking. If only he could find that everlasting peace.

* * *

"Where are you going now?" Beverly's father asked after she'd changed out of her sleek wool dress and into flannel-lined jeans and a heavy Icelandic sweater. "Jeff's on his way over. I thought we could make clam chowder, put together a jigsaw puzzle, maybe watch *It's a Wonderful Life.*"

"I have plans, Father. I told you that this morning."

"Going to lunch with your girlfriends." He chuckled. "You could always get out of it. After all, it's not like they're a date."

"Jeff isn't a date either, at least he's not my date. You invited him, not me."

Beverly jumped when she heard the heavy knock on the door.

"That must be Jeff now," her father said. "Are you going to stick around with us, or go gallivanting?" He winked.

"I'm going gallivanting." Her girlfriends—as her father liked to call Margaret, Shelley, and Diane—were good friends, the closest friends she'd had in a lifetime. She wasn't about to stand them up. Not for anyone.

"Well, you tell him; I'm not going to."

Beverly shook her head in mock exasperation.

Beverly pulled open the door, but before she could say a word, she noticed the exhaust from Jeff's still-running car engine kicking up big puffs of white clouds. He wore a worried look on his face. "I know your dad was expecting me to come by for lunch this afternoon," Jeff said, "but—"

"But what?" Beverly's father poked his head around her. "You have better plans?"

Jeff shrugged. "I've been trying to call my grandfather all day, but he's not answering. I'm sure he's fine, but I'm going to head into Augusta to check."

"Want some company?"

Beverly glared at her dad. "I have plans, Father. As much as I'd love to go with Jeff—"

"I'm talking about me," her father said, his eyes twinkling. "Beverly's having lunch with her girlfriends and I'd love to get out for a drive. Wouldn't mind going into Augusta if you wouldn't mind me going with you."

Jeff chuckled. "Don't mind at all."

"Good. Let me put on a pair of boots and I'll be right back."

"You'll call me after you get to your grandfather's, won't you?" Beverly asked. "I'll worry if you don't."

Jeff smiled. “If the weather holds, we should be there in an hour.”

“You don’t think you should call the police, do you? Have them do a quick welfare check to make sure nothing’s happened?”

“He’s fine. Call me crazy, but if he wasn’t, I’m sure I’d feel it in my gut.”

Beverly’s father opened the entryway closet and pulled out a parka. “I’m ready as I’ll ever be.” He gave Beverly a quick peck on the cheek. “See you later.”

“I’ll probably be upstairs wrapping Christmas presents when you get home,” she said, standing in the open doorway as Jeff and her dad walked down the stairs and headed for his Jeep. “Drive carefully.”

She waved as they drove away, then grabbed her own parka and headed for the Cove and lunch with Diane, Margaret, and Shelley. After that, they’d take a wreath out to Orlean Point. Candles too, if Diane had remembered to bring them. They planned to say a prayer for those affected by the crash of *Newcastle*. And they were going to pray for Edward Maker, asking God to take away the anguish and guilt that had haunted him since 1935.

Thinking of Jeff and her father headed to Augusta, she only hoped that they wouldn’t need to offer another prayer for Edward Maker.

Chapter Twenty-Five

Margaret huffed and puffed as she, Diane, Beverly, and Shelley climbed the stairway leading up the rocky cliff to the lighthouse. "Remind me to never again eat one of the Cove's triple-decker club sandwiches before making this hike. Right now I just want to lie down and go to sleep."

"I've wanted to lie down and go to sleep since I finished my marathon revision session at three this morning," Diane said, trudging up the stairway right behind Margaret. "Never in my life did I think the perfect book I'd written, with the perfect mystery and the perfect characters, would need fifty-three totally new pages, six new scenes, three deleted scenes, and—" Diane blew out a sigh of frustration. "Some of the writers I've gotten to know tell me that's not all that uncommon. That you eventually get used to it, but I'm not so sure."

"I have to revise budgets ad nauseam," Beverly added. "And to tell you the truth, I'm so tired of budgets that the first chance I get, I might sit down and dream up some kind of business I can do from home."

"Home as in Augusta?" Shelley asked. "Or home as in Marble Cove?"

Beverly laughed. "Home as in Marble Cove—now and always. This place grows on you."

Margaret thought her legs would give out before she made it up the last ten steps. "Be careful. This step"—she stomped on it a couple of times, holding on tight to the railing—"is feeling a little wobbly. First thing tomorrow I'll call the powers that be and make sure they get someone out here to fix it."

"You might have better luck getting Allan and Dan to fix it up," Diane said. "There's no telling when the powers that be can get around to it, especially if the storm that's been threatening actually shows up."

Margaret looked out at the ocean, at the black clouds that were rolling in. "That storm looks like it's a good hour or two away. Chances are it'll dissipate before getting anywhere close to shore."

"Well, just to be on the safe side," Beverly said, "let's not spend too much time up on the Point."

It was nearly three o'clock when they reached the top of the stairs. The wind had whipped up all of a sudden, making Margaret wonder if the storm was actually going to dissipate, or grow stronger and faster instead. Coming up here might not have been the wisest of ideas, especially today. But she'd felt compelled to come, just as she'd felt compelled to come to this place the day she first saw Caleb. She glanced up at the lighthouse, half expecting to see a flash. As she did the first fat raindrop hit Margaret's nose. She held out her hand and three more raindrops hit. "Maybe we should get our service started."

"Good thinking," Shelley said.

Together they walked out to the very tip of the Point, one of the prettiest vantage spots in all of Maine, a place from which you could see forever...on a good day. Today, however, was quickly growing dark.

"Wait." Beverly was staring at her cell phone. "Is anyone getting any reception up here? I was hoping Jeff might have called about his grandfather, but I'm getting nothing on my phone. The battery might as well be dead."

"I didn't bring mine," Margaret said, watching both Diane and Shelley dig into their pockets to check their own cell phones.

"Nothing," Shelley said. "I'm sure I've made calls from up here before."

"Maybe it's the storm," Diane said. "I'm not getting any signal strength, either."

"Oh well, I'll try to call when we get back down the stairs," Beverly said. "Hopefully it'll work then. I'm getting kind of anxious."

"Mr. Maker's fine," Margaret said, her faith strengthened by the reunion of Caleb's family, a reunion that came about all because of the mysterious lights. She peeked again at the lighthouse, but it stayed silent and dark.

"Think we'll have any luck lighting candles?" Diane asked, pulling four short yet thick candles out of her coat pocket, along with a box of wooden matches. "I should have brought my leftover trick birthday candles—you know, the kind you can't blow out."

"We'll never know unless we try." Shelley took one of the candles from Diane, plus the box of matches, struck one once, and its blaze burned bright. She touched the wick to the fire and the candle was suddenly alight.

Diane, Margaret, and Beverly touched their candles to Shelley's, and together they stood at the Point, solemn at last.

"Where should we begin?" Margaret asked. She'd never performed any kind of memorial service. She wasn't all that good at praying out loud either. She looked to Shelley and Diane, both of them with faith to spare. "You're a woman of words, Diane."

"For mystery novels, sure, but there's nothing that says we need to be formal about this. We just need to say what's in our hearts."

Shelley started. "Dear Lord, a long time ago, a ship crashed on our rocky shore, sending men and women to their deaths. I know that You clasped those people and those who loved them in Your loving arms. Still, there are those who continue to grieve for their loss, family who never knew the truth about their deaths. Be with these people, Lord. Console them, comfort them with Your strength and love. And, dear God, be with Mr. Maker, who was just a boy at the time, who believes their deaths are on his hands."

A violent gust of wind caught at the wreath Margaret held, trying to drag her across the Point, but she stood steady. The flame on each candle sputtered and disappeared.

The dark clouds rolled in fast, and fog rolled in like a wave.

"Should I throw the wreath now?" Margaret asked.

"I think you'd better," Diane shouted over the wind. "And then we'd better get out of here."

Margaret added a quick and silent prayer of her own. *Watch over Mr. Maker, Lord. Watch over us too. Please.* She tossed the wreath, but it blew right back onto the very edge of the Point.

"I'll get it," Shelley shouted through the sudden gale.

"No!" Beverly's voice was strong and adamant. "Leave it, and let's get out of here."

They ran for the stairs, fighting against the wind, which was doing everything in its power to sweep them over the edge of the Point, down onto the rocks, and out to sea.

"Hurry!" Shelley called out.

Margaret was the first one to the stairs. They were already slick with salt water from the waves that were crashing against the cliffs. She held on for dear life as she put a foot on the first step, then onto the second and third.

"Hurry," Margaret yelled back. "The waves are starting to roll onto shore. I've never seen them so high."

Shelley reached out and grabbed Margaret's hand as she took one more step. "Wait, Margaret. Let's stay here. It might be safer."

"Not if we hurry."

Margaret took one more step, and the stair let loose beneath her foot, the wooden board splintering in half. She screamed.

"I've got you," Shelley called out, her gloved hand gripping Margaret's wrist.

"I've got you too," Diane shouted.

Together the friends pulled Margaret back to safety.

"Let's get to the lighthouse," Beverly yelled, as a wave crashed over the Point, the water rushing toward them as they ran for the safety of the lighthouse. But the secret door was locked. The main door was locked. There was no way to get inside and the waves were now hitting the Point from all sides, the water ruthless and powerful.

The women huddled together in the lee of the lighthouse, though the wind whipped stinging pellets of water at them from every direction.

Holding hands.

Praying.

Their words washed away with the wind and salt water, but God would hear them. He'd saved them before. He'd save them again.

Minutes went by. Long minutes. Maybe an hour.

Margaret lost her sense of time entirely. All she knew was that it was dark and cold. Sea water had nearly frozen on her lips and brows. Her boots were full of sea water, and it was freezing.

She was even too cold to shiver.

"Did you hear that?" Shelley asked. She was probably shouting, but to Margaret it sounded like only a whisper.

"Hear what?" Diane asked.

"I don't know," Shelley said. "A horn maybe. The Coast Guard. The sheriff. Dan and Allan."

Margaret could hear the tears in Shelley's voice. "Please, God, don't let us die. Please."

"We'll be okay," Margaret said, pulling Shelley close to her chest, holding her tight. "We have to get out of this. Christmas is coming and you have to get that burping truck for Aiden and, and..."

"You ladies okay?"

Margaret spun around. Through the rain and crashing waves she could just barely see the silhouette of a man—a big man; no, several big men—walking toward them, dressed in yellow slickers.

"We've been better." Somehow Margaret managed a quick laugh. "I hope you're here to save us."

"My buddies and me are here with ropes and ladders. It was an old man who called us. Some guy named Edward. Said he had a premonition. A hunch there were a bunch of women up here on the Point. If it hadn't been for him, well, there's no telling what the next hour would bring."

"Is he here?" Beverly's eyes were filled with tears, though from emotion or the stinging cold, Margaret wasn't sure.

"Yeah, he's down at the bottom of the stairs, or what's left of the stairs. Said he wasn't gonna leave until you were all safe and sound. Then he said something funny."

"What do you mean?" Beverly asked.

"Said God had given him a second chance, and he wasn't going to blow it this time."

* * *

They sat together in Margaret's living room, wrapped in blankets and wearing Margaret's stockpile of old flannel pajamas and gowns.

"Can we get you anything else?" Allan asked, walking around the room with a pot of coffee in one hand and a box of tissues in the other.

"All I want to do is warm up," Margaret said, holding on to her cup of coffee for dear life, letting the heat from the mug soak into her hands.

The front door burst open and Jeff and Mr. Wheeland rushed inside. "What on earth happened?" Jeff asked frantically. Unlike Allan and Dan, he and Mr. Wheeland hadn't had a chance to absorb the fact that Beverly, Diane, Margaret, and Shelley were safe. That they'd survived the storm and would be just fine. "Are you all right? Should we take you to the hospital?"

"We're going to be good as new as soon as we warm up," Beverly said, nodding to the elderly man sitting in Allan's favorite easy chair. "Your grandfather's perfectly fine too."

"Grandpa?" Jeff twisted around to see his grandfather bundled up and drinking hot cocoa that Adelaide had made. "What happened?"

Mr. Maker shrugged. "I spent a good hour driving here in a downpour. I—"

"Why?" Jeff asked. "I've been trying to call you all day. What on earth possessed you to come to Marble Cove?"

"You've been on my case about coming here for months, and now that I have, you're on my case for actually showing up." Mr. Maker shook his head, but his gruff words were softened by his twinkling eyes. "I'm in good health. I haven't lost any mental acuity. And I've survived well over eighty years. If I want to drive to Marble Cove on a whim, I will."

"He saved our lives," Beverly said, her father standing behind her now, his hands on her shoulders. "If it hadn't been for him, who knows what would have happened."

"One of the guys who rescued us said you'd had a premonition," Margaret said. "What kind of premonition?"

"I don't know that I'd call it a premonition."

"Then what was it?" Jeff asked.

"It was that lighthouse painting you gave me." Mr. Maker chuckled. "It was the strangest thing you ever did see."

"What was the strangest thing?" Jeff asked, his exasperation growing.

Mr. Maker held out his mug. "Care to give me another refill, Allan? This stuff doesn't taste all that great when it's cold."

Dan took the coffeepot from Allan and filled Mr. Maker's mug.

At long last, Mr. Maker looked from one person in the room to another, his gaze finally resting on Jeff. "I was sitting in the same old chair I always sit in, listening to carols on the radio, and all of a sudden the lighthouse painting fell off the mantel. Just like that. No wind. No earthquake. Nothing shook the house. My radio went silent for a good five seconds, right in the middle of 'Silent Night,' and that picture frame just toppled over. Sent a shiver running up my spine and I knew something was up. I missed my chance to save a bunch of people a long time ago. I wasn't going to let it happen again."

Chapter Twenty-Six

Beverly, Jeff, and Mr. Maker—she just couldn't call him Edward; it didn't seem right—were chilled to the bone, their faces splattered with ocean mist. "You're gonna like Cass McDuffie," Jeff told his grandfather, when the boat he'd hired two days before Christmas docked at Abenaki Isle.

"That's not really here nor there," Mr. Maker said. "I'm not out to become fast friends. I just want to tell her and her family members that I'm sorry for causing the shipwreck in 1935 and get back home where it's warm."

"You know, Grandpa, it wouldn't hurt to spend a little time with her. Get to know about her life; let her know about yours."

Mr. Maker shrugged. "Why don't we play it by ear? See how things go."

Jeff nodded. "This is your day, and I don't plan to get in the way."

The skipper of the boat climbed onto the wharf, tied up the boat, then helped Mr. Maker get out. He was in very good shape for an eighty-something-year-old man, but he seemed a little wobbly at the moment. Beverly couldn't help but wonder how much of that was nerves; after all, she was filled with anxiety, and she wasn't the one coming here to apologize.

Beverly took off the life vest she'd strapped on over her heavy waterproof parka before taking hold of Jeff's hand and letting him haul her up onto the wharf. She wasn't taking any chances of getting swept away by a wave or going down with this ship.

It wasn't all that often that she wore her hair in a ponytail, but she'd pulled it back before leaving home this morning. She'd left off her makeup too, knowing that the wind and sea mist would make a mess of mascara and eyeliner. She felt exposed without her tasteful makeup, but she doubted anyone else had noticed that she wasn't her usual self.

"Do you like lobster rolls?" Beverly asked Mr. Maker when they headed for the shops along the main street in a town of fewer than a hundred inhabitants.

"Haven't had any in a month of Sundays, or longer, but yeah. They're not bad."

"Well, when I called Cass to tell her we were coming today, she told me that's what she'd serve us. Clam chowder too, and one of her favorite pies."

"Why? She doesn't know me, and I killed—"

"Stop it, Grandpa," Jeff said, his admonishment harsher than it probably needed to be. "That's history. Once this day's over, we're never again going to talk about what happened in 1935, unless—" Jeff shook his head. "No, never mind."

"Never mind what?"

"I know you don't want to talk about the shipwreck and I don't either, but there are other memories I'm sure you'd like to talk about, and I wouldn't mind checking out some of those caves you told Beverly and me about, the ones hidden in the cliffs below Orlean Point Light."

Mr. Maker chuckled. "I don't know if I can scramble up and down those rocks quite as fast as I did back when I was a kid, but I'd be happy to give you a run for your money."

"Do you think you can find the caves?" Jeff asked. "It's been a long time."

"Piece of cake." Mr. Maker looked at Beverly. "What about you? Once the warmer weather gets here, will you be open to doing a little rock climbing?"

Beverly nearly shivered at the thought. "I think I've experienced enough life-threatening events for one lifetime, but—" Beverly grinned. "Ask me again next spring. I might have a change of heart."

Beverly turned up the collar on her parka as she, Jeff, and Mr. Maker headed to Cass's restaurant. She had the uncanny feeling that people were hiding behind the windows in each of the buildings lining the street, staring out at the strangers in town. No doubt the people behind those windows knew who they were and by now even knew Edward Maker's story. She felt uncomfortable. Both Jeff and Mr. Maker had told her she didn't have to come, but nothing would have kept her away.

When they pushed through the door of the Lobster Shack, the men Cass MacDuffie had pointed out as her husband and son were sitting at one of the tables. The looks they sent toward Mr. Maker were not friendly. Beverly felt her stomach take a tumble. When they'd talked to Cass on the phone, Beverly and Jeff had both believed that whatever animosity had existed would be long gone before they arrived on the island. Unfortunately, although Cass may have forgiven Mr. Maker, Beverly couldn't help but wonder if others on the island, ancestors of those who'd died on the *Newcastle*, would be as forgiving.

"You made it," Cass shouted out from her usual spot in the kitchen, sounding far more jovial than Beverly would have, given the circumstances. "Thought you might change your mind about coming out here today."

"It's pretty outside," Jeff said. "Couldn't think of a nicer place to spend the day before Christmas Eve."

"I can see an Abenaki Islander saying that, but not a mainlander," Cass said, talking over the sizzle of something frying on the stove. Sausage, maybe, considering the strong yet heavenly scent. Beverly didn't eat sausage, but that didn't mean she didn't love the smell. "Still," Cass continued, "I'm glad you're here."

Cass pushed through the kitchen's swinging doors and walked straight up to Mr. Maker. She stared him down for the longest time, her face expressionless. Mr. Maker looked back, as if trying to read her expression. Finally, he swallowed hard. Could Cass have had a change of heart about forgiving him?

"So," Cass said at last, her Lobster Shack apron tied around her middle, nearly covering up the Santa Claus face on her bright red sweatshirt, "you're the one I've been hating all these years."

Mr. Maker nodded slowly. "That would be me."

Cass frowned, studying Mr. Maker's sorrowful eyes. "You wouldn't have been much older than my youngest grandbaby when the *Newcastle* went down."

"Seven. Barely," Mr. Maker said. "Just lost my second front tooth."

Her frown deepened. "And your daddy had you running the lighthouse?"

Again he nodded. "It was my job."

"Boys of seven should be outside playing, not manning the light in a lighthouse, but that's neither here nor there anymore."

"Yeah, it was a long time ago."

"Sit down," Cass said, dishing out orders and expecting everyone to obey. She pulled out a chair for Mr. Maker and once he lowered his body into the seat, she sat across from him. They were silent for a long time, sizing each other up. Then, without a word, Cass took Mr. Maker's hands in hers. "I hear your daddy was a bootlegger."

"Yep, that he was. No telling how many other villainous things he did. I never bothered to keep count, and when he ran off, well, he just wasn't worth caring all that much about."

"It's all kind of sad. Your daddy ran off and left you to grieve for the people who died, and to blame yourself for their deaths too. And my family set about hating anyone who'd had anything to do with the accident, even though they didn't know who they were hating. Seems like an awful lot of time was wasted being bitter and guilt-ridden."

"It happens in the best of families." Mr. Maker chuckled for the first time, but it was an uneasy laugh, and Beverly noticed that he focused on the table more than the woman he was speaking with. "I ended up with a great wife and a grandson who drives me crazy at times, but who I love half to death. Doesn't make the rest any better, just gives me good things to think about."

"Someday, when it's not so cold out," Cass said, drawing her hands from Mr. Maker's and shoving up and out of the chair, "and you've got some time on your hands—"

"That would be most all the time."

"Good." Cass smiled. "Tell you what. First thing next spring, when the wildflowers start popping up all over this island, you'll have to come for a nice long visit. I can tell you stories about my family, the ones who settled this island back in the day, the ones who've come and gone, and... and my grandparents—" She sighed heavily. "Excuse me a minute. Chowder's gonna stick to the bottom of the pot if I don't give it a good stir."

"I'll give you a hand," Beverly said, following Cass through the swinging door and into the kitchen. She needed to make sure Cass was okay, that coming here hadn't been a mistake.

"Are you all right?"

"Fine."

Cass's one simple word was brusque. Beverly knew from her own personal experience that you couldn't push someone when they were dealing with a strong emotion like hate, or the guilt she herself suffered with.

She leaned against the refrigerator in the cramped and cluttered kitchen, watching Cass's back as she took the lid off an over-large pot. The steam that had been trapped inside spilled out and the scent of chowder chock full of clams and potatoes permeated the room.

Cass dipped a teaspoon into the chowder and tasted it. "Forgiving's not all that easy," she said, shaking pepper from an aluminum shaker into the pot, then stirring it all with a big wooden spoon. "I've prayed about it. I've talked to my pastor. I even told myself to take a deep breath and just be nice to Mr. Maker, as if he's a long-lost friend. I thought that was working, but he isn't a friend and the only ones long-lost are my grandma and grandpa."

"I'm sorry, Cass. Maybe we shouldn't have come."

"No." She sighed. "You were right to bring him here. I know it wasn't Mr. Maker who killed them, and if coming here to tell me he's sorry will make him feel better, then..." Cass sighed again. "I want him to feel better. But my own hate's a pretty hard thing to tackle. It was bred into me and nurtured since I was a child for no other reason than that we wanted someone to blame."

"Maybe you're trying too hard. Mr. Maker isn't expecting your forgiveness. He just wants to apologize."

Cass picked up a ladle and filled four large blue pottery soup bowls with chowder. A few moments later she lifted a tray covered with bowls, cellophane bags of oyster crackers, big soup spoons, and napkins. "Mind getting the door for me?"

Beverly smiled, wondering what, if anything, Cass would say when they went back into the dining room. She opened the swinging door and followed Cass to the table. "You're in luck. Chowder didn't stick after all."

"Smells good," Jeff said.

"Mighty good," Mr. Maker added, his face filled with curiosity about why she'd left the room so quickly, Beverly imagined, and with the desire to say something nice, to make Cass feel better. "In fact, my stomach's been growling ever since you left the room."

"Well," Cass said, setting out the bowls of chowder, "eat up. I've got pots and pans to wash up right now, but once you're finished, there's an old church in the middle of the island you might like to see."

She said nothing more before disappearing back into the kitchen, leaving Beverly completely perplexed. Was Cass trying to make the act of forgiveness harder than it needed to be?

And what was it about that old church that fascinated Cass so much? She had made a point of telling Beverly and Jeff about the place when they were last on the island, and they'd gone there so Jeff could take pictures, but other than the fact that it was little more than a pile of old, broken-down boards, Beverly hadn't seen anything special about the place.

There had to be more. But what?

Cass's husband and son walked out of the Lobster Shack not more than a few minutes after Cass went back into the kitchen, and suddenly Beverly, Jeff, and Mr. Maker were alone, each looking at the others, trying to find something to say. For the most part, they remained quiet. Even Cass was silent in the kitchen, until she came out about twenty minutes later wearing tall rubber boots and a heavy yellow slicker over a thick wool sweater.

"Chowder was mighty good," Mr. Maker said. "Best I think I've ever had."

"People tell me that all the time," Cass said, staring down at the empty bowls. "My son'll come in and clean up in a bit, but if you're ready, why don't we head out to the church?"

She didn't wait for a response. She pushed through the door and they followed, out of the restaurant, between it and another building, past a few old houses that needed painting and any number of repairs, and out into the woods.

They'd been marching for nearly five minutes, with Cass leading them along the half-mile trail through patches of crusty snow, mud, and fir trees that did their best to keep the sunlight from shining down upon them. "Grandpa was a minister, and so was his grandpa," Cass said, breaking the silence. "It was my great-great-grandpa who built the church I'm gonna show you. My folks worshipped there when I was just a babe, but a hurricane took it down in 1944 and with the war going on, making repairs wasn't much of an option."

"Beverly and Jeff told me it was built of wood from old shipwrecks." Mr. Maker tramped along, his arms swinging back and forth in an effort to keep up with Cass. "Is that true?"

"Could be," Cass said, turning around, her cheeks red, a smile on her face. "Stick around this island very long and you'll hear the same tall tale told with a dozen different endings, but I believe that one's true." Her smile faded. "After all, you know as well as I do that there've been far too many shipwrecks on our shores."

"Far, far too many." Mr. Maker picked up his pace, until he could place a hand on Cass's shoulder and draw her to a halt. Beverly and Jeff stopped too, watching and waiting to see what was coming next.

Cass didn't turn around, and Mr. Maker didn't let go of her shoulder. "There's no way on God's green earth I can make up for what happened all those years ago. But I am sorry." His voice was strong, but Beverly heard a quiver in his voice. "Truly, deeply sorry."

Cass turned slowly. She didn't smile; she didn't frown. Instead, her eyes were red and her face was full of sadness. "I know you're sorry."

If Mr. Maker was expecting Cass to forgive him, he didn't show it. He seemed to expect that she'd turn and continue up the path without saying another word. Beverly wished Cass had said something more, if not that she forgave him, that at least she'd try. Hadn't Mr. Maker suffered enough?

At least another five minutes passed before they reached the church. It should have looked forlorn, with its beams twisted and turned and resting on fallen walls, the wood now black as night. But instead it looked serene, happy to have had a long and good life, and now a place for people to visit, to think about the past, about loved ones, and to ponder the words—old ones and new—carved in decaying oak and pine.

Jeff had taken endless pictures when they were here before, but Beverly was seeing it anew through Cass's eyes.

"My mama told me she'd jump down my throat and wiggle if she ever caught me carving my name in anything around here, but if you look hard enough, you might find Cass loves J.L. or Cass loves R.C." Cass laughed, the sound coming a little easier now. "I used initials to keep anyone from guessing who I was in love with, even though there weren't much more than a handful of boys on the island for me to fall for. But over here..."

Cass started to work her way over a pile of timbers, when Mr. Maker stepped up next to her and offered her his hand. "Here, let me help you."

Her head whipped around. "I don't need—" Cass shook her head. She looked frustrated with herself, agitated that she might appear to need help, especially from Mr. Maker. She didn't smile at him, and Mr. Maker didn't draw away. They stood there in limbo, but at last she took his hand. "Thank you."

"You're welcome."

Beverly and Jeff followed Cass and Mr. Maker over the timbers into an area where the chapel must have been. Now there were ferns growing on the wood, berry vines slithering in and around everything they could, and moss everywhere.

"I imagine over the years I've made note of most every carving in the wood, some of it dating back well over a hundred years. My mother hated to admit it, but even my grandfather carved a heart in the apple tree over there." Cass pointed out the gnarled, leafless old tree, still bearing a few pieces of unpicked fruit. "You can't see it all that well anymore, but Grandpa carved his name and my grandma's inside. Mama told me that Grandma and Grandpa always said they'd never be separated, that they'd go to their Maker together, hand in hand, and I guess they did."

"That's my fault," Mr. Maker said. "I wish I hadn't fallen asleep. I wish—"

"I wish all sorts of things too," Cass said, brushing off a timber and sitting down. She patted the spot beside her and Mr. Maker sat too. "I wish I'd known my grandparents, but—" She hesitated, contemplating her next words. "There aren't many old-timers left around here, but ask any one of them and they'll give you an earful about Grandpa's good deeds. Grandma's too. I'm lucky—and thankful—to have had that."

Mr. Maker nodded. "I never heard much of anything good about my dad."

"And I was blessed to have one of the best."

Beverly picked a bunch of red berries from a twisted vine, feeling like she was eavesdropping on a private conversation. Jeff appeared uncomfortable too, absently roaming through the ruins.

"You know, it wasn't just the church I wanted to show you, but something else that my grandfather carved when he was a boy...with his own grandfather's blessing. You can see it from just about anywhere inside this old tumbled-down place," Cass said, standing, "but I kind of think a close-up look might be better."

"All right." Mr. Maker pushed himself up rather slowly, pressed his hands into the small of his back and stretched. "Let's have a look, but mind you, my eyes aren't nearly as good as they used to be."

"Doesn't matter. I've got the feeling you've said the words before but maybe didn't give them all that much thought. As much as I hate to admit it, the same could be said for me."

Beverly and Jeff followed along, stepping over ferns, slipping on moss and mud as they made their way to the place where the altar might have stood long ago. She had good eyes, but no matter how much she stared, she couldn't see anything other than dark crumbling wood and the flora that was rapidly taking over this part of the island.

"Come in close," Cass said. "Take a look."

Jeff and Beverly hung back, looking over Cass's shoulder as Mr. Maker stepped within a foot of the weathered wood—a downed part of the wall. Beverly could see Mr. Maker squinting, then slowly turn and look at Cass. "It looks like a piece of Scripture."

"It is." Cass sighed, then reached out, touching a word with an index finger, tracing the first letter, then the next. Finally that word came clear to Beverly.

Forgive.

Mr. Maker turned slowly toward Jeff. "Most of it's gone, but... It's the Lord's Prayer. 'Forgive us our trespasses—'"

"'As we forgive those who trespass against us,'" Cass added. "I don't know how I could have forgotten those words, when I've said them so many times in my life. I don't know how I could have been filled with—"

"I'd forgotten too." Mr. Maker blew out a breath of pent-up air. "I can understand your hatred. I would have felt the same if it had been my grandparents who were killed. And forgiveness doesn't come all that easy, even if we've prayed for it again and again."

Cass frowned at him for the longest time. She'd looked tough, like a woman who could easily take on the world, but the emotion of the moment got to her. She turned away from Mr. Maker again and touched the carving on the tumbled-down wall. She traced the letters. She drew in a deep breath, and whispered so softly Beverly could just barely hear her say, "Forgive us our trespasses as we forgive those who trespass against us."

"Can you forgive me?" Mr. Maker asked.

Slowly, ever so slowly, Cass faced him again, looking into his eyes. Then she offered him the slightest smile and nodded. "Yes, Mr. Maker, I forgive you."

Chapter Twenty-Seven

Something tells me we're going to hit the sack early tonight," Allan said, walking up behind his wife, slipping his arms around her waist, and giving her a hug. "This gallery has been hopping since you hung the Open sign this morning."

"And you and Adelaide are probably exhausted." Margaret gave her husband a quick peck on the cheek and pulled away, needing to clean up the mess she'd made while wrapping gifts. "Why don't the two of you head home and get some baking done? Didn't you say you wanted to make something special to take to Beverly and Mr. Wheeland's get-together tomorrow night?"

"Chocolate pecan pie," Adelaide chimed in. She was dressed in one of her favorite Christmas sweaters, decorated with three fuzzy, snowy white kittens, each sporting a colorful Christmas ribbon and jingle bell around its neck. She'd known the truth about Santa for years and years, but she was still bright-eyed with excitement, anxious for the big day to arrive. "And we're making peanut butter cookies to leave for Santa Claus tonight."

They'd long ago decided that Santa would stay a tradition in the Hoskins household, no matter how old they got. They had endless amounts of fun pretending that the Jolly Old Elf came during the night, and when tomorrow morning dawned, there would be surprises for everyone under the tree. Right now, though, Margaret had to make it through the end of the day, and as another customer came in the door, Margaret shooed Allan and Adelaide out of the store before they were trapped and couldn't get to their baking.

For the next hour, she buzzed around the gallery, wrapping a necklace and earrings here, a trinket there, even the biggest painting in her store. When her first free moment came, she clapped a hand over her mouth and yawned. Allan was so definitely right. They would be making an early night of it.

The jingle bells rang on the front door, and even though she wanted a few more minutes alone to hang a new picture or two, she was thrilled to see Beverly and Diane walk in. "Thought you might like a little extra help for an hour or two," Diane said, instantly unwrapping the scarf from around her neck and slipping off her coat.

"And some banana-nut bread fresh from the oven. It's from one of my mother's secret recipes." Beverly smiled. "I don't bake very often, but I couldn't resist making this for a few of my special friends."

"I don't have time to sit down or drink a cup of coffee, but my stomach's been rumbling, my feet are killing me, and, oh my, the offer of help ranks right at the top of the best Christmas gifts ever."

"You aren't coming down with something, are you?" Diane asked, concern written clearly on her face. "Not the flu, I hope."

"Just overwhelmed with last-minute sales and too many gifts to wrap." Margaret laughed lightly. "I think a number of people came in here and bought presents because they could get them wrapped for free." She put her hands on her lower back and tried to stretch out the kinks. "I'd forgotten how backbreaking gift wrapping can be."

"Let me take over for a while," Diane offered, always ready and willing to lend a hand.

"I'll cut the banana bread, and since we're the only ones in the gallery at the moment," Beverly said, heading for the kitchenette, "I'll tell you all about my trip to Abenaki Isle with Jeff and Mr. Maker."

Margaret had completely forgotten about Mr. Maker going to the island, and it was something she and her friends had talked about ever since that horrific incident at Orlean Point.

"It was beautiful on the island," Beverly began while unwrapping the bread, cutting it into thin pieces, and placing two slices each on the napkins Margaret found for her. "We'll have to go over in the spring—"

"That would be lovely," Margaret said. "But what about the woman whose grandparents died in the shipwreck? Did Mr. Maker talk to her? Did she forgive him?"

Beverly grinned. "Obviously I don't tell a story quite as poetically as our author friend Diane."

"It's not that, Beverly. I've just been in such a rush all day and there's so much I want to know."

"I'm teasing," Beverly said, laughing lightly.

Feeling tired and maybe a little overwhelmed, Margaret at long last allowed herself to sit down and rest her feet. "Okay, why don't you begin again? I promise I'll relax."

The jingle bells on the door ceased to ring as Beverly told Margaret and Diane everything, right down to the touching moments where Mr. Maker held out a hand to help Cass climb over some downed timbers, and Cass tracing the letters on the word *forgive* carved into the old oak.

"So Cass forgave him?" Margaret asked.

"Yes. Most definitely."

"You didn't by any chance find out why there's no historical record of the shipwreck, did you?" Diane asked, standing at the wrapping station at the back of the gallery, making up all sizes of gold and purple bows in case they were needed before Margaret closed for the day. "Not that it matters any longer, when we've learned so much of what we wanted to know about the mysteries at the lighthouse. I just can't help but wonder why we didn't find any records of it anywhere. Details like that might fit into a book sometime."

Beverly shook her head. "We didn't talk about the shipwreck details at all. It didn't seem important any longer, definitely not as important as Mr. Maker finally making peace with the people who were hurt by his father's recklessness and...and his own very innocent action."

"Such a shame so many people had to suffer," Margaret said, picking at the last bits of banana-nut bread crumbs on her napkin. "I just hope Mr. Maker and Cass and the rest of her family can put it all behind them now and move forward."

"They will," Beverly said. "You could see it in their faces. They've even talked about getting together in the spring, so the day ended on a good note."

Another note rang just then, the jingle bells on the front door, bringing in yet another customer, forcing Margaret to scramble up from her chair and get back to work.

Beverly and Diane stayed an hour longer, wrapping small gifts, finding packages for customers who had put items on layaway, and adding their cheerful smiles to the warmth inside the gallery. Things were quieting down by the time they left. The traffic out on Main Street was almost nonexistent. Most people were at home now, watching *It's a Wonderful Life* on TV, wrapping gifts, cleaning house before guests arrived, or checking their lists, not once but twice.

Margaret tried to stifle a yawn when she heard the front door bells ringing again—she hoped for the last time today. "May I help you?" she asked, stepping out from behind a partition displaying paintings by another local artist.

Caleb stood just inside the gallery, stomping snow off his boots as he'd done many times before.

"I brought back your casserole dish," Caleb said nonchalantly. "The chicken and biscuits were awfully good. Not as good as my mom's, but"—he grinned—"not bad."

"I'm glad you liked it, although you know it was Allan who cooked it, not me."

"Yeah, I know." In his usual style, he strolled around the gallery, hands behind his back, looking at the paintings. She hadn't seen him since last Saturday night during the Christmas Stroll, when he'd proudly introduced his dad, when she'd watched from afar as Caleb, his mom, and his dad held hands, laughed, and maybe even cried. That was a night she'd never forget; a night when she'd witnessed the miracle of Caleb's family getting back together.

For some odd reason she'd thought she'd never see him again. She'd done her part; she was no longer needed in Caleb's life. But he was here. Now. And it felt wonderful.

"Are you looking forward to Christmas tomorrow?"

Caleb nodded, the widest grin she'd ever seen brightening his face. "I haven't peeked, but I think my mom and dad might have gotten me paintbrushes and paints. Some canvases too. Dad says a lot of sun shines into his apartment in Portland. It's kind of small, but he says it's the perfect place for an artist to work."

"He's going to start painting again?"

"Yeah. That's all we've talked about—me and him painting together. He knows some techniques that he says are really cool and he thinks they'd be perfect for the kind of stuff I like to paint."

The miracle had worked even better than Margaret had imagined.

"So your dad's going to spend more time here in Marble Cove?"

"Nope. Mom and I are moving to Portland. Right after Christmas."

Margaret thought for sure her heart had stopped, and then it started again, beating rapidly.

She was losing him after all.

"What about school?" she asked, hoping her words didn't sound as distressed as she suddenly felt.

"There's one just a couple of blocks from the apartment, and Dad says he and Mom can enroll me the first day after winter break."

She couldn't cry in front of him. She had to be positive; after all, wasn't this all she'd wanted for Caleb? "That all sounds great. I'm glad that you're all going to be together."

"Yeah, me too."

He was silent a moment. He sighed. And then, in a style that was so unlike Caleb, he put his arms around Margaret in an awkward embrace.

He quickly backed away and looked at Margaret self-consciously. "Thanks. For everything."

"I'll miss you," Margaret said softly, her hand already held up, waving good-bye.

He waved without speaking, then turned and ran out of the gallery.

Chapter Twenty-Eight

I heard the bells on Christmas Day, their old, familiar carols play, and wild and sweet, the words repeat, of peace on earth, good will to men."

Margaret stood near the fireplace in Mr. Wheeland's living room, listening to Bing Crosby crooning an old favorite song, although most of the tune was muffled by the chatter of good friends sharing tales of their day. She held a mug of hot mulled cider close to her lips so no one would see her yawn. Christmas Day had been wonderful; so had the entire Christmas season. She hated to see it go and already longed for the next eleven months to go by so she could begin to celebrate all over again. But goodness, she was tired.

Beverly crossed the room and stood at Margaret's side. Uncharacteristically, she linked her arm through Margaret's.

"So," Beverly said, leaning close so Margaret could hear, "did you find a digital camera with all the bells and whistles under your tree this morning?"

"Did I ever, and so much more." Margaret grinned, remembering the way her fingers had trembled when she tore off wrapping paper, one gift after another. A flannel nightgown; a ceramic birdbath to hang in her garden next spring; a pretty red silk flower to clip in her hair; and...the camera. She'd flung her arms around her husband as she'd done those first years of their marriage, and felt his heart beating next to hers.

"What about you?" Margaret asked. "Anything special, or maybe something unexpected?"

"A pair of creamy kid leather gloves that couldn't be any softer, and a pair of hiking boots." Beverly shook her head, laughing lightly. "It seems Mr. Maker told my father that I wanted to go with him when he showed Jeff all the hiding places in the cliffs below Orlean Point Light. He said I'd need to wear more sensible shoes on an adventure like that—so Father bought me hiking boots. Thank goodness he has good taste, because, really, they're not all that bad to look at. I couldn't believe how comfortable they were when I slipped my feet into them."

Margaret chuckled. "Before you know it, we'll have you dressing down in flannel-lined jeans and yellow slickers for business meetings. Turn you into a real Mainer, not a citified one."

"We'll see about that."

Beverly patted Margaret's hand. "Looks like it's time for me to pass around the hors d'oeuvres again and make sure everyone's glass is full."

"I'll help," Margaret said. "I need to move around anyway. I was on the verge of nodding off a few minutes ago. It's been quite a day; in fact, quite a few weeks."

Shelley looked happy tonight, Margaret thought, as she wandered around from guest to guest, refilling their mugs from a carafe of hot cider that Mr. Wheeland had brewed from a recipe that his wife had served every Christmas. She'd dressed up in a red knitted dress. Her long blonde hair was pulled back into a French braid and sparkling red rhinestones dangled from her ears. She was chatting with Mrs. Peabody and her sister Coral, laughing at some story or other, while Emma curled up in her lap, sound asleep and already dressed in her jammies, ready for bed when she and Dan decided to call it a night.

"Dan gave me the most beautiful Christmas gift," Shelley said to Margaret, holding out her mug. "Of course, you probably know about it already."

"Not I." Margaret shook her head. "Allan knew, but said he'd promised to keep it a secret from me, even though it was hidden in our garage."

"Dan doesn't trust me," Shelley said, laughing. "Of course, I really can't blame him. I do try to find my presents long before Christmas, and when I do, I carefully unwrap them, take a peek, then wrap them up again and pretend I'm totally surprised on Christmas morning."

"Guess you didn't have to pretend today."

"Not at all, but, oh my gosh, Margaret, I was really surprised." Shelley looked across the room, where her husband stood, a dead-to-the-world Aiden hanging over his dad's shoulder. "Dan made me a cookbook stand out of the most beautiful wood I've ever seen. He carved a few small lighthouses into it too."

Margaret smiled. "It'll look great in your kitchen."

"I already know exactly where I'm putting it," Shelley stated. "But all in good time. First I have to wait until the new kitchen's ready, and with any luck, that won't be long."

The front door opened, letting in a rush of icy air along with Diane, her son and daughter, and Mr. Maker and Jeff Mackenzie, each of them bearing plates full of goodies.

"Merry Christmas, and sorry we're late," Diane said, shrugging out of her coat. "Justin and Jessica didn't get into town until noon, but having them here—" Diane grinned from ear to ear. "Having them here, well, it's just wonderful."

"That painting we got you wasn't all that bad either," Justin added, laughing at his mom, slinging an arm around her shoulder. Tall, muscular, and good-looking, his blond hair cut in a buzz cut and his brown eyes sparkling, he was the typical soldier boy, and his mother's pride and joy—one of them, at least.

Pretty and willowy, just like her mom, Jessica gave Margaret a big hug. "Why don't you let me take that off your hands," she said, slipping the carafe away from Margaret. She leaned close to the spout and inhaled. "Mmm, smells wonderful. Hot cider with cinnamon, cloves, nutmeg, and—"

"And a bit of brown sugar," Beverly added, greeting the newest arrivals. "If you like it, I'll give you the recipe."

A few moments later, Beverly had Mr. Maker's overcoat and Jeff's parka hanging over her right arm, and Margaret joined Allan, who was standing next to the rocker where Adelaide was sitting "Let's sing carols," Adelaide suggested.

"Sounds like a wonderful idea," Mr. Wheeland said. "What should we sing first? Anyone have any ideas?"

"'Jingle Bells,' Adelaide called out, and immediately started to sing.

Nearly everyone in the room joined in. It took them a few measures to find the melody together.

Mr. Maker's voice was subdued, but he looked joyful and at peace. He stood next to Mr. Wheeland, and Margaret could imagine them as boys playing baseball together. As she scanned the room, she found her attention caught by two other people. Beverly and Jeff stood in the entry, her arms empty now, no coats, no tray of hors d'oeuvres. She was smiling and Jeff was laughing, and everyone else was finishing up their song.

"*Oh, what fun it is to ride in a one-horse open sleigh.*"

Suddenly Jeff took Beverly's face in his hands. Her smile turned to shock. "We're under the mistletoe," Margaret heard Jeff say, even though he'd said it so quietly that Beverly should have been the only one to hear. And then he kissed her lightly.

Beverly pulled back. Margaret could see the blush flowing up Beverly's neck, staining her cheeks a bright red.

Jeff was smiling, but Beverly looked shell-shocked. She spun around, took a deep breath to regain her composure, let it out quickly, and smiled as she walked to the center of the room. "Let's not stop so soon," she said. "How about 'It Came upon a Midnight Clear'?"

"Perfect," Margaret said. "And totally appropriate when you consider how beautiful it's been the last few nights."

Margaret watched with rapt attention as Beverly, dressed in pearls and a soft and beautiful green cashmere sweater, slipped onto the piano bench. An instant later, lush chords filled the room. No one spoke; Margaret almost forgot to breathe. The sound was full and beautiful.

Beverly finished playing the introduction, and then she added her voice to the tune she played. *"It came upon the midnight clear..."* She turned, smiling at her friends and loved ones. "Come on, everyone. Don't let me sing by myself."

"That glorious song of old..."

Jeff crossed the room and stood beside the piano, Diane hugged her children close, Dan and Shelley rocked their little ones, and Allan slipped his arm around Margaret's waist, keeping her at his side, as he always had. Suddenly the roomful of people, both young and old, became a choir, friends and loved ones joined together, arms linked, singing beautifully.

"From angels bending near the earth, to touch their harps of gold."

Once more, Margaret looked around the room, her heart filled with joy as she memorized the faces of her friends and loved ones. This was one of the best Christmases of all, filled with one miracle after another. God had clearly blessed them. Yet as she looked at Beverly, playing the piano like a virtuoso, she couldn't help but smile.

What other secrets waited in store for her and her friends?

Author Bio

USA Today best-selling author Patti Berg began penning stories while in elementary school, when she wrote the script for a puppet show that she and her friends put on at a local hospital. Thirty years later, one of her dreams came true when the first of her many warm and lighthearted novels appeared in bookstores.

Scared of dogs until the age of fifty, Patti now goes out of her way to pet every dog she gets close to and would happily bring home all of the puppies in the pound if her less impulsive husband would only let her. He's had less success keeping her from saying *yes* when family, friends and others ask her to volunteer. A past president, secretary and newsletter editor of the Sacramento Valley Rose chapter of Romance Writers of America as well as past president, Web site and conference coordinator for RWA's Published Authors' Special Interest Chapter, Patti is currently volunteering with the Ada County Idaho Sheriff's Department.

She lives in southwestern Idaho with her husband of thirty-three years and a huggable Bernese mountain dog named Barkley. To learn more about Patti, go to pattiberg.com.

A Conversation with Patti Berg

Q. *Each of the four women in Miracles of Marble Cove is starting over in her life or career. If you were not a writer, what would be your choice of career?*

A. Anything that involves travel. In my teens I wanted to be an archaeologist. To this day, I don't know why I didn't pursue that dream. I love antiquities and history, and can easily see myself on a dig in Egypt's Valley of the Kings, Jordan's Petra, and, of course, most anywhere in Greece or Rome. Accompanying Indiana Jones on any of his adventures would definitely be fun—though, of course, he's fictional, and I'm not.

Q. *The four friends of Marble Cove gather frequently at the Cove for coffee. If you were to join them, what would you order and why?*

A. Well, it definitely wouldn't be coffee. The two of us don't get along and never have, which is odd, since I was raised by a mom and dad who drank coffee from morning till night. In winter, I'd go for hot cocoa—and not the instant variety. I like the real stuff, made with whole milk, sugar and cocoa powder. Yum! And I'd have to sprinkle a few marshmallows on top. (As a matter of fact, Margaret did that for Caleb in *A Midnight Clear.*) A big and fat cinnamon roll would be awfully good too.

Q. What was the most interesting experience you've had while doing research for your books?

A. Every instance of doing research is an interesting—and exciting—experience. But I have to say the most thrilling research experience occurred on a trip I took to St. Augustine, Florida, which is the oldest continuously occupied city in the United States. While strolling through red brick lanes, past centuries-old churches and ancient forts, I ducked into a quaint bookstore and immediately spotted a pirate's skull and crossbones on the front of a very large book. Totally intrigued, I bought the book, became engrossed in the tales and pictures, and, on my flight home, created the outline for a new story. I sent off the idea to my editor the next day, and a day after that—it was a go. That book became one of the easiest to write and one of my favorites, *Looking for a Hero,* about a time-traveling pirate.

Q. What do you want your readers to take away from A Midnight Clear*?*

A. Warmth. Generosity. The compassion and joy of friends. The love of family. These are the things that make my life so worthwhile. I hope everyone can experience them!

Baking with Shelley

Margaret's Christmas Snowballs

1 cup softened butter
⅓ cup granulated sugar
2 teaspoons water
2 teaspoons vanilla
2 cups sifted all-purpose flour
1 cup chopped pecans
Confectioners' sugar

Preheat oven to 325 degrees. Cream butter and sugar, add water and vanilla, and mix well. Blend in flour and nuts. Chill four hours. Shape into balls. Bake on ungreased cookie sheet about eighteen minutes. Remove from cookie sheet and cool slightly. Roll in confectioners' sugar. Makes about three dozen.

From the Guideposts Archives

This story by Cliff Snider of High Point, North Carolina, originally appeared in the December 2008 issue of *Guideposts.*

Christmas begins early for me. In the fall, I take my red suits out of storage and get them cleaned. Then I start lifting weights and doing crunches. I need to get strong, so I can lift kids up on my lap. By November, I bleach the roots in my beard and hair. My hair is gray—what's left of it, anyway—but to make it that straight-from-the-North-Pole snowy-white, I need a little help. I get out the little leather-bound book I use for writing down children's names. But the book, the beard, the fur-trimmed suits—they're not what make me a real Santa. That comes from something I discovered years ago.

I grew up right here in High Point, North Carolina. I was a shy, overweight kid, the third-string tackle on the football team and third-chair violinist in the orchestra. I was content to stay in the background. The one person I really talked to was my father. Dad was a kind, gentle man, who ran the print shop in town. I didn't need to be Mr. Popular when I had a best friend—my dad.

Then one Labor Day weekend, he rode with my uncle to Camp Lejeune to pick up my cousins who were being discharged from the service. They were hit by an oncoming car. Dad was killed instantly.

I was fifteen and determined to be brave and strong for my mother and younger brother. *You've got to take care of them now,* I told myself. At the funeral service, I held back my tears. I went back to my routine, but I knew life would never be the same.

That December, everyone in my youth group was excited about the Christmas party we were putting on for children at the local mission. The others set to making paper chains and wrapping presents, but I just sat at the table, not feeling like celebrating. Our youth leader cornered me. "Cliff, we've got a special job for you at the party. We want you to be our Santa this year."

I couldn't muster the energy to argue. I was sure he picked me because I was the fattest kid in the group—very little padding necessary.

The day of the party I put on the rented red suit and hat, the wig, and the cotton beard. I cinched a black belt around my waist and looked in the mirror. The awkward fifteen-year-old was gone. In his place stood a jolly, smiling, kindly man. Santa.

It was so easy at the party. I didn't have to start a conversation. The kids came to me, and my shyness melted away. After a child told me about what he wanted for Christmas, I said a prayer for him. And with each smile I got from a child, my grief receded and Christmas felt more real.

Almost every year after that, I was Santa at Christmas gatherings. I went into the printing business, just like Dad, and played Santa at our holiday party. Still, I wondered if there was something more I could do. I learned about the Charles W. Howard Santa Claus School in Midland, Michigan. The school was rigorous—accepting only ten students per year. "I want to go to this school," I told my wife Janie.

"Go," she said. "It's important to you."

At first I was intimidated. The other student-Santas were so convincing with their beards, jolly voices, twinkling eyes. "I'm not sure I'm cut out to do this," I said to Tom Valent, the dean of the school.

"Cliff," he said, "here's the secret. When you get back to your hometown, you *are* Santa. Just be the best Santa you can be." Soon enough I'd earned my degree.

Every year I listen to hundreds of children tell me their hopes and dreams. Once I noticed a young boy waiting in the back of a crowd until the others had finished. Then he walked up and whispered, "Santa, all I want is for everyone to quit calling me names on the bus."

I looked at him and saw the boy I'd once been. "I know exactly what you're going through," I told him. "What I'm going to do is write your name in my book, and when I get home, I'll ask God to help those children be as nice as you are."

Sometimes people tell me, "You know, Jesus is the real reason for the season." I totally agree. We celebrate the miraculous birth of our Savior. But Santa represents the spirit of giving, and that's important too, even miraculous sometimes. Because, as I discovered at that youth group Christmas party so many years ago, bringing joy to others brings out the best in you.

Read on for a sneak peek of the next exciting book in *Miracles of Marble Cove*!

Shining Bright
by Anne Marie Rodgers

Beverly Wheeland-Parker smiled as she saw the familiar sign: Marble Cove: 10. As she turned off Maine Route 1 onto the smaller road that wound along the coast, anticipation rose. As soon as she came around the next bend, she'd be able to see the lighthouse.

The sign and the sight of the lighthouse had become a part of her weekly landscape as she made the drive from her office in Augusta, Maine, to her new home in the tiny coastal town.

Although she hadn't grown up in Marble Cove, her parents had moved there many years ago, and her aging father still lived in the same house they'd shared. Beverly had recently moved in with him. With her boss's blessing, she had found a way to do much of her work from home, only traveling to the office one, sometimes two days a week. Today was the first Wednesday in January, the kind of bleak winter day that made her really glad she wasn't making the daily drive anymore.

She steered into the curve, her eyes on the spit of land where the lighthouse stood, stark against the steely sky. She suspected there would be snow by morning, and she was grateful she'd be settled back in Marble Cove this evening.

The world appeared in shades of black and white during these short days of midwinter, and the ocean was a dark, gunmetal gray boiling with whitecaps that foamed up around the rocks along the shore. When she'd decided to telecommute, she hadn't considered how grueling the drive to and from Augusta could be when the winter weather turned bad.

And heaven knew the weather in Maine could be unpredictable. What appeared to be a dazzling sunny day when she left in the morning could turn to a howling blizzard by the time she headed home. So far, she'd been fortunate that she hadn't been caught in anything too terrible. And she'd been working hard to limit her travel.

Wait! What was that? A light had flashed from the window at the top of the lighthouse that housed the Fresnel light—the light that had been deactivated for nearly sixty years now. It flashed again, and she caught her breath as an insistent presentiment of danger rolled through her. Adrenaline surged, and she sucked in a breath as her fingers tightened on the wheel.

A blur of red whizzed around the sharp turn *in her lane*!

Instantly, Beverly wrenched the wheel to the right, reflex kicking in milliseconds after she perceived the threat. The red car's brakes screamed, and it fishtailed, the rear of the driver's side sliding inexorably toward her.

Lord, help! It was all the thought she had time for. As her car shot off the road and bounced into a rocky ditch, the undercarriage scraped and clanged over small boulders. Just when she was sure she was going to be hit, the red car fishtailed again and missed her by inches. As Beverly jounced to an abrupt halt, the red car roared past. And her airbag exploded into her face with a sound like a shot.

Stunned, Beverly didn't move for a moment. The car's engine was still running, and she automatically reached for the key to shut it off, but her arm was pinned. Then she realized her eyes were closed. She opened her eyes and blinked at the cloud of dust swirling around her. Smoke? Her pulse surged. Moments later, though, she realized that it wasn't smoke but the powder from the airbag that had deployed.

Coughing, she fought her way free of the rapidly deflating airbag enough to turn off the engine. She stopped then and took a careful inventory of herself. Nothing seemed broken. *Thank You, God.*

Relieved to note that she didn't feel pain other than some deep aching where the seat belt had restrained her, she reached down and unbuckled herself. The door handle was blocked by the remains of the airbag, so she had to grasp handfuls of the thing and shove it out of the way until she could open the door and step out.

Whoa! To her shock, she stepped into thin air. She landed on her hands and knees on the ground with a jolt, still coughing as she blinked to try to clear the airbag powder from her eyes. When she looked around, she saw that her car had come to rest at an angle, the left front corner off the ground with the tire in the air. It explained why she'd fallen so hard when she stepped out of the car.

Slowly, she stood and straightened. She hoped the other driver hadn't been injured.

And then she realized she was alone on the side of the road. He didn't stop! Beverly couldn't believe it. She could be injured, or worse, and that careless road hog hadn't even stopped!

Quickly, she took stock of her aches and pains again. Knees and palms stung from the fall in addition to the bruises she'd noted earlier, but thankfully, she hadn't been badly hurt. She shuddered, recalling a red fender sliding inexorably across the road straight at her. It could have been much worse.

She shivered as she buttoned up her coat. The temperature was January-frigid: she'd heard the high today had only reached eighteen, which probably explained why there were so few people on the road.

Squinting against the snow-brightened landscape, she checked the highway in both directions. Nothing coming.

She sighed. She really didn't want to call 911. She wasn't injured. But she sure wasn't going anywhere until she got her car off those rocks.

She patted her coat pocket and drew out her cell phone. Grimly, she smiled as she hit her list of contacts. It paid to be prepared. She had both the nonemergency number for the state police and the number of a body shop just outside Marble Cove. After two short conversations, she slipped the phone back into her pocket and pulled out her elegant leather gloves.

Slipping on the gloves as she walked, she returned to the car. Fortunately, she could reach the back door on the driver's side, where she knew a warm hat and scarf lay on the seat. Moments later, she was swaddled in both.

To keep warm, she paced back and forth along the berm of the roadway. She supposed she might be able to get back in the car and turn on some heat, but given the odd angle at which the car was perched on the rocks, that might not be smart. The ground dropped away on the far side of the stranded vehicle.

She hoped there was no significant damage to the undercarriage. The car was still in excellent shape, a dark metallic gray Ford Fusion she had purchased in 2010, and although her insurance would cover most of a repair bill, she worried that a damaged-and-repaired car might never be the same.

A car with flashing lights atop had come around the bend while she was engrossed in her dismal thoughts. Moments later, the state police cruiser drew to a halt near her, and an officer emerged. As she was giving him the story and the limited description she had of the red car, a minivan rounded the curve. It slowed to pass and then suddenly pulled over to the side of the road just beyond the cop's car.

A short, rounded woman bounced out of the driver's seat. "Beverly! Are you all right?"

A flood of relief spread through Beverly as she recognized her friend Margaret Hoskins, who lived just down the street from her. She excused herself from the policeman and went to meet her friend, accepting Margaret's warm embrace with far less reserve than she normally would. "I'm okay." She explained how the accident had transpired.

"Let me drive you home," Margaret urged. "It's freezing out here."

"Thank you, but I need to wait for the tow truck."

The officer overheard the comment. "If you'd like to go on home with your friend, I'll supervise the towing." He pointed down the road. "I think that's the truck coming now."

Beverly hesitated. It went against the grain not to handle her problems herself. But it was *cold* out here! Finally she handed the officer her keys. "Thank you."

Quickly Margaret hustled her to her van.

"Wait," Beverly protested. "I've got to shake off this powder."

"Forget the dirt," Margaret told her. "This van has seen worse."

All the same, Beverly brushed down her stylish, lined trench coat to remove the residue before Margaret bundled her into the passenger seat. Margaret hurried around to the driver side and hopped in. She turned up the heat until the welcome warmth was blasting out at Beverly's chilled cheeks.

"Wow," she said. "I didn't realize how frozen I was getting."

Margaret nodded. "It's deceptive. By the time you figure it out, you're one icicle away from frostbite." She put the vehicle into gear and, after a cheery wave to the helpful police officer, accelerated onto the road toward Marble Cove.

"Thank you for stopping. It's lucky you were traveling this way today."

Margaret nodded. "We have Louellen Lumadue to thank for that."

"Lou...who?"

Margaret chuckled. "Louellen Lumadue is an artist. Her work inspired me when I began to paint again. The first time I went to a showing of her work, I was absolutely captivated."

"What appealed to you?"

Margaret shrugged. "She's an impressionist, and there's just something about the way she uses color that's unique. I could look at a lineup of paintings and instantly pick out a Lumadue." She smiled. "It sounds rather mystical to say that her work called to me, but there was something in the paintings she created that I couldn't stop thinking about. And from there, it was a short step toward trying it myself."

"But I don't understand what that has to do with your being on this road."

"Oh, sorry." Margaret shook her head. "I forgot where I was going with that story. I read in the paper last week that Louellen is exhibiting during January and February at Colby College's Museum of Art. They have a nice collection that focuses on American artists. So I thought I'd go up to Waterville to see it."

"How was it?" Beverly was eager to distract herself from the unsettling memory of metal scraping over rock as she veered off the road.

Margaret sucked in an enthusiastic breath. "Oh, it was wonderful! She still has such a unique command of color, although she's moved from impressionism into expressionism." She made a face. "I have to say I prefer her earlier pieces. Why, I still can recall one series she did in which she incorporated hidden images that reflected the theme of the painting. Very, very subtle, and absolutely riveting. Her newer work doesn't speak to me like that, but the exhibit was fascinating all the same. And here's something even more wonderful: she's going to be giving a lecture at the art museum next week."

"Are you going to attend?" Beverly rubbed her hands together. She could feel her fingers and toes thawing, tiny pinpricks of sensation stinging her extremities.

"I'm hoping to. Though I wouldn't dare commit to something without checking my calendar first." Margaret made an exasperated noise. "Enjoy your memory while you've got it. This aging stuff is for the birds."

"Oh, Margaret, I'd say you're aging as gracefully as anyone."

They shared a laugh as the lighthouse loomed large on its rocky promontory near the town limits.

The sight triggered a memory. "Margaret." Beverly caught her breath. "I saw a light."

Margaret glanced across the console between their seats. It was obvious she'd made the connection between Beverly's words and the solitary structure. "Do you think it was a warning?"

"I do," Beverly said in a wondering tone. "Right before the accident, it flashed twice."

Margaret appeared unsurprised. She smiled. "Another miracle to add to our collection. Wait until Shelley and Diane hear about it." Her smile faded. "Thank heavens for that light. Your accident might have been much worse."

"You're right. Because it caught my attention, I was looking that way when the car came around the curve. If I hadn't seen it as soon as I did, it probably would have hit me head-on."

"It does seem there must have been an angel on your shoulder." Margaret glanced over at her friend and raised her eyebrows. "If you'd spun a little farther, you'd probably have flipped over going down that embankment."

A Note from the Editors

We hope you enjoy Miracles of Marble Cove, created by Guideposts Books and Inspirational Media. In all of our books, magazines and outreach efforts, we aim to deliver inspiration and encouragement, help you grow in your faith, and celebrate God's love in every aspect of your daily life.

Thank you for making a difference with your purchase of this book, which helps fund our many outreach programs to the military, prisons, hospitals, nursing homes and schools. To learn more, visit GuidepostsFoundation.org.

We also maintain many useful and uplifting online resources. Visit Guideposts.org to read true stories of hope and inspiration, access Our Prayer network, sign up for free newsletters, join our Facebook community, and subscribe to our stimulating blogs.

To order your favorite Guideposts publication, go to ShopGuideposts.org, call (800) 932-2145 or write to Guideposts, PO Box 5815, Harlan, Iowa 51593.